MW01258759

Altared
a novel

Sharyn Kopf

Book Three of the *Spinstered* Series

LoJo Publishing
2017

ISBN-13: 978-1975822255
ISBN-10: 1975822250

LoJo Publishing
803 E. Sandusky Ave.
Bellefontaine, OH 43311
www.sharynkopf.wordpress.com
www.girlsnightin40.com

Special discounts are available on quantity purchases by corporations, associations, educators, and others. For details, contact the publisher at the above listed address.

U.S. trade bookstores and wholesalers: Please contact LoJo Publishing, tel: (937) 407-7943 or email sharynkopf@gmail.com.

To all of my friends who inspired so many of the characters and events within these pages.

And to all those dreams we hold close to our hearts.

Prologue
Uli

September 1981

He stood in the doorway, grinning, his hands behind his back.

"Daddy!" I ran to him, but he didn't swoop me up into his arms like he usually did.

"Hello, sunshine," he said. "I brought you a surprise." Then he held out a big yellow flower like a scepter.

Round petals surrounded a large brown center. "What is it?"

"It's a dream."

I giggled. He couldn't fool me. "No, silly. It's a flower. But what kind?"

My mother came in from the sunroom, using a rag to wipe purple paint off her hands. "That's a sunflower, Uli. Haven't you ever seen a sunflower before?"

I shook my head. Since I was only seven, they could hardly expect me to know everything yet. "Does it have the sun in it?"

Mother laughed, but Daddy said, "Of course it does! That's why it's a dream."

"Don't fill her head with foolishness, Mark," Mom said before strolling back to the sunroom and her art.

Daddy put his hands under my arms and lifted me up onto the shelf opening between the hallway and the living room. He liked to put me there. He told me it was so we could be at eye level. But he was tall, and I had to raise my eyes to see his smile.

"You have to promise me something, Uli," he said, and I nodded. "Use your words, sweetheart."

"I promise, Daddy."

That seemed to be what he wanted to hear. "Okay, I want you to promise you'll follow your dream."

"What's my dream?"

"That's what you have to decide."

"You tell me."

He tickled my chin and laughed. "I can't tell you your dream."

"Why not?"

"Because it has to come from your heart." Then he patted my chest over my heart, so I closed my eyes and tried to hear something, but all it said was *thud, thud, thud.*

Well, that doesn't help. I opened my eyes. He was still smiling, though his face looked tired. "What's your dream, Daddy?"

"You're the only dream I need, sweetheart."

"Can that be my dream?"

"Now who's being silly?" Then he wrapped me in his arms and picked me back up.

"What is a dream?" Because all I knew was that sometimes they were strange and sometimes they were scary.

"Hmm," he said, and tapped his chin. "It's anything you hope for that will make you super happy."

"You make me super happy."

He smiled. "You're a good girl." But his eyes seemed sad as he hugged me.

I snuggled in close and whispered, "You're a good daddy."

Three weeks later he was gone, taking all of my dreams with him.

Chapter 1
Uli

𝒜 balmy, misty breeze floats over my skin, and I breathe it in. The air is warm and spicy and sweet, like cinnamon toast. Nothing can touch me here except the fabric of paradise.

I push the ground with my feet, setting my swing into motion at the small open-air cantina we settled on for supper. We already ordered—fish or grilled chicken with rice and beans and coleslaw, which seems to be a standard meal on the Belizean island of Ambergris Caye.

The waitress sauntered away several minutes ago, yet we sit in silence, sighing and smiling and occasionally rubbing aloe onto sunburned shoulders.

Slowing the movement of the swing, I stir my pina colada and take a sip. I had to get it sans alcohol because my stomach is still sensitive thanks to a bout of food poisoning that hit me hard five days ago. I'm not even close to being back to normal, but at least I no longer feel like I'm dying. And I've already lost almost eight pounds. If I can keep this up, I might actually have a slimmer figure on my wedding day.

I never thought I'd actually thank God for food poisoning.

"Well, I guess we should figure out what we want to do tomorrow," Catie says, almost reluctantly, as if she's not happy about bringing a schedule to such a peaceful place. "Maybe a bike ride?"

It's Sunday night and the six of us have been in Belize just shy of two days. Adjusting to island life means we've spent most of that time lounging on pastel-colored chairs at the beach outside our condo, reading or talking about minor things like music or recipes or whether swimsuit cover-ups could be worn as shirts. (We decided they could, which is why I donned my favorite aqua one over white capris for dinner tonight.)

I say, "Some exercise would be good," and mean it. Jolene laughs, but it doesn't bother me. I hardly believe it myself. It's like my brain has reset. I don't say anything to my friends, though. I'm focused on making one person happy ... and he's in Colorado.

Besides, if things go wrong and this mindset switch doesn't last, I don't want my friends wondering why I'm not losing weight anymore and asking me how the diet is going. Best to keep it to myself for now and make sure it sticks.

Kate, the youngest of our group at thirty-four, adjusts her seat. With hips too wide for one of the swings, she had to sit on the chair side of the table, next to Jolene. "I'd like to sign up for parasailing at some point," she says, then chuckles with a shrug and a shake of her head. "If I'm not too big, of course."

I admire her courage to admit it out loud.

"Well," Becca says, "we can at least ask." Becca is athletic and so cool she brought her hand-painted Fender guitar as her carry-on. Last night we sat around a small campfire, eating watermelon and pineapple and chatting about life while Becca strummed our very own background music. It was like being in a movie. A small, independent film that can't afford any male actors, sure, but it had a Hollywood feel. Without the romantic storyline.

What am I saying? I have my romantic storyline. He paid for my vacation and promised to love me forever. Maybe our relationship has been light on the romance for some time now, but a girl takes what she can get.

The final member of our party, Libby, is our travel agent and one of the funniest women I know, something I hadn't realized until this trip. She's also full of information and has made every part of our vacation easier. It's a great group, actually. I can already tell I'm going to enjoy the new camaraderie that will grow out of this week as much as I already cherish my friendships with Jolene and Catie.

I'm very blessed, friend-wise, something staying at my mom's townhome in Iowa for over two months made intensely clear. Maybe it's my respect for these two women that has prevented me from mentioning my reconciliation with Cole. I've opened my mouth to tell them a dozen times, but the words weren't there. It's obvious they believe I'm better off without him, so if hearing the wedding is back on will bring them down, I might as well wait until our trip is over.

Besides, Jolene has enough love-glow for all of us. Her ringless finger implies Trevor hasn't proposed yet, but her eyes sparkle like a woman with a hot secret, and I have to wonder. Though I'm tempted to ask, I keep my mouth shut. Why ruin a perfectly good vacation?

Once the platters of food arrive, Libby offers to say grace before we dig in. Well, the others dig in. I'm still not able to do much more than nibble on my rather bland bowl of rice, which is saved only by a pad of butter and some salt. Even then, I'm not sure how much I'll get down.

Jolene notices. "How's your stomach?"

"It's still pretty angry at me."

"I'm surprised you'd go on a vacation after just going through something like food poisoning."

"Yeah, I'm a little surprised myself, but I wasn't about to let a little nausea ruin an opportunity like this." I reach toward the bowl of tortilla chips in the middle of the table but pull my hand back when my gut churns in disgust. Guess I'll stick with the rice and, if I'm hungry later tonight, snack on some of the saltines I bought at the local market.

Catie takes a chip and all I can do is watch her enjoy it, imagining the salty corn flavor on my tongue. She swallows and says, "I'm even more surprised you were able to afford it."

9

Ignoring the question in her eyes, I glance toward Kate. "I'd be up for parasailing. Want to check it out in the morning?"

Fear and worry mingle in her eyes as her gaze darts pointedly at my safe but boring meal. I add, "I promise I won't throw up on you." Everyone chuckles, including me. "I haven't thrown up in four days if that helps."

"Still," Libby chimes in, "you might want to take it easy."

"I know." *Boy, do I know.* "But I'm on this gorgeous island, and I want to take advantage of what could be my last tropical trip." A couple of the girls protest, and I hold up a hand. "Hopefully not, but you never know. Besides, I need something to make up for not being able to join you all on Tuesday."

The rest of the group signed up for a day trip Tuesday that will include taking a boat to the mainland where they'll visit the Belize zoo, then board a bus and journey deep into the jungle. Once there, they'll hike about a mile carrying inner tubes, which they'll use to float down the river as it snakes through a series of caves. I'd love to go but decided being away from easy access to a bathroom for a whole day isn't such a good idea. So I'll have to settle for reading and relaxing and tanning on the beach while they're out exploring.

It's a sacrifice, but I think I can handle it. Plus, it will save me over fifty dollars.

Jolene's phone chirps and she takes a peek. Again. This has been a near-constant distraction since we arrived. She smiles and sends a response before looking up to find five pairs of eyes glaring at her. *Okay, I'll say it.* "Can't you put that thing away for one meal?"

Her expression tells me she feels sheepish but not sorry.

Libby adds, "Maybe we should try that rule where the next person to look at her phone has to pay for dinner."

Everyone agrees except Jolene. Probably because she's the only one who actually has people who miss her and want to stay in touch, which means she's the only one in danger of losing that game.

It's been four days since Cole surprised me by showing up at my mom's and three since he kissed me goodbye before jumping in his truck to drive home to Colorado. And the only contact I've had with him since then was the message from PayPal letting me know he'd transferred money into my account. So, technically, it was from some PayPal guy named Albert, not Cole.

How sad is it that I would even remotely consider that "contact"?

Becca asks, "Who is it, anyway?" at the same time Catie says, "Can't you and Trevor be out of communication for one week?"

Jolene takes a deep breath. "It isn't just Trevor. I mean, it's mostly Trevor. But also my mom or one of my sisters or—" She pauses. And blushes. I'm almost certain I've never seen Jolene blush before. "To be completely honest, we're planning a wedding."

Catie and I scream and jump up to hug our friend. Libby seems surprised, while the other two glance around in confusion. Kate asks, "Whose wedding?"

A light dawns on Libby's face and she shrieks at Jolene, who almost falls off her swing. "You're getting married?!"

With a grin, Jolene reaches into the v-neck of her black sundress and pulls out a gold chain necklace. A sparkly diamond ring dangles from the end, catching the rose color of the setting sun and winking at us with almost as much delight as what's emanating from Jolene's eyes. All she says is, "Yep."

Half a dozen questions hit her at once, and she chuckles as she slides the ring on the finger where it belongs. "Okay, okay, one at a time, please. This is what I know: We've tentatively scheduled the wedding for October 18 and it *will* be in Colorado."

We all cheer, though I wonder if I'm the only one who's

11

simply glad I won't have to book a flight to Nashville. It's not like Cole would pay for another trip.

Wait a minute. We'll be married by then. I will attend Jolene's wedding as Mrs. Uli Moretti. Wow. His money will be my money, and I'll finally know what it's like to not have to constantly worry about finances. Something lifts and it suddenly feels like I lost another eight pounds. It's glorious. Why shouldn't my friends share in my joy?

I dig my feet into the sand and clear my throat. "As long as we're talking about weddings ... Cole and I are back on."

This announcement does not garner shouts of joy and hugs all around, and I feel their disappointment all the way to my sandy, sandaled toes. I catch a grimace from Catie and pure disappointment from Jolene.

"Come on, guys, this is good news." I put on my best happy face and add, "It's what I want ... and we should celebrate."

As if to confirm my words, the waitress stops by to see if anyone wants dessert. Since one of our goals this week is to try the key lime pie at every restaurant we go to, everyone orders a slice. Except me. But I will at least get a taste. The girls promised to take turns giving me a bite.

The minute the waitress walks away, though, Jolene turns to me. Well, turns *on* me would be more precise. All she says is, "Why?"

"Why what?" My voice sounds clipped, but I don't care.

"Why would you ever go back to planning a life with that ... that jerk?"

Apparently, "jerk" was the nicest word she could come up with.

"He's not a jerk." I put my fork down. Suddenly, not even a bite of pie sounds good. "And I love him."

Jolene's eyes spark frustration, maybe even anger, and Catie has her business face on, which usually means she's trying to make sense of something she finds nonsensical. The other three women share a look of confusion mixed with what seems to be a desire to escape this conversation and talk about something less divisive, like politics.

After studying me for a moment, Jolene nods. "Love. Yeah, right."

And just a few minutes ago I was thinking about what great friends I have. Now I wish they'd all hop on a boat to Neverland and leave me alone. In the meantime, I'm more than happy to respond to Jolene's snarky assessment. "What do you know about love anyway?"

"More than you, apparently, if you think what you have with Cole is love."

Argh. I want to throttle her. Miss Goody Two-Shoes social worker with the dream-come-true fiancé. "We can't all have your perfect life, Jolene. And what I have with Cole *is* love. In fact, it's because of him that I can pay for this trip."

More stunned expressions. I continue, "That's right. He bought my ticket and gave me spending money." Then I return Jolene's glare. "Because he *loves* me, and he wants me to be happy."

"Oh, well, why didn't you say so?" Jolene laughs without a hint of humor. "I didn't realize love could be bought."

I grab her left hand right near that glistening ring and say, "No? What do you call this?"

A throat clears and Catie says, "Um, girls? Maybe this isn't the right time or place for this." She glances around the restaurant, and I realize we've become the center of attention. Not that I care what a roomful of strangers think. Still, for the sake of the rest of my friends, I let go of Jolene's hand and say, "I'm going for a walk."

After dropping more than enough money to cover my food and tip, I push myself off the swing and stomp out the door. I

13

hate stomping, but I'm too angry to walk in a more lady-like way. A few wooden-slat steps take me to the beach, and I turn in the direction away from our condo. Maybe I'll sleep on the sand tonight. Anything to not have to deal with my former roommate for a few hours.

A salty breeze tousles my hair as sand scratches and scrubs between my feet and sandals. The waves crash against the shore, but in a gentle, come-to-me kind of way. So I do, letting the water splash around my legs. I smell the ocean and suntan lotion and fried fish.

I just want to breathe it all in. I don't want to think about Jolene and whether or not she's right. I've told myself Cole loves me so many times. And only love could have given me the ability to forgive him for his fling with that tart, Merryn, right? He's not like other men, and I shouldn't expect him to be. That's love.

Right? *Cole loves me* ... (breathe) ... and then, out of nowhere, an intense feeling of aloneness. Though the sun hasn't quite set, a few stars are already slightly visible, reminding me of the vastness of our universe. Reminding me how small I am. How small my life is. As I stare, the sky turns into a master blend of colors, from the dark blue of the sky above to a vibrant orange-pink at the horizon. So much beauty telling of a creator. A creator who seems as far away as those stars. Farther, even, because I can't see or feel Him. Haven't for a long time.

God doesn't love you. He doesn't even care.

I turn in circles. Left. Right. Nowhere to run. Tears pulsing. So I take a deep breath and dive into the ocean, clothes and all, and let the water wash away my thoughts.

Chapter 2
Catie

It's quite possible I will always think of this Belize trip as the time Uli and Jolene got into The Fight. I just hope we can someday look back on it and say something like "Remember when?" and "What a silly thing to fight over." But it's been twelve hours now … and as far as I can tell neither has said a word to the other since. Amazing how easy it is not to talk to someone when you're stubbornly committed to not talk to her.

Uli came back to the condo late last night, her clothes and hair damp and mascara streaked. Before anyone could ask what was wrong, though, she stalked past us and hurried to her room. I didn't see her this morning.

Whatever's going on with Uli, it's a lot more than being upset at us for not liking her fiancé, though that's big enough, and I hate that I feel that way. She's my friend. I want to support her. I want her to find happiness. I want that for all of us. But happiness sometimes seems so elusive, especially if you define it based on your relationship status rather than anchoring it in your position as a child of God.

I'm still working on that … and there's been progress. Like that night barely a week ago when a handsome but married man knocked on my door, and I rested my forehead on the doorjamb and wondered what would happen if I let him in and if that would be so bad. Then I prayed and, miraculously, God answered. Yes, a part of me still wonders what could have been, but at least I can fall asleep with only a tinge of regret, which is a much lighter load than guilt.

My sleep has been especially sweet the last few nights, with fresh air blowing in from the ocean and rustling the white curtains until they swirled around like ghosts trying to break free from the curtain rod links. And the humidity has put so much moisture back into my skin it feels like butter. I can't stop touching my arms. Too bad I'll be flying back to my Colorado alligator skin on Saturday. Still, in the meantime, I'm enjoying the best sleep I've had since I was diagnosed with uterine cancer.

Of course, it also helps if I don't think about the hysterectomy and subsequent cancer treatment I have to go through the Wednesday after I get home.

Yeah, Catie, don't think about that now. Because today I'm on a boat racing across the waves toward the main island of Belize. We're eating the best pineapple and mango ever, and the young men driving the vessel are telling us funny stories about the area and pointing out anything of interest. I'm happy—happy!—to merely listen with my eyes closed and the sun on my face.

We finally reach the mainland, and the boat maneuvers into a waterway where it has to slow down quite a bit. A shout interrupts the gaiety, and I open my eyes. One of our drivers stabs his finger toward a large ripple in the water. At first I'm not sure what I'm searching for until I see it ... a lumbering mass that slowly breaks the waves about ten feet from us.

Kate leans against the railing beside me. "What is it?"

"A manatee." And then I add, "Actually, I see two more. And that one looks like a baby."

"Wow," Kate says, and Becca says, "Cool."

Definitely cool. In a big, ugly sea cow kind of way.

We see so much of the area wildlife, in fact, that I wonder if the zoo will be redundant. At last our crew pulls up to the shore, where we unload only to immediately climb into a bus that, to my disappointment, isn't nearly as rickety or adventure-promising as the one in *Romancing the Stone*. It's white with green stripes and bumper stickers that seem to be everywhere but on the actual bumper. All the windows are down, which is the only thing that saves us from completely melting in the stifling heat. But that also

16

means the noise from the air rushing in and the laboring engine drown out any attempt at conversation. I smile at Jolene, she shrugs, then we both sit back to relax and appreciate a view unlike any we've seen before. No, this isn't our first trip to Belize, but last time we didn't do any excursions, choosing to hang out at the beach for the most part and spend our extra money on souvenirs.

Though I wouldn't have thought it possible, the Belize Zoo is even worse than the bus, humidity-wise. It feels like someone threw a sopping wet, electric flannel blanket over the land and switched it to high. The only one in our group who seems unaffected is Becca. Kate holds up her thick brown hair and mentions, for the third time, her regret at not putting it in braids. Libby fans herself with a page of Arby's coupons she found in her wallet. Jolene just groans.

"Remind me again why we're doing this?" She tries to wipe the moisture off her forehead, but since her hand is just as sweaty, it doesn't do much good. "I don't think I've ever been this hot."

I'm almost too boiled to respond but manage to mutter, "I've made my peace with it. Since I can't do anything about how sticky I feel, I might as well let myself drip and remember in a few hours we'll be floating down a nice, cool river."

Jolene nods but adds, "That's assuming I can last a few more hours."

"I have faith in you," I say and throw an arm around her. Then immediately pull it back. Sweat on sweat isn't good for a friendship.

Our guide takes off with our three friends and the rest of the tour group close behind. Over the next ninety minutes we see—and learn about—pumas and ocelots, white-lipped peccaries, and more monkeys than I can count. Plus, multi-colored birds like parrots and pelicans, and the venomous pit viper . But the true

17

standout is the rather repulsive tapir. The guide suggests we keep our distance because of its tendency to spit. Ew.

And then we're back on the bus, which now feels like heaven thanks to the fresh air rushing in.

Jolene gulps it in. "This might be the first time I'm so grateful for open windows that I couldn't care less what it's doing to my hair."

The other females on board agree, and a blond woman with a British accent who's probably in her sixties and looks more impeccable than anyone should in this weather, turns around and smiles. "At least we're all in the same boat ... or bus, as it were."

"Oven," Jolene says. "I think you mean oven."

"Furnace," chimes in Kate.

"Incinerator," I say.

Libby laughs. "It's not a competition ... but if it was, Catie wins."

And so we brave the inferno as we journey deep into the Belizean jungle, the road becoming more ragged the farther we go. My knuckles are white from clutching the seat in front of me, and I release my grip, stretching and wriggling my fingers to get the aches out and the blood moving again. At that moment, we hit a particularly deep rut—about the size of a canyon, I imagine—and I fly into the air, hitting my head on the top of the window and slamming into Jolene on the way down.

It's not hard enough to knock me out, but I sit there, stunned, trying to organize my thoughts past the pain thudding through my skull. Everyone turns around, and Jolene touches my arm lightly, as if afraid too much pressure will make it worse.

"Whoa," she says. "That was a doozy. Are you okay?"

"I ... um ... I think so." I gingerly touch the side of my skull just above my right ear, and can already feel a knot forming at about the same pace as the headache now working its way across my forehead. A wave of nausea rolls through me, and suddenly I can't get off the bus fast enough. Moaning, I lean forward and rest my head on my knees.

"Catie," Jolene whispers, "do you need some water?"

Unable to speak, I nod. It's a feeling I'm not used to—weakness. Jolene hands me a bottle of water and I try not to guzzle it down too quickly. It's warm but helps me feel a bit more settled and less queasy.

When we finally arrive at the small restaurant in the middle of the jungle about twenty minutes later, the throbbing has mellowed to a dull ache. Stepping off the bus helps, as does the fresh air breezing through the outdoor seating area. To no one's surprise, they serve grilled chicken with rice and beans plus the ever-present coleslaw. Only this time, the meat has a mango and red pepper salsa-like topping. Not too spicy and I savor every bite.

"This," I tell Jolene, "might be the best thing I've ever eaten."

She nods with a sigh. "You might be right. And I might have to put this on my wedding reception menu."

Yes, another of my friends is planning a wedding, and I get to smile and hear all about the cake and the flowers and the dress. And the honeymoon. I take a deep breath. *It's not about you, Catie.*

Again. Because it never is. How many times will I have to repeat that in order to hide my hurting heart? It's not like marriage is even possible anymore.

Okay, there was that inexplicable incident with my co-worker, Adam Sinclair, but I'm more and more convinced that was nothing more than a drunken booty call. The thought that I actually considered it has been the worst part, and I'm still trying to forget my moment of weakness.

Yet why should I be surprised that I was tempted? I'm human; I have needs. And it was wonderfully nice to be wanted. Everything inside me felt pent up and on edge, and in that moment I couldn't think of a reasonably good reason to say no. I had my hand on the doorknob … when my phone rang.

It sometimes seems like God has a fairly mean sense of humor. Because it was Tess on the phone, wondering how my date with Mafia Dave had gone earlier that night. It certainly seemed like a cruel joke. A timely call from the one person who most reminded me of the no's of my life: No, you won't fall in love. No, you won't get married. No, you won't have sex.

And definitely *no* children. Ever.

All blessings that many women, like Tess, take for granted. While I get to look forward to a painful surgery along with the radiation and chemotherapy that will forever end my chance to be a mom and, for all I know, marry, she has a whole life of love and family ahead of her.

Unless, by some miracle, God brings a man into my life who doesn't mind a broken woman with a damaged body. The biggest problem there, of course, is that I stopped believing in miracles a long time ago. Funny how I can be just as sure God loves me and has a plan for me as I am that His plan doesn't include romantic love.

And I'm still having a hard time reconciling the two. I don't want to feel like He's dealt me an unfair blow, but I do.

Our guides let us know it's time to go, so we finish our meal, grab our inner tubes, and start our trek even farther into the jungle. As we walk, Jolene tells me more about her wedding, and it sounds lovely. What else can I do but keep pretending all is well and all I feel is delight for this friend who's found her true love? As hard as it is to believe, what started out as four friends meeting for our Accountability Monday dinners, three are now looking forward to married life. I, on the other hand, have surgery and weeks of chemo ahead of me.

My head starts throbbing again as we hike our way through the jungle, and I take one deep breath after another. But my thoughts won't leave me be. Why do I continue to feel I have no worth without a husband? How can I know God is enough one minute and question His love the next? Will I ever really understand who I am in Him as a single woman?

Jolene has quit talking, and it might be because she asked me a question and is waiting for a response. I glance toward her. She seems to be concentrating on breathing and her face looks flushed. It's my turn to ask, "Are you okay?"

She whispers, "I can do this," and I'm fairly certain she's not talking to me. But I still respond, "Yes, of course you can."

My inner tube bumps against hers and she drops it just as we're stepping over a rather large log across the path. As we watch, it skitters down the slope behind us with, it would seem, no intention of stopping. I turn to Jolene, and it's obvious she's no more interested in chasing after it than I am. If we weren't at the back of the group, someone could have grabbed it for us, but everyone seems a lot more energetic, and they all keep trudging onward while we stare at the annoying tube now resting innocently against a mound of dirt about a hundred feet below us.

"I'll get it," I say, because it was my fault.

"No," she says, her voice heavy with heat and exhaustion. "I'll do it."

Yet neither of us moves. Then she glances at me. "You look a bit pale."

"I do?"

"And your face is red."

"I'm fine."

"Of course you are. And I'm full of youth and vigor."

Despite the situation, I laugh. The sound echoes around us, and I realize how quiet it's become. I can't even see our group anymore. "Hmm," I say, "perhaps we need to get moving or we'll find ourselves alone in the jungle."

21

Jolene looks up the hill and gasps as fast footfalls break the jungle quiet. One of our guides, tall, bronzed, and bare-chested, comes crashing toward us. He leaps over the log like a gazelle and, barely a minute later, is coming back up the hill, tube in hand. He holds it out toward Jolene with a grin, then says something I don't quite catch but interpret as along the lines of "lazy Americans."

"Let's go," he adds in his cute accent as he brushes past me. "We're almost there."

As soon as I'm able to breathe again, I whisper, "That might have been the most beautiful thing I've ever seen."

Jolene nods. "Sometimes God gives unexpected good gifts."

Yes. Yes, He does.

Chapter 3
Jolene

Surprisingly, it turns out I actually enjoy floating through river caves on an inner tube. Partly because being in the water is the coolest I've been all day and partly because it's so incredibly peaceful. At one point a guide asks us to turn off our head lamps and we sit there in the pitch black, listening to water as it drips off the rock walls and swirls around us, accompanied by the rhythm of our own breathing.

All in all, it's an unforgettable excursion.

Our return trip to Ambergris Caye is, for the most part, a reversal of what we'd done on our journey away from it earlier today. A hike to a bus then to a boat. And, at long last, we're racing across the Atlantic toward our little island, basking in the fresh, cool air. Breathing is nice. Other than that, this part of the journey is fairly uneventful ... until the guides start making rum punch and appease our need to snack with a beautiful box of Snickers bars.

Hmm. I wonder if I can convince Trevor we need to pursue some kind of island life.

It's been a fun and wonderful day, but my first thought when we finally reach our condo is talking to my man. I snatch a Coca Light—as they call it here—from the fridge, then hurry to my room. Shutting the door behind me, I grab my phone and a pillow and settle against the headboard of the rock-hard queen bed I'm sharing with Becca. Since she's currently resting in one of the lounge chairs on the beach, I have some time.

As if he can sense my desperation, Trevor answers before the second ring.

"Hey, gorgeous."

"Stud."

23

He chuckles. "Are you sunburned yet?"

"No, but my skin does have a lovely pinkish glow to it. And it's soft, like apple butter."

"Oh yeah?"

"Yeah, warm and spicy."

"Spicy?"

"Sure. Cinnamon and nutmeg and maybe a little cayenne."

There's a breath of silence, then, "I think I'd like to see that."

"I'd like to see you."

"So come home."

I grin and tease, "Do you miss me?"

"You have no idea."

I make slurpy kissing noises and he laughs again. After taking a drink of Coke, I say, "On a more serious note, I've been thinking about where we're going to live."

"Really? Does that mean Colorado isn't a foregone conclusion?"

"How could it be?" I settle a little more into the pillows. "Especially now."

"Because you have a daughter in Tennessee."

"And grandkids." With a shake of my head, I add, "And that's still weird to say."

"You want to move to Nashville?"

"I don't know. That's the problem. I think of the Springs as my home, but so is Tennessee. And then there's Cocoon House, which I can't even begin to imagine leaving. What do you think?"

There's silence on the other end, and I picture him rubbing his hand over his bald head while he considers my question. Then, "Well, my job is here too, but my home is with you."

My heart melts like peanut butter fudge ice cream on a hot day. I fiddle with the ring on my left hand and take a breath. "We'll figure something out."

"Sure we will. You can move in with me here to start, then we'll see what happens."

And the thought of living with him stirs my emotions and makes me wonder if ... "Do we really want to wait until October?"

"No, we don't. But your mother would kill you."

"She would. And my sisters. And Catie."

"And Uli." When I don't say anything, he adds, "Or not Uli?"

"We've had a bit of a ... falling out."

"Over?"

"Cole."

"Cole? I thought that was over."

"Nope, definitely not. And that's the problem. I think he's a jerk and she should kick him to the curb, and she thinks that's incredibly disloyal and an indication I don't want her to be happy."

"That's ironic."

"It's incredibly ironic! She's never been happy with that jerk. How could she possibly believe wedding vows would change anything?"

"From what you've told me, she wouldn't be the first woman to think marriage would fix her life."

He's right. Most of the single girls I know have had the same thought at one point or another, including me. Now that I'm about to join the ranks of the Mrs., I'm looking forward to how it *will* change my life. How could it not? Trevor has incredibly strong shoulders for me to lean on—literally *and* figuratively. And considering the financial struggles Uli has had most of her adult life, she has to see Cole's good, steady income as a source of relief. Since she's been barely getting by for much of her adult life, who could blame her?

"I think," I tell my fiancé, "she believes it has to be better

25

than her life now. And do I have proof it won't?"

"You have proof he cheated on her. And so does she."

"If only that were enough." I set the now-empty soda can on the bedside table just as someone knocks on the door. I tell Trevor to hang on and call out, "Come on in."

Catie opens the door and peeks around it. I cover the phone as she says, "We're going to head into town for supper in about fifteen."

"Sounds good. Thanks." Bringing the phone back up, I say, "That was Catie."

"And you need to go?"

"Yep. It's time for our nightly stroll into town for dinner."

"What's on the menu this time?"

I laugh. "Um, probably some kind of seafood."

"With coleslaw?"

"You know it."

"And tomorrow?"

"Tomorrow?" I walk over to the closet and pull out a soft pink and black flowered sundress. Cool and comfortable. That's my main wardrobe standard for the week. "What about tomorrow?"

"I … um …" he hesitates, and I pause in my preparations. "I like knowing what your plans are so I can imagine what you're up to."

That makes me smile. He makes me smile. And it hurts my heart that Uli doesn't have what I have since that's what she longs for. But it hurts my heart even more that she hasn't figured out how to find what she longs for in God instead.

On Wednesday, after a lunch of ham and cheese sandwiches,

fresh melon, carrot sticks, and tortilla chips with salsa at the condo, we trek down the beach toward town for parasailing. We've all decided to give it a go. Though I'm not a big fan of heights, I've seen the can't-miss-it yellow smiley-faced parasail wing—at least, that's what someone told me it was called—floating peacefully above the ocean. How bad could it be?

Since we're going in pairs, I grab Libby. She's the most likely to make me laugh, and that's just what I need. Kate and Catie go first at Kate's persistence. We were stepping onto the boat when she said, with a slight tremor in her voice, "The sooner I go, the less time I have to get nervous about it."

"Is there a reason to be nervous?" Libby asked, looking at me. I shrugged because of course we should be nervous. Scared even. But I take a position opposite to Kate's—*please let me go last*.

The powerfully built, dark-skinned man driving the boat said, "It's perfectly safe," to which Uli added, "Of course it is," like we were a bunch of idiots. The wish that she had stayed at the condo scrolls across my mind, which I immediately feel bad about. But the coldness between us has kept a cloud hovering over my beautiful beach vacation.

It's not the best way for two friends to behave, and at some point we'll have to work it out. I'm ready, but I can tell by the way Uli avoids me that it's the last thing she wants. After years of living together as roommates, I'm well aware how different we are in that respect. I always wanted to get things out in the open and taken care of as quickly as possible. Uli preferred to stew about it until she exploded with a list of grievances. I learned early on to rip off the bandage. Those blow-ups were a little tough to take.

Now, as we sit in the boat while it races across the waves, watching Kate and Catie dangle above us like a big, yellow bird with four bare feet, I can tell by Uli's expression every time I glance her way that she's had too much time to simmer already.

27

Well, I won't let her go to bed angry one more night. I'll have to pull her aside at some point and get this settled.

As if she can read my mind, Uli glances my way and scowls. I smile because she's my friend, and she turns her back to stare across the ocean. Wow. There's so much more going on here than just feeling like I don't support her relationship. It goes deeper than that, and I need to find out what's really going on.

Way too soon, it's my turn to strap into the harness next to Libby. Though it seemed to be a fairly slow process when the other girls lifted off the back of the boat and rose up into the sky, it feels like they shoot Libby and me into the atmosphere like a rocket. My nightmare of soaring into space—untethered and lost—seems about to come true, when the cable connecting us to the boat at last catches and holds.

Then, just as the brochure promised, we float above the ocean surrounded by the peaceful rush of island air, which is so different from what we breathe back in Colorado. I can see our entire island of Ambergris Caye and, in the distance, the mainland. The many shades of blue in the ocean and sky remind me of a paint palette, only stunningly displayed. It even smells wonderful, pure and tropical, like coconuts. No wonder the other girls had seemed so much more relaxed when they were done. Even nervous Kate and angry Uli.

Libby and I both sigh at the same time, and she giggles. "This is fantastic. I could stay up here forever."

I nod. "It's heavenly."

She glances my way. "Do you think …" she pauses and bites her lip. "Do you think God intended us to fly?"

"Fly?"

"Sure. I sometimes wonder if, before the fall, Adam and Eve could have if they wanted to."

"You mean, actually fly … like a bird?"

"Why not? Don't you ever feel like you could, but you just

28

forgot how?"

"No, but …" I look across the vast expanse of water, the air brushing my face and lifting my hair like a caress. It does feel almost natural. "It's a lovely idea."

"Maybe in heaven."

"Maybe." Then I grin. "Why not?"

All too soon we feel the cable begin to shorten as they draw us back toward the boat. I'm so disappointed, it occurs to me I will probably never be afraid to travel by plane again.

Later that night, as we stroll back toward the condo following a delicious meal of shrimp tamales, potato salad, and the requisite rice and beans, I throw my arm around Libby. She has interesting ideas, and I want to hear more.

The other girls are close enough that when she asks, "So, what is it you love about Trevor?" they all move a little closer to hear my answer. Well, all but Uli, who stretches her legs to move away from us.

"What's not to love?" I say, and they laugh. "He's just an amazing person."

"Oh, sure," Libby says, "but I'm going to need specifics."

"Mmm. I guess you want more than 'he's hot.'"

Libby grins. "That's only the beginning, honey."

"Oh, but what a beginning," Becca adds, and everyone chuckles again.

As I watch Uli pull farther away, I say, "Well, he's a good person—not just a good man but an all-around good person. He cares about people. He's strong but doesn't make a big deal out of it. He makes me laugh and will do just about anything to make me happy. And he loves me."

I glance around at the smiling faces. They don't seem to mind how corny I sound.

Catie says, only a little sarcastically, "Is that all?"

I stop short. "Have I mentioned he's a fantastic kisser?"

Becca punches me as Catie groans and says, "Now you're just rubbing it in."

Sensing a note of truth behind her teasing grin, I decide it's a good time to change the subject. We spend the rest of the walk discussing tomorrow's plans.

Soon we're back at the condo, and I go in search of Uli.

It's time.

Chapter 4
Uli

I know it's Jolene as soon as I hear the uppity knock on my door. The way she's been watching me all day, I had a feeling a confrontation was coming. It's actually a miracle she hasn't cornered me about it yet.

Well, I might as well get this over with.

As I open the door, I try to keep my expression neutral. "Do you want to talk here or outside?"

"I'm sure we can find a quiet spot on the beach."

"Lead the way." Before heading out, I grab a sweater from a chair as the nights can get a little cool. We don't say a word until we get to two plastic chairs stuck in the sand and take a seat.

"The main problem for me," Jolene says, jumping right in, "is that I'm not entirely sure I know why you're so upset."

"Not liking my fiancé isn't enough?"

She scratches her cheek and shrugs. "I've never liked him. You know that."

"But you don't know him. Not like I do. He's good. He'll take care of me." She glances my way and, because I can tell what she's thinking, I add, "And he loves me."

"I'm glad."

"Are you?"

"Uli, of course, I am. If that's what you want."

"I want to be married."

"To Cole."

"Yes, to Cole. Do you really think there's someone out there who's better for me?"

Jolene shakes her head, and I sense her frustration. "That's not the point."

"You want me to trust that God is going to give me a perfect life if I end things with Cole."

"No, that's not it." She pauses and is quiet for so long I wonder for a second if she's okay. Then, "I want you to trust that what He has planned for you is good, with or without a husband."

Ugh. "That's easy to say when you're engaged to an 'amazing man.'" Because I did hear some of what she said to the other girls about why she loved Trevor.

Jerking her chair out of the sand, Jolene turns it to face me a little better. "You're right." I barely have time to be shocked when she continues, "It *is* easy to say, but not because I'm engaged."

Now that she's looking right at me, I make an effort to not roll my eyes, but she knows I want to and she laughs. "Come on, Uli. You're so focused on this one area that you miss everything else."

I wasn't expecting that. "Like what?"

"Okay, let's start with the fact that all you see is my engagement ring. You don't see the years it took to get here or what I've lost along the way. You don't see me, Uli, or the sacrifices of my life." Her voice catches and the sliver of moon reflects off tears filling her eyes. "All you see is a ring."

"Jo—" and I don't know what else to say.

She looks down at her hands for a second then glances back at me. "There's so much going on in our lives, and you haven't even noticed. Catie has cancer and is facing a surgery next week that will end forever her chance to have kids. Have you asked her about it? Have you prayed for her? Have you even thought about what she's going through?"

I can't respond. She knows I haven't.

"And last week, I …" Jolene shakes her head like she's telling herself no. "Last week I had to deal with some … issues that were pretty tough."

"What happened?"

The increase in tears tells me it's something big, but all she says is, "It's a long story." She puts a hand on my arm. "I'll tell you and Catie all about it. Soon. This just isn't the time."

"Jolene, I'm sorry." We both stand up and move into a hug, and now I'm crying too. After a few seconds, I pull away. "I know I've been acting like a baby this past week."

Needing to move, I walk toward the beach, and Jolene follows. A breeze brushes across me, lifting my hair and making my sundress twirl around my legs. I love the salty, spicy, balmy scents of island living. It makes me feel like I'm in the middle of a suntan lotion commercial, without the great tan and perfect bikini body. Slipping out of my sandals, I step into the water. It's warm and inviting. With a sigh, I say,

"I feel trapped, Jo, between fear of what is and fear of what's to come. No matter how much I insist Cole will be a good husband and we can make it work, deep down, I don't really believe it. I'm scared I have to make a choice between being miserably unhappy with him or miserably unhappy alone." I turn toward her. "I don't have your smarts or business sense. You've seen how hard it is for me to find work and hang onto it. Every day is a strain as I wonder where I'll get the money to pay my bills. I'm stressed all the time."

Does she get it? I don't know but continue anyway. "At least being married to Cole would take some of that strain away. Maybe then I'll be able to breathe again … long enough, I hope, to figure things out and maybe get a better idea of what God wants from me." I'm talking with my hands more than usual, but this is important. "Think of all I could do if I didn't have to worry about money. I could volunteer to help the church and different ministries, like Cocoon House. Maybe then I could actually do something that makes a difference."

She smiles at me then. "You have a good heart, Uli. A

confused, love-starved, good heart. But all this tells me is you still trust Cole more than God."

I let go of her hand and look out across the ocean. "No, you're right. I don't trust God. How can I? He doesn't care about me. Not really. If He did, He would care just a little more about my broken heart and how lonely I feel almost all the time."

"Why would you say that?"

And it hits me. I know when this started ... and why. "Because of my dad."

She steps back. "Your dad? But—"

"Yeah, he's been gone a long time. I didn't even know he was sick until they put him in the hospital. He was there a week and, finally, Mom told me how bad it was. So I prayed day and night, begging God to let my dad be okay and send him home. I told God that Mom and I couldn't make it without him. I promised anything—everything—if only I could have my dad just a little longer." I choke down a sob. "And then he was gone."

I close my eyes, memories hitting me like the waves at my feet. I can't hear Dad's voice anymore or remember what he smelled like, but I have a sense of him—his presence, his love for me, the way his laugh was a deep rumble that was felt more than it was heard. It wasn't until years later that I understood HIV and learned how Dad had contracted it when he received blood during an appendectomy. A routine appendectomy killed my dad.

Once again, Jolene rests a hand on my arm. "It doesn't mean God doesn't love you or want good things for you."

I turn back to her. "Don't you understand? How can I not think that?! Despite my pleas, God ripped my dad from my life and left me with a mother who was too busy trying to find her next husband to care about her lonely daughter. I didn't think He would do that. And what it taught me was that He could take anything—anyone—from me. No one is safe. I don't trust Him because I can't. No matter how much I want to."

34

Jolene wraps an arm around me but doesn't say anything. We stand there staring at the dark ocean with only the dim light from that tiny bit of moon winking at us as it moves across the midnight blue curtain. It's like Jolene and I both decide to take a break from talk of heartache for a moment. And that's when we hear the other girls coming from the house.

"There you are," Kate says as she bounds toward us. With a twinkle in her eye, Libby adds, "We have a plan."

That's when I realize they all have swimsuits on, even though it's now well after midnight, and three of them seem rather chipper. Catie does not. In a monotone voice, she warns, "They've decided it's a good night to go skinny-dipping."

I'm so surprised I can't respond, but Jolene laughs. "Why not?" The next thing I know, she's slipped her sundress over her head and has thrown it, along with her underthings, on a nearby beach chair. With a flash of shiny, bare skin, she turns and races into the waves, shouting over her shoulder, "Last one in buys everyone key lime pie tomorrow!"

In an instant, Becca, Kate, and Libby have followed suit and are splashing into the water after Jolene, buck naked and giggling.

I look at Catie. She's taken off her cover-up but still has on her modest, one-piece swimsuit. "Well," she says, "what do you think?"

Glancing one way down the beach, then the other, I note it is rather dark and deserted. And yet … "I don't think so." Because even after over a year of sleeping with Cole, I still don't want anyone to see me sans clothes. Not so much out of a sense of modesty but more because I'm ashamed of the rolls of fat draping my mid-section. Cole finally quit complaining about my lights-out rule sometime before last Christmas.

Catie, however, doesn't have to worry about fat rolls and, before I know it, she's doing her own little striptease. "We might as well, Uli. It's not like either of us wants to be left out of this

35

story." With a grin, she kicks her suit to the side and skips in after our friends.

And that's when I realize taking your clothes off alone on a public beach is infinitely more difficult than stripping in a group. I shouldn't have waited. But the girls are clearly having fun, so I shed my dress and underwear and wade in. Unfortunately, my goal to get under the water as soon as possible is hindered by about fifty feet of shallow, rocky terrain. Since I'd been swimming in this area for several days now, I should have known and can only blame myself.

As I gingerly make my way toward my friends, I'm torn between not being exposed and not scraping my feet or twisting my ankle or doing anything that might cause pain and even more embarrassment. All I can do is move as quickly as possible and, at last, I reach my goofy, shameless friends.

With the water deep enough, I duck down to my shoulders. Jolene is telling the girls about another skinny-dipping adventure in college, and I say, "Are you kidding? You've done this before?"

She waves a hand at me. "Oh, sure. Twice in college and once while on a camping trip. In fact, we—"

Just then, Becca interrupts her with a "shush" and points down the beach. I don't see anything at first, only darkness and a few random house lights … until I realize one of those lights is moving. It's someone with a flashlight heading straight toward where the clothes and swimsuits of six women litter the beach. My heart jumps, and we all dip as low into the water as possible.

Libby whispers, "Do you think they'll be able to see us?"

"Nah," Jolene says, "it's too dark."

Kate backs up a little more as the light moves even closer. "What if it's the police? What if we're arrested?"

"It's not illegal," Catie says, then pauses. "Is it?"

Libby, our travel agent and tour guide, shrugs. "I have no idea. I hope not."

The thought of being thrown into a foreign prison for skinny-dipping is too terrifying to imagine. As the light reaches our part of the beach, we all duck even deeper at the same time until the water hits just below our noses. At that moment the light stops moving, then, to my horror, suddenly swings out toward the water, sweeping back and forth.

Nobody moves.

Nobody breathes.

Thanks to the rocky shore, we're too far back for the light to reach us, so we just wait. Quietly. The light moves a few feet farther down the beach, points out our way again, then clicks off.

We all take deep, frightened breaths. Becca says, "Is he still there ... waiting?"

"I think so." There's a slight tremor in Jolene's voice. "Looks like we're trapped, girls."

And the shiver that trickles up my spine has absolutely nothing to do with the coolness of the night.

Chapter 5
Catie

Exposed. That's the best word. I've put some effort throughout my life into not being caught naked, yet here I am, crouching in water that's barely five feet deep, hoping some stranger lounging on a beach isn't the first man to see me in my birthday suit.

Birthday suit. The fact that I might still describe nudity that way makes me so sad, I giggle. Out loud.

"Shh!" Kate nudges me and everyone glares, except Jolene. She grins like this is the most fun she's ever had. Though that might be true of me, I already know it's not the case for my adventurous friend. She seeks out crazy fun. I have to fall into it. Or wade, as the case may be.

I'm not even sure how long we've been waiting, but I can tell my fingers are getting prune-y. All I want is a warm robe and a hot cup of coffee. Unfortunately, we've all stared intently at the beach for at least half an hour and, as far as I can tell, our peeping Tom is just sitting there, waiting patiently for a free show. Well, let him wait. The only thing that will get me out of this water besides watching that flashlight continue down the beach would be …

Dawn. Eventually the sun will come up, exposing us all and showing Tom right where we are. We certainly can't stand here in the ocean for another five hours or so only to have, potentially, an even bigger audience. We have to do something. *Think, Catie. Think.*

I glance up and down the beach, but there's not much to see. It's not like there's a building or rock outcropping or even a close-enough dock to use as cover. And the water is so shallow near the beach, we can't even sneak up on him. So, that's it. We're just going to have to let this guy see us naked.

Great.

At that moment, Jolene turns around and gestures us all closer. "Okay," she says. "I'll be the bait."

Libby laughs at that. "What do you mean, bait?"

"I'll swim that way," she points to the dock about a quarter of a mile from us, "and make a lot of noise. Hopefully, he'll follow me down there and give you all a chance to get to shore and take cover."

Becca shakes her head. "We can't let you do that."

"You're not *letting* me do anything," Jolene says. "I volunteered. And I really don't mind."

"Ha!" Now it's my turn to laugh. "You might not, but I'll bet your fiancé would."

She waves a hand at me. "Oh, he'll be fine. In fact, he'll probably think it's funny. Besides, one of you can throw on your suit, grab my dress, and bring it out to me."

"It could work." Kate shrugs. "I don't see that we have much choice."

Becca says, "I'll go with you so he thinks it's a group," and the two brave, not-so-shy women strike out toward the dock.

Thanks to plenty of splashing and laughing, they do make quite a bit of noise. The rest of us hold our breath, our eyes trained on that spot on the beach, waiting and hoping. Then, sure enough, the light comes back on and seeks out our friends. As it starts to move away from our things and toward the dock, we quietly make our way for the beach.

We're about to the spot where the water shallows out. I can't see our stalker or the flashlight and can tell Jolene and Becca are almost to the dock. Okay, it's enough. I'm ready to get out, come what may. Squaring my shoulders, I whisper, "I'm just gonna go for it."

They all nod and, after a deep breath of courage, I step toward the beach, moving as quickly as possible across the stony

39

sand. In seconds, I'm almost completely out of the water. I can't stop shivering, though I'm not sure if that's from fear, embarrassment, or because I'm actually cold. But I don't see anyone, and my cover-up is only ten feet away.

And that's when the light switches on. He's there, only twenty feet or so down the beach, shining that stupid thing on me like a spotlight. Well, then, let him enjoy the show. Someone might as well. It doesn't slow me down, though, and, within seconds, I'm throwing my cover-up over my head and pushing it past my hips. It's low-cut and short but suddenly feels like the most modest thing I own.

Once I'm covered, I turn and look right into that light. I straighten my shoulders and just stare. Finally, the light wavers, then does a one-eighty, and he walks away. I can tell now that it's a young man, a boy even. I'm sure he'll enjoy telling his friends about the free peep show.

A splash catches my attention and I turn to see my friends coming toward me, dripping wet and laughing. I grab clothes and towels and start handing them out, and we all run down the beach a bit to meet up with Jolene and Becca. Soon, we're all decent again and make our way toward the condo.

"Catie," Libby says, "that might be one of the coolest things I've ever seen. And by 'cool,' I mean you didn't lose yours."

Jolene slides an arm around my waist. "To tell you the truth, I didn't know you had that in you. You've always been so … shy."

"Honestly?" I say. "I didn't know I had it in me either. But I realized I was more angry than embarrassed. What a jerk!"

"No kidding." Uli steps up onto our condo patio but doesn't go in. None of us do. We're all dripping saltwater and, apparently, no one wants to clean that mess off the tile floor. Fortunately, there are several beach towels hanging on chairs and railings around the patio after an earlier swim. We each grab our own and dry off as we talk about our adventure.

"Well," Becca says, "I think we should all chip in for Catie's dinner tomorrow as a thank you for sacrificing herself for the rest of us."

Jolene rubs her towel down her legs. "Absolutely. She's our hero."

"A naked hero," Libby says, "but that's a good way to save money on your costume."

Everyone laughs, but I just shake my head. "Does that mean nudity is my superpower?"

"It certainly was a good distraction." Becca grins and pats me on the shoulder like a football coach. "He was so focused on you he forgot all about Jolene and me."

"Yeah, well, that's peachy, especially since you two were supposed to be the bait."

"You were pretty amazing, Catie." Uli hangs her towel back over a railing and plops down on one of the patio chairs. "If I hadn't seen the whole thing, I wouldn't have believed it."

"I just wanted it to be over," I say and hold up my prune-y hands. "I'm not fond of wrinkly skin, even of the temporary variety." The coffee pot is calling me, but as I step toward the door, a low, familiar rumble in the distance stops me. "Sounds like there's a storm coming."

Everyone groans, and Kate says, "Well, that could ruin our fun in the sun tomorrow."

And just like that, the party's over and we scurry inside for the evening.

A fierce tropical storm does, in fact, hit our vacation island in the middle of the night. Around four that morning, a bright flash of light followed by a violent clap of thunder jolts me from my sleep. It's so startling, it takes a moment to separate my crazy, being-chased-by-a-flashlight dream from the reality of what woke me up. I take a few deep breaths to calm myself down.

Uli, my roommate for the week, rolls over and whispers, "Are you okay?"

"Yeah, I'm fine." I lay my head back on the pillow. "I've never minded storms before, but that was intense."

"I love storms."

"Really?"

"Yeah. My parents would let me crawl into bed with them when I was little. One of the few occasions when my mom was actually okay with that. Daddy would put his arm around me … it's the only time in my life I've ever felt really safe."

I turn toward her. "Is that something you struggle with? Feeling safe?"

"Sure. Don't you?"

No. Well, I say, "I suppose there are times I worry about getting hurt or that I might find myself running naked across a beach with a stranger staring at me, which can be a little disconcerting." She laughs with me, and I continue, "But I've certainly never been worried about living alone. It's never occurred to me to think I'm *not* safe there."

"But you've lived alone a lot, right?"

"Most of my life."

"That probably makes a difference. Other than one summer during college when I rented a studio apartment, I've never lived alone."

"Seriously?" I push up onto one elbow. "Just three months? In college? How is that even possible?"

She sits up next to me and runs her fingers through her hair. "I'm not sure. I guess I've always looked for a place I could share. It's a good way to save money."

42

"That's true." Another lightning strike hits close with the clap of thunder almost right on top of it. Then the rain starts—immediately, fiercely—and it sounds like someone's shaking a sheet of metal. Uli sighs and lies back down, but I'm not ready to sleep yet. Sliding out of the bed, I pad over to the window and watch the storm wreak havoc on our beach. The palm trees bend away from the wind as foamy waves batter the dock and shore. It occurs to me there might still be a few beach towels on the patio.

Since I haven't heard another word from Uli, I take that as confirmation she's already asleep again. Over the last few nights, I've been surprised by how quickly she can pass out considering her legendary history with insomnia, and I wonder if it's because she's getting married or because she won't have to worry so much about finances anymore. Possibly both. Maybe she finally feels safe.

After slipping on a hoodie, I tiptoe out the door, shutting it behind me as quietly as possible, then make my way to the back patio door. The tile floor is cold on my feet and for the hundredth time I wish I'd brought a pair of slide-on slippers. But the chill keeps me moving.

I step outside into a hurricane. At least, it feels like one for someone who hasn't spent a lot of time ocean-side. The wind practically pushes me over, but I manage to make my way to where I see a few towels flapping and barely clinging to the railing, which makes me wonder if some have already sailed to parts unknown. Grabbing the towels and a pair of flip-flops left by the door that I recognize as Uli's, I'm about to go inside when something stops me and I turn back toward the ocean.

It's fascinating, really, watching nature when it's this angry, and it takes my breath away. I want to be a part of something this wild even as I admit I'm not really sure what that would be. Yet this vacation has been full of these moments—moments that remind me I want more passion in my life. But what does that look like for a single woman? All I've ever known feels like false passion … or what I can experience vicariously through others. Books and movies and the romantic entanglements of friends. But sometimes I feel on edge, like I'm standing in the middle of a storm I can't feel. There's so much life swirling around me, and I'm missing it.

I don't want to miss it anymore. Something needs to change. Something significant—so significant that things like skinny-dipping and storm-watching and parasailing over ocean waves seem minor by comparison. A passion that might even point people to God.

By the time I get back in the house, I'm soaked. I drop the flip-flops by the door and toss the towels over a rack in the main bathroom. While there, I pull a clean one out of the linen closet to dry off.

As I rub the towel over my hair, change into a different t-shirt, and finally crawl back into bed, I ask God to get me through my surgery and give me a life of significance. Because there has to be a place for me to put what I'm feeling to use. A way for me to make a difference.

All I need is for God to lead the way. And to give me a heart that wants to go there when He does.

Yeah, that should be easy enough.

Chapter 6
Jolene

We're stormed in for our last two full days on Ambergris Caye. No more swimming. No more walks on the beach. We're trapped in our condo, eating leftovers and peanut butter sandwiches and imagining what we'd be doing if the weather was better. Catie's happy because there's plenty of coffee and the condo has wi-fi. Uli has read at least five of the short romances stacked on a bookshelf. She spends the rest of her time taking close-up photos of raindrops and editing the dozens of other pictures she captured during the week. Though she mentioned several times at the beginning of our stay that she wished she'd left her Mac at home, she's putting it to good use now.

As for the others, Becca told us she's writing a song, and Kate and Libby go back and forth between playing Mexican Train with a case of dominoes Libby found in a cupboard and binge-watching old movies on the TV in the living room.

In between messaging Trevor, my mom, and each of my sisters at least once as we make wedding plans, I've certainly kept plenty busy. Which doesn't mean I've stopped wondering how things are with Uli. Though I feel we're at a better place now, the relationship feels as strained as a violin string. It might take a little longer to get things back to the way they were than I thought.

On Friday, my daughter, Vala, calls. Since this is the first time she's phoned me, I hurry to my room before swiping it on.

"Hello?"

"Hi, Jolene, it's Vala."

"It's great to hear from you! How are you doing?"

"Good. Good. I mean, we're okay. But this isn't really a social call."

Working hard to keep the disappointment out of my voice, I

45

say, "Oh, that's fine." I take a breath, then add, "I'll take any excuse to talk with you."

Silence on the other end leads me to hurry and interject, "I'm sorry. It's hard for me to keep an arm's-length perspective. I'm always ready to just jump right in … emotionally, at least."

Now she laughs. "It's okay. My husband would tell you I'm the same way."

"You don't think so?"

"Well, I like to think I'm a little more level-headed."

"Me too." I chuckle, then add, "But over the years I've had to accept that I'm not."

"My youngest, though, is a different story."

"Olivia? Are you saying you have a level-headed daughter?"

"Level-headed. Stubborn. Brilliant. She's really amazing."

At least she didn't take after her ne'er-do-well grandfather. How blessed am I? The wonder of it all overwhelms me— again—and I can barely contain myself. I'm ready to lift my hands and praise the Lord for His goodness when Vala continues,

"That's why I'm calling, actually. Livvie is sick. I would have told you last week, but it seemed weird to bring that up when there was so much going on."

"Sick?" My heart races at her words. I don't know if I can handle watching another loved one with an illness after my sister Freddie's bout with cancer and, now, Catie's. Yet even as "I can't do it!" scrolls through my head, I know I can … and will. Because this is my daughter talking about my granddaughter, and I would do anything for them.

Anything.

It's a funny thing, love at first sight. People act like it's a romantic notion, but it's a blood one. I didn't even have to see my daughter to love her. And I don't have to spend time with my grandchild to know I am willing to die for her. So I say,

"What do you need, Vala?"

A shuddering breath travels across the phone line. "I'm so sorry to lay this at your feet," she says, "but it's such a God thing that you're here now. Just when we need you. Just when Livvie needs you."

The pain coming through her voice is almost too much. What I wouldn't give to be there with her now instead of thousands of miles away! Suddenly, the thought of returning to Colorado seems childish. I belong with my family—close enough to do some good.

"I believe in God things. And don't think of it as laying something at my feet but as taking some of your burden and putting it on me. You'd be surprised how strong I am. Whatever it is, I can handle it."

"All right." Another deep breath. "We'd like you to be tested to see if you could be a kidney donor for Olivia."

And that's when I realize how serious this is. "Her kidney?"

"She was in a car accident earlier this year. We all were, but Livvie was hurt the most. One kidney had to be removed and the other is severely damaged. We've tried everyone here without success. But you … maybe other members of your family … if there's even a chance. . . ."

"Yes, of course there's a chance. We're leaving Belize tomorrow so I'll call on Monday to set up an appointment to get tested as soon as possible. And I'll let the rest of the family know too so they can get right on it."

"Are you sure? I know it's a lot to ask a stranger."

I try not to let that word, "stranger," bother me and say, "Honey, I would give her both of my kidneys if I thought it would save her."

Her response is so palpable, I can almost feel the relief radiate toward me. I add, "We'll do whatever's necessary to save your girl, Vala. You're family now."

And even though she thanks me in a mostly detached, professional way, the wall between us seems to drop just a few more inches.

After I hang up, I make my way back to the living room. My friends are all engaged in their various activities and having a good time. But there's something I need to tell them. I've already taken too long. And though I'd rather tell Catie and Uli privately, I don't mind sharing the news with the others.

I clear my throat to gain their attention. "Um … you need to know what happened while I was in Nashville last week." They all turn to look at me. "I didn't just get engaged."

No one says anything, but they're definitely curious. I continue, "You see, I never told you—" and I specifically look at Uli and Catie—"but when I was young I had two abortions."

The surprise on my best friends' faces far eclipses that on the other three. Uli asks why; Catie seems too stunned to talk. So I share the whole story—about the abuse and the mistakes and the pain and how I sought forgiveness and healing. About discovering Vala and her family. I even tell them how my parents bought the old clinic building in order to destroy it, and I describe the day I watched it burn with a spirited woman of God named Nanny Rosa.

And lastly, I share my joy over God's perfect timing of bringing me into Vala's life just when her daughter, my granddaughter, needs a kidney. I tell them everything.

When I'm done, they're still surprisingly quiet. Finally Catie says, "That's amazing, Jolene. And wonderful."

"You think so?"

"Of course it is!" She smiles, tears in her eyes. "You're a mother."

I nod. "And a grandmother."

Then, much like when I told them I was engaged, my friends surround me in a giant hug. "This," Uli says, "is the best news."

48

With a grin, I say, "It really is."

The rain finally lets up Friday afternoon. Kate notices first, glancing up from a table of marching dominoes. "Hey," she says, "the sun's back out!"

We all scurry toward the wall of windows to see a brilliant sun clearing a path through the dissipating clouds like it's annoyed at the days it was kept hidden. Well, it's about time. Getting stormed out of your vacation kind of stinks. I mean, if I'm not going to be soaking up the sun and splashing through waves, I'd just as soon be in Colorado with my man.

Sadly, the storm doesn't clear soon enough to make our Friday excursion to the famous Blue Hole, a place where a sunken volcano created a shallow area in the middle of the Atlantic that's perfect for snorkeling. We had planned to spend the day there. Now, it's just after two, so not much time for anything.

And yet, Catie points out, we have to do *some*thing. That's when Becca shoots up a hand and says, "This is the perfect time to go kayaking!" Something she's wanted to do all week. Though paddling around a recently emotional ocean doesn't sound like much fun to me, I'm as willing as the rest of the group. So, we suit up. I throw jean shorts and a tank top over my swimsuit and, in a few minutes, we're strolling down the beach toward the little shop that rents kayaks and canoes.

Becca and Catie are all over being master of their own kayaks, but since Kate, Uli, and I are more interested in sharing the work, we opt for canoes instead. Libby doesn't care either way and offers to row with Uli while Kate steps gingerly into a canoe with me.

Really, I have no idea what I'm doing, but I settle on the seat in the back and hope for the best. "Any advice?" I ask Becca. "I'm new to this."

She seems a bit thrown by that and glances at Kate, who shrugs and says, "I went a few times when I was a kid at summer camp."

If I knew Becca better, I'd be able to tell if the look she gives Catie is one of curiosity or concern. But I don't, so I hope for curiosity. After all, how hard could it be?

"All right," Becca says, "Jolene, most of the responsibility to steer is on you."

"What?! Why me?"

"Because you're in the back."

"Right. You steer from the front."

"In a car, yes." She squints at Catie, who shrugs. Uli and Libby seem to know what they're doing because they're rowing in big figure eights while they wait for us.

"A canoe is different," Becca continues. "The person in the back determines which direction you're going by how she rows. If you want to go left, row on the right; if right, then on the left. But if you need to make a sharp turn, put your paddle in straight down on the side you want to go and push." She demonstrates with her own paddle. It looks simple enough.

Kate glances from Becca to Catie. "What do I do?"

"It doesn't really matter which side you row on," Catie tells her, "so your main job is to help keep the craft moving. If you feel the canoe going too much one way, that's the side you need to row on." At Kate's confused look she adds, "Because you row on the opposite side of where you want to go."

"But what Jolene does has the most impact on direction," Becca adds. She nods at me. "Why don't you practice? Row out toward Libby and Uli, then turn around and come back."

Okay. I square my shoulders and start rowing. I row. And

50

row. And row some more. My arms already feel exhausted, yet we're close enough to Becca that I could reach out and pat her on the hand if I wanted to.

I don't want to. I want to get out of this flimsy excuse for a boat, go back up on the beach, and stroll down to that cute little nail salon for a pedicure. But I keep paddling, switching the paddle from one side to the other, and so does Kate and, eventually, we reach the other girls. Now comes the hard part. Though I had planned to make a left loop around their canoe, I did it wrong and we find ourselves circling right. *Opposite, Jolene. Row on the opposite side of the direction you want to go.* Which kind of makes sense.

Even though I think I have it down, we still end up scraping alongside Uli and Libby's canoe. They laugh and Libby says, "Now I know how the iceberg felt when the *Titanic* hit it."

Ha ha. I say, "I'm laughing on the inside," as we make our way back toward Becca. Before we get too close, though, she says, "I think you're good. Let's get moving. We have less than an hour now!"

A quick glance at my watch tells me we've already been rowing for ten minutes. Only fifty to go. I can do this for fifty minutes. Then, pedicure time. So, I set my paddle to water and follow after my friends.

In about the time it takes me to paddle twice on each side, the rest of our group is so far ahead of us they're like specks in the ocean. "Come on, Kate, we need to go faster."

In between panting breaths, my companion says, "Do we … really? It's … not like … we'll get lost."

"Well, no. As long as we don't get swept out to sea." A look back tells me the dock where we started is now barely a speck against the shore, and I'm surprised by how far we've come. At least we're moving. And maybe Kate's right. It's not like this is a race, so I pull up my paddle and relax. The canoe seems to have enough momentum to keep floating in the right direction. Might as well take a break. We could even wait until we see the others coming back, then head toward the dock.

After a few minutes, though, Kate says, "Are we … going the wrong way?"

A three-sixty scan of our surroundings tells me she's right. And I'm not sure we have the ability to fix that. "Should we keep paddling?"

She shrugs. "Maybe. … Probably."

And the paddles go back in the water. I look around again, and we're even farther from shore than before. Our friends have gone around a bend and are no longer in sight.

"Let's go back," I say. "Let's just turn around now and go back. I don't like being out this far."

Kate nods and I get to work, rowing as hard as I can on the side farthest from shore. But no matter how many times that paddle goes in or how hard I pull, we don't move. We're still drifting.

And I'm not sure we're strong enough to do anything about it.

Chapter 7
Oli

I'd forgotten how much I enjoy canoeing. And I'm actually pretty good at it, considering how unathletic I tend to be. But it just seems to come naturally. Thanks to Libby's surprising strength, we're moving through the water at a fast clip. We're having a great time, until Catie rows up beside us and says,

"Um, where are Jolene and Kate?"

They're nowhere in sight. Granted, we've just rowed around a curve of the island. "I'm sure they're not too far behind," I say. "Considering who we're talking about, I'm not surprised they're having a hard time keeping up. And it's possible they turned around and went back to the dock."

"I'd better go check, just to make sure." Catie calls out her plan to Becca, who shouts, "I'll go with you!" and they start paddling back the way we came.

Libby turns and says, "We should probably go too."

"Why? They're fine. Just slow."

"Okay, but what if they're *not* fine?"

When she has a point, she has a point. With a sigh, I start maneuvering the canoe in a tight circle to turn around. Soon, we're on our way, only this time it's so much harder because now we're rowing against the current. In fact, I hadn't realized how much that current was helping us ... until it wasn't.

The added difficulty increases my worry for our friends. What if they got caught in a riptide? Or, worse, tipped over after being hit by a wave? Visions of Jolene and Kate frantic and crying out for help while the water drags them under overwhelm me, and I row even harder. I am going to be so sore tomorrow. But that's nothing if my friends are hurt.

We finally push our way around the bend and see ...

nothing. At first. Then, to my horror, I realize I'm not looking out far enough. There they are—at least it must be them—a little black dot in the distance. And the closer dots are Catie and Becca straining to reach them.

Since I don't see the benefit of Libby and I heading that way too and possibly joining whatever danger our friends are in, I say, "Let's go back to the dock. Maybe they can send a boat out."

Libby nods and we both put what muscle we have into rowing. It's too exhausting to talk. Besides, what would we say? *I hope they don't die?* That's something that doesn't need to be said.

It takes forever, but at last we reach the dock. My breath breaks out in gasps, and I take a moment. The shop owner runs toward us, helping Libby off the canoe, then grabbing my hand and pulling me onto the wooden planks.

"Our friends," I say, panting and pointing to where they can barely be seen. "They're in trouble."

His mouth drops and he yells, "Javier!" Soon another man comes racing down the dock. In a moment, they're jumping into a boat. Libby asks if we can go and Javier says, "Yes, quickly!"

And then we're off, bouncing across waves as we hurry toward our friends.

"If that's the scariest thing that ever happens to me, I can live with it."

Jolene shudders and takes another sip of coffee. It's not something she usually drinks, but apparently getting caught in a riptide and almost drowning gives a person the chills. And hot beverages aren't the easiest to come by on a tropical island, so she settled for coffee. She would have preferred tea, but we just went to the closest eatery we could find and they didn't have any.

Personally, I can't imagine being cold enough to drink that stuff, but then, Jolene and I are different in many ways.

The near tragedy has us all on edge—and hungry—so we order tacos, chips with guacamole, and I ask for a large glass of Mountain Dew. It's not diet, but I don't care. It's caffeine. Even though I seem to have mostly recovered from my food-poisoning disaster, my appetite hasn't fully returned. As a result, I've hardly eaten anything all day and will probably just nibble on chips with a touch of guacamole. So, why not enjoy a little extra sugar in my pop? Besides, it's the only thing that sounds good.

"It's my fault," Becca says. "When you told me neither of you had experience with a canoe, I should have switched things up so there'd be at least one person who knew what they were doing."

Jolene sets down her mug and puts a hand on Becca's arm. "It is absolutely not your fault. I should have listened to that little voice." She glances around the table and smiles. "It told me to get a pedicure."

Now, *that* we have in common. Kate says, "A pedicure would have been better."

"But this is a better story," I interject. "Add that to surviving a hurricane and our other adventures and there's plenty to tell."

Libby laughs. "Sure, if anyone believes us."

"I'm not even sure I believe it." Catie grabs another chip and, in-between crunches, says, "Especially the skinny-dipping story."

And she brings it up again. I have a feeling this is a tale I will hear many more times. Many, many, many more. Though perhaps I shouldn't begrudge her this, considering what she's facing.

Wow. Why am I not a nicer person? Everyone sitting at this table is kinder than me. Becoming engaged hasn't made me less bitter. Or less angry. I'd rather be happy, laughing, enjoying my

55

life. So, why aren't I? I have everything I've ever wanted … yet I look at Catie, who not only doesn't have the love she's longed for but is about to lose even more, including her chance to have children. And she's the one laughing. She's the happy one.

Why? Because she's content. She's found the secret, somehow, and it's not what I think it should be. It's God, of course, which just makes me more angry. God, who's done nothing but let me down since the day I lost my dad. God, who could do something but doesn't. God, who seems to care about as much for me as an ant under His shoe.

It's how I feel … and it's why I'm going to marry Cole and find my happiness on my own. Somehow.

Yeah. Right.

The waiter comes back to refill glasses and replace one empty chip basket with a full one. He's older than most waiters—in his thirties at least—and though pudgy, he has a full head of dark hair that has a nice sprinkle of gray at his temples. Best of all, he speaks with a charming English accent.

And he seems to be flirting with Catie. We're a fairly attractive group, but his eyes keep going to the redhead. I have to admit she does look cute in a brown- and pink-flowered sundress. The sun blushed her pert nose and cheeks in a way that somehow makes her eyes appear even bluer. She certainly doesn't look like a girl with cancer.

Or maybe this is what a girl with cancer looks like when she has nothing to fear.

It's funny, though, to watch this waiter, who introduced himself as Michael earlier, flirt with a woman who is completely clueless. Seriously, it's possible I've never met anyone with less game than Catie. He leans over and fills her glass first, smiling like a smitten schoolboy. She glances up and asks, "Where's the restroom?" and I try not to groan out loud. Then, to my amazement, he responds,

56

"You are beautiful."

The whole table—the entire restaurant, as far as I can tell—suddenly becomes silent. Almost like spectators watching a tennis game, we turn as one to look at our friend. She seems confused and says, "Um, I just … is there … a bathroom?" Like she thinks his comment is a diversion rather than a compliment. And she probably does.

"Of course," he says, unperturbed. "I'll show you."

She stands, still with that confused expression, and follows him to the other side of the restaurant. As soon as they're out of sight, we all explode into laughter, like someone just burst a balloon bouquet.

"What the …?" Becca begins, then, "What was that?"

Jolene wipes a tear from the corner of her eye. "I know she feels awkward around men, but I had no idea it was that bad!"

"I think she needs lessons in flirting," Libby says. "I nominate Jolene."

"Me?" Now Jolene's the one who looks confused. "Why not you?"

Libby holds up her left hand. "Let's compare ring fingers and then decide who's most qualified to help out our friend."

I wiggle my own engagement ring at her. "Um … hello?"

"Well, yeah," she says, blinking several times. "Of course, you too."

Yeah. Of course.

Though, since I sometimes have a hard time believing I'm engaged to Cole myself, perhaps I shouldn't be surprised when my friends forget.

"All I know," Libby continues, "is that I'd take advice from anyone on the fine art of flirting. I obviously have my own issues, or I wouldn't be known as the dateless wonder."

Kate nods. "Me too. Help us, Obi-wan." She giggles at me. "You're our only hope."

57

Catie returns in time to hear Kate's comment. "Who's our only hope?"

"Jolene," Kate says.

Libby smiles at me. "And Uli."

Catie takes her seat and sips from a glass of water as she looks from me to Jolene. "What are you our only hope for?"

"Flirting," says Becca. "You need help."

"I need help?"

"We all do," Libby interjects. "We've decided the engaged women need to help the single ones."

Becca grunts. "Speak for yourself."

Now we all turn to Becca, who shrugs. "I date plenty," she says. "Though I suppose advice on making a relationship last long-term wouldn't be a bad idea."

Everyone laughs but Catie, whose eyes are fixed on Becca. "You think I need help?"

"Well," Becca says, "you didn't even notice that Michael is completely into you."

"Michael?" She glances around the room as if some guy with a neon "Michael" sign will suddenly appear. "Who's Michael?"

All together we say, "The waiter!" and Jolene adds, "He was totally flirting with you."

And Catie looks confused again. "He was?"

Everyone grins.

"Oh, yeah," I say. "And you were completely oblivious."

"No," Catie says, shaking her head. "He was just being nice. That's his job."

Jolene says, "Is it his job to say you're beautiful?"

"It is if he wants a good tip!" Catie laughs, then seems to realize we're completely serious. "I still don't see it."

And it's obvious she means it, which makes me wonder if she's missed out on relationships because she simply doesn't know how to recognize when a man is interested. Maybe she

58

honestly can't see it. So I ask,

"Catie, can you tell when a guy is into you?"

She ponders the question for a moment, then says, "I suppose it's obvious because he wants to talk with you and spend time with you and actually puts an effort into it. And he shouldn't want anything else … not even a tip." Catie smiles, but it's a nervous smile. Because she doesn't believe that's possible. And I admit I kind of agree with her. The eager-to-be-with-me guy she's describing is not what I've gotten from Cole.

Does that mean he's not as into me as I am into him? He did come all the way out to Iowa to win me back. That has to mean something.

"It has to mean something," I say out loud, and all eyes turn to me. "Cole came to Iowa to tell me he loves me and can't imagine life without me"—or something to that effect—"and that means something. That is a major effort."

Jolene nods. "It is. But I don't know if it's a big enough effort to forget he cheated on you. Because you have to know, Uli, that if a man says he loves you and wants to marry you one minute then has sex with another woman the next, he's lying. How did he ever convince you otherwise, besides making the trip?"

"He apologized." Yet even as I say the words, I know it's not enough. How did he convince me his cheating on me was okay? Suddenly, I can't remember the conversation other than his sad face … and how sick I felt. And then he offered to pay for me to go to Belize.

"I guess it was a combination of things," I finally say. "He assured me it was a fling and a mistake and wouldn't happen again. Plus, he said he'd pay for this trip if I'd only come back to Colorado when it's over."

Catie says, "And will you?"

I turn toward her. "Yes. How can I not? We're getting

59

married next month."

And the true weight of that statement tightens the muscles in my neck and makes me want to throw up.

What am I doing?

Chapter 8
Catie

The trip back to Colorado on Saturday is uneventful. As soon as I get to my house, I drop off my things, then hurry next door to get my dog, Luna, from Colin, the neighbor boy who watches her whenever I travel. Luna loves that kid, and it's nice to know she'd have a loving home if anything ever happened to me.

After a long week of pretending I feel like my normal self, it's nice to have nothing to do. And that's exactly how I spend my weekend—vegging on the couch binge-watching the first season of *Chuck* on Netflix and napping. A lot. Meals consist of oatmeal or peanut butter and honey on an English muffin or a bowl of soup with crackers.

I'm so worn out I skip church on Sunday, even as a voice reminds me it might be a while before I feel up to going again. But I'm floating through a live-in-the-moment mindset right now and don't feel like making plans.

The phone rings around six that night and when I see who it is, I consider not answering. Tess Erickson calls about once a month, but the thought of talking with the girl who's engaged to the last man I had feelings for just seems awkward. Though I've accepted the fact that Brian Kemper is not—and never was—the right guy for me, it still hurts my heart to think of him and how he stirred my hope for the few weeks I thought he was interested. More than a month, in fact, of pining, only to learn in the most embarrassing way about his relationship with Tess. Here I'd imagined he was falling for me when, all along, he was already in love with someone else. And not just anyone. My friend, Tess. Young, beautiful, could-have-any-man-she-wanted Tess.

And I actually believed he might want me. I feel so foolish, I want to dig a hole and pretend it never happened. But Tess and

Brian are getting married, and she keeps calling. At some point I'm going to have to deal with it. Might as well be today. I answer the phone.

"Hey, Tess."

"Catie! I'm glad you answered!" Her voice is bursting with optimism, as usual. What is it like to be so carefree? She continues, "How was the beach?"

"It was wonderful. The week flew by, of course, but we had a great time."

"Oh, nice. I'm so glad you were able to make that work out."

"Um, thanks." Because I'm not sure how else to respond.

"Well," she says, "I'm calling about Wednesday."

"Wednesday?"

There's a pause and a rustling like a page in a book has been turned. "Isn't that when your surgery is? That's what I wrote down."

She wrote it down? The girl who's planning a wedding? Why would she do that? "Yes," I say, "I'm supposed to be there by nine-thirty Wednesday morning."

"Oh, okay. Well, I was wondering if there's anything I can do to help out."

"You want to help?" And again I'm thrown off-guard. Why would she want to do something for me? We hardly ever see each other anymore. "I'm not sure—"

"I could take you to the hospital. And once you're released, you could stay here while you recover. I have a spare bedroom that's really nice."

"Wow, Tess, I don't know what to say. I mean, Jolene already volunteered to drive me there, so I think I'm good, but …" Could I ask her of all people?

"But …?"

"No …" *I can't.* "It's too much."

"That's not possible." There's so much love and concern in

her voice, I really do believe her. But it *is* too much, and I don't feel right about asking. On the other hand, she might have a suggestion.

"Actually," I say, "I've been wracking my brain trying to figure out what to do with Luna." This is my biggest concern. I could be stuck in the hospital recovering from surgery anywhere from a few days to a week or more. Plus, I'll need to take it easy once I'm home, and Luna can be a handful. But I already talked to Colin, and he and his family will be on a camping trip for almost two weeks. And I don't know who else to ask.

"Oh, perfect!" Tess laughs. "I told Brian you'd need help with Luna, and he suggested we sign up as your dog sitters."

"Both of you?" How would that work?

"Well, me, mostly. The biggest problem being that neither of us has a place that would be good for a dog—certainly not one as big and rambunctious as Luna."

"Yeah, that's a problem. And she does better at home ... or close to it."

"Oh. Hmm."

I can practically hear the wheels turning. And there's clearly just one solution. I say, "Would you, um, be willing to stay here?"

She says, "Really?" and it's mostly sincere since we obviously both know it's our only option. "Because I'd be happy to take care of your dog and keep an eye on your home at the same time. For as long as you need."

I want to say no, though I should say yes. It would certainly ease some of my stress. But Tess? And Brian? In my home? And yet, what choice do I have?

None. With no other alternative, I tell her yes, then we plan for the two of them to come by Tuesday after work so I can show them around and start getting Luna used to having strangers in her home. I hang up and go back to the episode of *Chuck* I was watching. And wonder if Luna will be more amiable

63

toward Brian now than she was when we were spending time together last fall. Because if not, Tess will be on her own.

Though, I'm sure she can handle it.

I hope.

On Monday and Tuesday I go into work, even though my boss assured me it wasn't necessary. Mostly I want to take care of anything that came up while I was in Belize, straighten my desk, and return any necessary phone calls and emails. Knowing it's my last day at the office for several weeks, I work through lunch and make sure to send any information I'll need to take care of some projects at home while I'm out. If that's even a possibility. But I want to at least try. The more I can get done, the better my employer will feel about me working there. And I want to still be working there once this cancer business is taken care of. This is no time to be unemployed.

Shortly after six, everything seems as done as I can get it and, at last, I call it a day. As soon as I get in my car, my brain clicks on to the topic I've tried to avoid since Sunday—Brian and Tess in my home. I focus on being mentally prepared, though that seems as futile as thinking I'm prepared for tomorrow's surgery. I'm not ready for either but at least it will all be over with soon.

And then I remember the last time Brian and Tess were in my house: at Uli's birthday party in November. The night I realized he was, in fact, not at all interested in me because his heart already belonged to Tess. And I asked her to leave and promised we'd work things out someday … but we haven't yet had that conversation.

I'm kind of hoping she forgot about that. She *is* planning a wedding. Why would she care about our relationship?

Since I have over an hour after I get home to prepare, I finish packing for the hospital, make sure everything they'll need for Luna is set out, and use the last of my bread and cheese to make a sandwich for supper. I add a sliced apple and some mandarin orange sections to a bowl of cherries, making a simple salad with all the fruit I have left. I started purging my kitchen of perishable food items days before I left for Belize, and there's not much left now. Guess I'll see what Brian and Tess can use and throw the rest out.

Because thinking about food keeps me from stressing about the confrontation to come. Though perhaps thinking of it as a confrontation isn't the best way to look at it. We're just going to talk about taking care of Luna and picking up my mail and making sure nothing breaks down so I can come back to the same home I walk out of.

All too soon, the doorbell rings and, seconds later, I invite the man I thought I loved and his fiancée into my house. I start by showing them where I keep Luna's food and treats in the pantry, then give them a rundown of her day. After everything dog-related is taken care of, we leave Brian downstairs while I show Tess the guest room as well as the thermostat and the laundry area in the upstairs hall. I also give her the piece of paper where I'd written down important phone numbers and the wi-fi password.

Once we're back in the kitchen, I say, "And feel free to eat anything I have here." I point out a few things in the fridge and on the counter. "Especially any of this stuff that would go bad while I'm gone. And if you don't want it, feel free to toss it out."

"Thanks," Tess says. "I'll bring some basic things with me but will definitely eat the bread and veggies. I can't have dairy but"—she glances at her fiancé—"Brian can, so between the two of us we should be able to clear everything out."

Brian chuckles and adds, "It would be safer to tell us

65

anything we *can't* have."

Though I suspect he's joking, I feel it's important to point out, "Well, if you could leave some coffee and the English muffins I put in the fridge so I have something when I get home, that would be great."

Tess gives Brian a look that, I can tell, he understands, before turning back to me. "Don't worry. Our main goal is to help you during and after your surgery."

"Yes, I know. And I appreciate it."

We spend a good ten minutes talking about nothing, like what TV channels I get and how the DVR and BlueRay work. I might actually survive this. Until Tess says,

"So, we've discussed all the practical aspects of your surgery. Now, what about the spiritual and emotional ones? Do you have anything specific we can pray about?"

Well, that certainly feels more personal. "There's a lot going on." I glance at Brian, then back to Tess. "And a lot I'd rather not think about."

Tess catches the look. She pats Brian on the arm. "Honey, could you give us a minute?"

He nods and leaves. Just like that. Tess turns back to me. "Do you have any coffee?"

"Coffee?" That's unexpected. "If I make coffee this will take longer than a minute."

With a smile and a shrug, she says, "He'll wait. He brought work with him."

Does that mean she anticipated this? That she planned to have a chat with me? I mull that over as I put together a pot of coffee. Maybe it's because of everything that's been going on and because I'm tired and have health issues, but I just can't decide if it's good or bad that Tess came here thinking we'd have a heart-to-heart. When I turn back to her, though, her expression is so honest, open, and loving, I want to believe the best.

Before the Brian incident, I always found it easy to open up to Tess, even though I was never really sure how she felt about me. But I feel that way about quite a few people. How can you tell if someone truly cares about you? I'm not sure. Almost fifty years old and I'm not sure. All of which makes me wonder if I'm capable of close relationships ... and if maybe that's why I'm still single.

Do I want to share my thoughts with Tess? Not really. Not the deep stuff anyway. While we wait for the coffee, I say, "I'm sure everything will be fine."

"But it won't be the same."

Well, that's a weird thing to say. "What do you mean?"

She seems surprised by the question. "This is a significant surgery—not just the cancer but the hysterectomy. That ... changes things."

"I suppose." After I pour two mugs of coffee, I ask if she wants milk or sugar. She shakes her head, then follows me to the dining table where we sit across from each other. Since it's clear what she's getting at, I say, "But it's not like children were a possibility for me anymore. Not really."

"No, I guess not."

At least she can be honest.

"What about you?" Because I need to *not* talk about my situation. "Do you and Brian want children?"

She gives me a half-smile that doesn't go all the way to her eyes. "Brian, yes. Definitely. And ... I do. I didn't, but now I do."

"What made the difference?"

"A lot of things changed with Brian. I never thought I'd get married, so I didn't let myself consider the possibility of children. There's a lot I'm looking forward to." She stares out the window toward the backyard, her face soft and covered with love. To be that young and that pretty and that happy—it's hard to look at. For a moment, I can barely breathe, the ache of what I've missed

67

out on too overwhelming.

But I push it all aside and, within ten minutes, I've said goodbye, see-you-in-the-morning to Tess. As soon as they're gone, I crawl into bed. I don't cry because it won't do any good. And I'm just too exhausted anyway.

Chapter 9
Jolene

As promised, on the Monday morning after I get home I schedule an appointment to have myself tested to be a potential kidney donor for my newly discovered granddaughter. It's a much more complicated process than I had imagined—not that I've spent much time imagining what kidney donor testing is like. Since the earliest appointment they have available is over two weeks away, I send Vala a quick text to let her know before starting my first day back at work.

Next, I post to our family's private Facebook page begging them all to do the same. Within minutes, most of my relatives have promised to get right on it.

It takes the rest of the week to get back into the swing of things at Cocoon House. Fortunately, my staff handled the minor issues that came up like the pros they are, meaning I can concentrate on meeting with my residents and seeing how each one is doing.

No surprise, I'm mostly worried about Benita, who's been at the home since last September but has been having trouble with her former boyfriend, Diego, for several months now. Over eight years ago, Benita gave birth and has hidden their son, Luis, from Diego ever since, worried—scared even—as to what he might do if he knew he had a child. To prevent that from happening, she's stayed away from Luis, trusting he's safer living with Benita's mother in Pueblo. I've been working with her parole officer on trying to find a way to reunite mother and son safely when it comes time for Benita to leave Cocoon House a few months.

It hurts my heart to think of what the pretty schoolteacher has gone through since she made the mistake of falling for Diego Chavez so many years ago. But going to prison for being an accessory to armed robbery seems mild when compared to losing your baby. The events of the last month in my own life have given me a new perspective on the bond between a mother and her offspring, and oh, how I long to give Benita something I destroyed for myself—the chance to raise her own child. But Benita made the noble choice. She gave her baby life. I took life away.

But God in His mercy has forgiven me. And, amazingly, He didn't stop there. He's giving me a second chance. A chance to have a real future with the people I love. What's funny is how being this happy can be rather stressful, though in a good way. I can't just focus on my own needs anymore because I have invited new people into my life and gleefully given them permission to need me.

It's a "burden" I'm more than happy to take on.

In the meantime, I'm taking on a different kind of burden that doesn't make me quite so happy—Trevor and I have promised to go on a double-date with Uli and Cole Saturday night. Between wanting to show support to my friend along with Trevor's suggestion that we not spend too much time alone, we decided dinner out would take care of both.

Which would be great if I wasn't dreading every minute of it.

At least there's a lot of week to get through first, including visiting Catie at the hospital as soon as possible. I called her Wednesday, and she told me the doctor said she's healing nicely. But when Trevor and I arrive Thursday evening—the first time Catie's cleared for visitors—she looks pale and tired. It doesn't surprise me, though it does twist my heart a little, and I'm reminded once again of Freddie's cancer journey several years ago. "Cancer" really is more of a verb than a noun.

We promise the nurse we won't stay long. She tells Catie to let her know if she needs anything, then leaves.

"Hey," I say, sitting on a folding chair near the bed and

putting my hand on Catie's. "How's it going?"

Catie takes a sip of water. "Ugh. I want to go back in time a week."

"That was a good vacation. It went by too fast."

"It did." She sighs and slumps back against the pillows before smiling at Trevor. "Congratulations, by the way. You chose wisely."

He grins back, picks up my hand, and fiddles with the sparkly bling on my ring finger. "Thanks. I've been blessed."

"Yes, you have."

I don't like the sadness behind the exhaustion in Catie's eyes. She needs to know she's not alone. Pulling my hand from Trevor's grasp, I sandwich her fingers between my own. "You are the strongest, most amazing woman I know."

A tear sparks in her eye, so I go on. "Never stop believing that God has an incredible plan for you."

"Thanks, Jo." She trembles a bit and her other hand flutters up to cover her heart as she takes several deep breaths. "I hope so."

The three of us are quiet for a moment, then Catie says, "Tess and Brian are watching my house and taking care of Luna while I'm here."

"Really?"

She nods and takes several more gulps of water.

I ask, "How did that happen?"

"Tess volunteered."

Well, that certainly sounds like Tess. "And you're okay with it?"

"I'm okay with knowing my dog is in good hands."

"That's certainly true," I say. "But how awkward was that?"

She laughs. "So awkward. But good awkward. I feel things are better between the three of us now."

"I'm glad to hear it."

71

Trevor adds, "And we know Tess is happy to help you. Brian's mentioned how much she misses you."

What? I turn to my fiancé. "When did you talk to Brian?"

"We've hung out a couple times."

All these years and he still throws curveballs. "You have? When?"

"I don't know." Because he doesn't know why it should matter. "We got pizza once while you were in Belize."

A glance at Catie tells me she's beyond exhausted. I can find out how Trevor and Brian became friends later. The woman needs her rest. We say our goodbyes, and I hug her for as long as seems appropriate. When I get to the door, I glance back at my friend. She's already asleep. We step into the hall, and I turn to Trevor, who pulls me into his arms without a word.

I am a blessed woman.

Saturday night comes, and Trevor picks me up for our double-date with Uli and Cole. I have no idea how this night is going to go, and I've been trying to prepare myself mentally for just about anything. Then I realize how crazy it is to think that will do any good.

We decided to meet at a small local diner that's known for its ribs. It always looked a bit like a dive to me, but I keep hearing good things, so why not?

The restaurant is incredibly small with enough seating for maybe thirty people, including a handful at the counter. We end up waiting over half an hour for a table. Well, Trevor and I wait because Uli and Cole show up about five minutes before they let us know our table is ready. I choose not to believe that was intentional. Uli and I slide into the booth opposite each other, and Trevor sits beside me. Only then do I realize Cole is gone. A quick glance around the room and there he is—talking with a guy drinking from a ginormous beer stein. Seconds later, Cole has one of his own. I turn to Uli, who also noticed. She looks at me and waves it off.

"I swear he knows everyone," she says. "No matter where we go, Cole finds someone to talk to."

Since the only thing I can think to say is, "Someone besides you?" I choose to change the subject instead. Picking up the menu, I check out the various options. But the whole restaurant is bathed in the aroma of slow-cooked meat and tangy barbecue sauce, which kind of makes my decision easy. "I don't know about the rest of you, but I'm ready to try the ribs."

Trevor drops his menu. "I'm in."

Uli says, "Yeah, that sounds good to me, and Cole loves ribs too. I'm fine just going with that."

The waitress arrives and we order two full racks along with hand-cut fries and coleslaw, which makes Uli and me laugh. "I was sure I'd never eat coleslaw again after Belize," she says, "and here I am only a week later."

"Just goes to show you can't fight fate." I take Trevor's hand as Cole and his recently refilled beer mug join us. "We might have to accept that coleslaw will always be a part of our lives."

"It certainly was a memorable trip," Uli adds, which makes Trevor chuckle. He knows all about Belize—the good and the bad—because I kept him as updated as possible while we were there and filled in the blanks when we met for dinner the night after I got home. But when Cole says, "Coleslaw is memorable?" I wonder if Uli was as open about all that happened with *her* fiancé.

I say, "It's a staple with meals down there. At least, it seemed to be. That and rice with beans. Every meal."

"Well," Uli says, "not every meal." She laughs. "Sometimes

73

we had potato salad."

Cole leans back against the seat and gulps his beer. "Sounds boring."

I'm about to say something snarky about Cole's ability to recognize a good time that doesn't include alcohol when Trevor squeezes my hand. It's a cautionary move because he knows it's way too early in the evening for me to confront Uli's fiancé like I long to. But perhaps before the night is over I'll get my chance. Because if anyone needs a good talking to, it's that boy my friend plans to spend her life with.

Glancing across the table, I catch Uli's eye. I expected her to be embarrassed by her rude fiancé but no. Her head is up, and she's staring at me as if she dares me to say anything negative about her man. It's the craziest thing. I have no idea how to respond because she just seems completely blind to the character of the person she's decided to marry. Sure, he's good looking … if you like the blue-collar type. I'm more of a button-down shirt and tie girl myself, though I can see the appeal of someone more rugged. But there's a big gap between rugged and uncouth.

Well, if vacationing on a tropical island is "boring," I'll find another topic. Again. Something I have a feeling I'll be doing throughout dinner. Taking a deep breath, I ask, "How are your wedding plans coming along?"

"Slow," Uli says. "I can't seem to decide on anything."

I smile at my friend. "That's your creative mind. Too many great ideas to settle on one."

"I suppose."

The waitress arrives with glasses of water and a loaf of bread with cinnamon butter before hurrying away. I cut off a slice and spread a nice layer of butter on it. Mmm, carbs. Uli takes one and nibbles on it plain. She must really be sticking to that diet. I'm impressed. In fact, her face looks a bit slimmer. Good for her. A twinge of jealousy courses through me, but that warm bread with real butter just tastes too good. Besides, Trevor likes me the way I am.

Meanwhile, Cole takes his own slice and says, "Uli's doing a better job than she lets on. She keeps asking for money," he says with a laugh, "so it certainly seems like things are moving forward."

Uli giggles and nudges him with her elbow. "You're going to regret not making me keep receipts."

"It's only money." He puts an arm around her, pulls her close, and kisses her head. "Whatever makes my baby happy."

Well ... that was sweet. Just when I think he's one-hundred percent pure jerk, he does that. I study them closer. Maybe he really is in love with her.

"He's not in love. Not with Uli anyway."

"What? How can you say that?"

We're driving home, stuffed and satisfied with the most succulent ribs I've ever had—outside of Tennessee anyway, and I told Trevor maybe I was wrong about Cole all along ... and that's how he responds. I grunt, annoyed. "There's definitely more there than I thought."

"Hmm." He rubs his head. "Okay."

Sheesh. It's my fault, though, falling in love with a man of few words. "You have to explain yourself now."

"He feels ... comfortable with her. She probably reminds him of his mom."

"Oh, that's romantic." I lean my head back and close my eyes. *Poor Uli.* "Are you sure?"

"Pretty sure."

Great. "How do I help her?"

"You don't."

I turn toward him and try not to glare. Unsuccessfully, because he laughs. "I'm sorry, sweetie, but you should know how blind a woman in love is."

"Well, yeah. *I* know. But how do you?"

He chuckles again. "This isn't my first rodeo."

"I don't want to talk about your ex-girlfriends."

"Actually, I've learned this mostly from you. You do know a lot of women, love, and you tell a lot of stories."

It's true. I do that. And mentioning that women in love make bad choices sounds like something I would say. "But I really hate seeing someone I love make a mistake this big. It would be nice if she could see it *before* the wedding."

We pull into the driveway next to Cocoon House, where I've been living since giving up the apartment I used to share with Uli. Trevor puts the car in park, then turns to me and takes my hand. "Just keep praying for her."

"I know."

"God loves her more than you do."

I lean over and kiss his cheek. "You're a good man. Why am I so blessed?"

He pulls back. "Don't start feeling guilty."

"Guilty?"

"Because you have what she wants."

"Oh?" Trying not to grin, I plaster a confused look across my face. "And what's that?"

He waggles his eyebrows at me. "A dreamy fiancé."

I shrug. "Yeah, I suppose."

Then he grabs me and kisses me and nibbles on my ears and my neck until I push him away, jump out of the car, and race inside.

October is forever away.

Chapter 10
Oli

After dinner with Jolene and Trevor, Cole offers a few kisses and a quick goodbye before he drops me off at Mel and Lynn Baker's home. I've been staying in a spare room in the elderly couple's basement ever since Belize. Considering most of my stuff is in storage or at my mom's, including my car, I'll need to find my way back to Iowa sooner or later. I just keep putting off trying to figure out when ... and how on earth I'm going to pay for it. I'd rather wait until the wedding. I even asked my mom if she could drive my car out then, but she wasn't keen on that idea. Mom's never been a fan of long road trips.

Fortunately, I took two big suitcases on the trip, so I have enough to get by on, for now.

In the meantime, I'm job hunting and wedding planning. I barely have a hundred dollars in the bank—and wish I'd saved a little more of the money Cole gave me—so I have to be tight with spending. Which is why this free basement room, though small and practically window-less and clearly a welcome hideout for spiders, is ideal for the moment. In one month I'll be married and moving in with Cole. And making his house look like the home I've always dreamed it could be.

The first thing I do when I get to my room is check for those eight-legged monsters. I learned that lesson the hard way when a fuzzy black minion of evil jumped at me as I switched on the light my second night here. My heart hasn't yet returned to a normal beat.

To my relief, there's nothing to greet me tonight but Chilly, the Baker's gray and white cat. This was his room first, making me the interloper. I suppose I should be glad he lets me sleep on a section of the double bed at all. It didn't take him long to get used to me, though, which is good since we seem stuck together. As I pass the bed, I run a hand over the soft kitty fur, setting his motor running.

At least someone's happy to see me.

Since it's only nine at night, I watch a little TV while finishing up some work for my one remaining client, then hit the sack early. Because, really, what else is there to do?

Three uneventful weeks speed by, and I'm still living at the Baker's, still looking for work, and still planning a wedding no one cares about but me. Which means I'm keeping it so simple and cheap it's just one level above eloping to Vegas. An idea Cole found immensely appealing, by the way.

But before my wedding, I have Tess and Brian's today. The ceremony is at the church at five followed by a reception at a country club. Because, it turns out, Tess's mom put away money for her only daughter's nuptials. My main goal is to enjoy the day and celebrate my friend's happiness and not spend even one minute comparing my life to someone else's. I wish it wasn't easier said than done, but it is.

Since Cole merely laughed when I asked him to come with me, Catie and I are going together. I've seen her several times over the last few weeks and each time she seems a little stronger. But because I don't know how that will change once she starts chemo, I'm determined to spend as much time with her as possible.

Nothing like cancer to make you realize how precious someone is to you.

If it weren't for my fiancé, I'd be stranded without a vehicle, having left my car at my mom's before flying down to Belize. But

Cole managed to borrow a beat-up old Chevy from one of his construction buddies so I could remain mobile. Thank goodness. The big maroon monstrosity isn't the most visually appealing, but it will do. But since it would be nice to have something a bit more presentable, I give it a good cleaning—even taking it to a car wash where I vacuum and wipe down the inside before running it through the sprayers. At least it's shiny, and I'm not quite so embarrassed to be seen in it.

Catie's ready to go when I arrive at her place twenty minutes before the wedding. I mentioned a few weeks ago how surprised I was to hear she wanted to attend, and she replied, "Tess is my friend, and I love her. Nothing else matters."

"That might be," I said, "but I saw how hurt you were when you found out about them."

"I was." She shrugged. "But I'm not anymore." She didn't say anything else for a moment, then, "Brian wasn't right for me, but he is for her. I see that now. And I'm happy to celebrate with them."

So now she's coming down her walkway wearing a soft, sleeveless aqua dress cut in a 1950s style. It's a little June Cleaver-like, but Catie pulls it off. Even the strand of pearls around her neck work, which surprises me. That, along with her short hair, really emphasizes her long, elegant neck. Catie's always been more practical than stylish. It's nice to see her trying new things, fashion-wise.

As for me, I'm happy to have fit into a bright pink, new-to-me dress I found at a secondhand store that's a size smaller than what I wore a month ago. Somehow, I've managed to not only keep up healthier eating habits, but I've added a regular workout routine, usually a brisk walk with some running around the neighborhood and a little weightlifting. Though I could barely make it a mile without wanting to collapse from exhaustion when I started, I'm now able to go almost two miles. Considering the

79

way I was not three months ago, doing anything that works up a sweat is a win in my book. And it's nice to feel better about myself for a change.

It's especially lovely when someone notices, as Catie does soon after she gets in the car. "Wow. You're looking thinner every time I see you, Uli."

"Thanks. I have a ways to go that's for certain, but it feels good to be heading in the right direction. Hopefully I'll drop at least another ten pounds before the wedding."

"Well, don't get your hopes up. That's a lot to lose in two weeks."

"Hmm ... yeah ... I actually have almost two months now."

I catch her glance my way but concentrate on maneuvering through Colorado Springs traffic. She says, "Two months?" like she's not sure she heard me right.

"Yes. But it's good. Cole and I decided to wait until Labor Day weekend for several reasons, but mostly because that's the earliest my mom said she could get out here."

"Oh. That's nice." Her voice is small, and she doesn't say anything until we're almost to Academy Boulevard. Then, as if there hadn't been that long pause, she adds, "I guess it's nice to have more time."

"I have to go back to Iowa for a couple weeks anyway, and it's easier to do that before the wedding."

Catie's quiet again for a few seconds before asking, "Have you talked to Jolene? She's been working on plans for your wedding shower for several weeks now."

"Yes, she knows. We're just bumping it up until later in August."

And then more of the silence that's starting to feel like her trying to decide what she can say because she doesn't want to say what she feels she should. Since that's fine with me, I add, "Plus, it gives me more time to grow out my hair."

She says, "You're growing it out?" since she can't say, "And more time to change your mind," which is what I'm sure she's thinking. And what Jolene's thinking. For all I know, it's what everyone in a sixty-mile radius is thinking. Maybe even me. All that doubt has a tendency to confuse a girl.

"I found a nice up-do I'd like to try," I say, and spend the next fifteen minutes of our drive talking about wedding hairstyles and a few guesses as to how we think Tess will do her hair and what we hope they'll serve at the reception. And other thoughts on how the happy couple will celebrate their union.

They are, indeed, a happy couple and in a short time Brian and Tess become Mr. and Mrs. The two beam joyfully at us as they practically skip down the aisle. I turn to Catie and whisper, "I don't like it when the minister pronounces them '*man* and wife.' If she becomes a wife, they should acknowledge that he is now a husband. Because he was already a man ..." And I intend to say more, until I see how Catie's hands are clenched and her face looks a bit pale. I motion to Jolene on the other side of her, and we both help our friend sit down.

"Are you okay?" Jolene says and, surprisingly, Catie giggles.

"Why does it seem you're always asking me that?" she says. "Do I seem that fragile?"

Jolene tilts her head. "I'm just worried about you."

"Don't be. I'm not sure what that was, but I'm fine."

"You don't look so fine," I say, though it does seem like some color has come back into her face. If only I didn't also get the impression there's something she's not telling us. But I do.

When I catch Jolene's eye, the concern on her face lets me know she feels the same way. Whatever's up with Catie, she's not ready to talk about it with us yet. I only hope it's not residual feelings for Brian because that kind of heartbreak is hard to get over. But, for whatever reason, I don't think that's what it is.

For the rest of the evening, I try to keep an eye on my

friend. And go back and forth as to whether she's tired or sad or simply doesn't feel good. Or all three.

Once we get to the country club, we sit down to a meal of chicken marsala with rice and broccoli along with several other tasty side dishes and, of course, plenty of sweets. I limit my portions because it makes me feel better, and because I'm saving up for cake. A gorgeous orange and cream concoction that caught my eye the minute we walked into the reception room.

Then the dancing starts. But there's no chicken dance or "Electric Slide" for Tess. She went with classic ballroom dancing, and as the couples glide across the floor in their flowing skirts and sharp suits, I go back and forth between being glad Cole isn't here and wishing he was. Really, though, it's better that he's not. The man wouldn't glide across a floor with me if it was coated in ice. Dancing, he's told me several times, is for sissies.

The charmer.

Trevor and Jolene, however, look like they're competing on *Dancing with the Stars*. Not so much because they have the moves—though they certainly have a few—but because they're so right together. Yes, they have something Cole and I don't. It doesn't mean what I have is wrong. It's just different. I can't waste time comparing my life with Jolene's. What's right for me isn't necessarily right for her.

That said, it would be nice if my friend and her fiancé would dial back the Hallmark movie clichés a bit.

Well, I have better things to do than stare at a roomful of happy pairs. Where's Catie? I promise to keep an eye on her and, just like that, I've lost her. She'd be a good person to talk to about something besides weddings, but I was so caught up in the dance performance I didn't see her leave the table.

A quick scan of the room doesn't show me where she is … until I finally spy her through the large windows looking out over the golf course. She's sitting on the patio sipping punch, alone.

And it's unclear whether she chose to be away from everything or would appreciate company. Hoping it's the latter, I grab a few choice snacks from the buffet table, refill my own punch cup, and slip through the French doors to the patio.

Catie smiles as I walk toward her. A good sign. As I set my contraband down, she says, "It's just too nice a night to be stuck inside."

She's right. It's a gorgeous July evening. The air has a smoky quality, which can be disconcerting this time of year, but it melds with the setting sun, spreading a pinkish glow across the lush green hills around us. Considering the intensely dry summer we've had so far, I can only imagine how much they paid to keep the grounds watered. And I feel a bit pampered, sitting here enjoying something so extravagant without it costing me a cent, other than my portion of the large toaster Catie and I went in on as a wedding gift.

We sit silently for a moment, munching on delicate hors d'oeuvres, including pinwheels with turkey, cream cheese, dill, and other bits of heaven that I could eat forever, and staring at the morphing colors of sunset. Then Catie says,

"I am happy for you, Uli." Her eyes glisten a bit, and she closes them with a sigh. "At least you don't have to do all this alone anymore."

Yes. At least there's that.

Chapter 11
Catie

Weddings. This is my year of them. One after another. Next is Uli's in August, followed by Jolene's in the fall. That will mean every one of our accountability group will soon be married except me. But now that I've made it through Tess and Brian's, the others should be a breeze. I've kept my emotions under control today by reminding myself Tess is not marrying my man. He's not for me, and he never was. I saw in Brian something that wasn't there. It's not the first time I've fallen for the idea of someone rather than the real person.

Why do I keep doing that?

Though I'd decided a month ago to spend time in Ohio after the weddings, with the date change of Uli's ceremony it occurs to me that I could actually leave for home as soon as possible. And I don't miss how telling it is that I think of Ohio as home. With months to go in my recovery, my family encouraged me to spend more time there so they could help me through chemo. Another plus—we'll be able to start it earlier now.

After quietly enjoying the sunset over the golf course with Uli, I hunt down Libby. As expected, she's sitting with a group of friends from the singles group, joking about who's brave enough to join the catch-the-bouquet crowd.

I put a hand on Libby's shoulder and lean down. "Do you have a minute?"

She seems surprised but says, "Sure." We move to an empty table, and she asks, "What's up?"

"I found out tonight that Uli's changed her wedding date to later in August, which means I could leave for Ohio two weeks earlier."

"Oh, nice. The sooner the better, right?"

"Exactly. How hard would it be to change my flight?"

She taps a fingernail on the table. "You're flying into Columbus, right?" I nod, and she continues, "There's a good chance you can catch a flight that's not full, but you'll have to pay a fee. Let me work my magic, though, and see if I can keep that price down. Considering the circumstances."

"That would be great." I pause for a second, then, "I can't tell you how much I appreciate your help with all this."

"It's no problem. That's why I get paid so much." She grins and pats my arm. "But seriously, I'm happy to do whatever I can. I love my work, especially that aspect of it."

And she means it. I've met only a few people in my life who always mean what they say and say what they mean, and Libby is one of them. She gives me a hug, then giggles when Brian gets up and announces it's time to toss the bouquet.

As Libby stands, I say, "You're going up there?"

"Why not?" She laughs again with a shy shrug. "Even if it doesn't mean I'm the next bride, I could leave with a very pretty flower bouquet. Nothing wrong with that."

True. Tess's bouquet of peach-hued peonies and orange calla lilies is gorgeous. Libby saunters over to join a group of mostly younger women. Girls, actually. Huh. Well, I want a shot at it too. It's a rather small group of females with various degrees of desperation on their faces. Keeping my expression as neutral as possible, I wiggle my way up next to Libby and give her a competitive nudge. She throws her arm in front of me, so I push forward and do the same, laughing along with her. Soon, everyone is jostling for a better position … including Uli, who suddenly shows up at my side.

"Hey," Libby says, "not fair! You're already engaged."

Uli bares her teeth in what's either a grin or a snarl—probably the latter—and says, "What's wrong with a little insurance?"

85

Oh, sure. "I don't think so." I wave my hand at Tess. "Help me out here, friend." She nods and turns around. Seconds later, an explosion of orange and peach flies over her head, aimed in a perfect trajectory for ... Uli. Not willing to give up that easily, I reach out my hand. A ribbon catches in my fingers, and I pull back. The momentum causes the bouquet to fly up into the air and plop down ... right into my hands.

Everyone stares at me, almost as astonished as I feel, and someone starts to clap. Soon, the room is applauding. Uli shakes her head with a slight grin. "Couldn't happen to a better person," she says. Then she hugs me. And Libby hugs me. Then Tess, and Kate, and Jolene. For a moment, I feel like I'm in a wedding receiving line what with all the good wishes and congratulations.

If only catching a bouquet had any power over my marital status. But seeing as this is my third one and the first catch was over twenty-five years ago, that seems unlikely.

Oh, what difference does it make anyway? The flowers are beautiful and smell a little like heaven must, and they'll look lovely on my dining table until I leave. Maybe I'll even take them with me.

When it's time for the garter toss, I wait in anticipation since everyone knows I have to dance with whoever catches it. Not that I have many options as I'm pretty sure I know all the single guys who'll participate. Mafia Dave, Scott, even Wes—the man I had a two-day crush on in May but who's now dating single mom Heather. Stunning in a tight deep blue dress, she smiles sweetly at Wes as he takes his place with the other men.

Wow. This could be bad.

Except it's not. Well, not as bad as it could have been. A chubby-faced boy who can't be more than fourteen makes the catch like he's outfielding at a Little League game. And he's not embarrassed at all but takes my hand and leads me to the middle of the floor. We sway to the Celine Dion song, "That's the Way

86

It Is," my hands on his shoulders, his at my waist. I could kiss Tess for not choosing something cheesy and romantic. And I would if she wasn't waltzing with her husband, who seems happy to handle all the Tess kissing for me.

And longing hits my heart again. How I wish I could keep it at bay, but it's like an air bubble inside me that occasionally works its way to my heart and makes it thump out of rhythm for a moment. It's an emptiness that feels fillable. Like there should be someone there. As soon as the song ends, I thank my grinning dance partner and scan the room, hoping to find Uli. Hoping she's ready to leave as soon as they cut the cake. But it's Jolene who captures my attention when she beckons me over.

She's alone, surprisingly, so I join her at a table near the edge of the dance floor.

"That was adorable," she says.

"Oh, yeah? I think he might be a tad too young for me though."

"That's too bad." Jolene lifts her eyebrows at me. "He was kind of cute."

I laugh. "And not a bad little dancer." Then we both say, "Oh well," at the same time and laugh again. Just as I've decided to get up and snag my water glass from my table, Jolene hands me one from hers. "It's mine," she says, "but I've been drinking tea."

"Thanks." After taking a few sips, I ask, "Where's Trevor?"

She gives me a "what-are-you-gonna-do" grin and says, "He found out they're showing a Rockies game in the lounge and went to check it out."

"And you don't mind?"

"Eh." She lifts one shoulder. "I decided some time ago that if I'm going to be in a relationship with a man who likes sports, I'd better be okay with it. Which means I don't begrudge him his games, and every once in a while he goes antique shopping with

87

me."

"Sounds like a fair trade." And though I try to stop it, a sigh slips out. "The mystery of how relationships work amazes me. Even though I don't believe in soul mates, there's still something magical about it."

"I suppose." She watches me for a few seconds. "Wait. What's going on? You look like you're about to cry."

And just the words make a few more tears fill my eyes. Do I dare say it? Will she think I'm crazy? Yet, it seems if anyone might possibly understand, it would be Jolene. I take a deep breath. "I miss him," and my voice breaks.

"Who?" Her eyes track the room, then come back to me. There's dismay in her voice when she asks, "Brian?"

That's comical. "No. Definitely not Brian."

"Then who?"

"Him. Whoever *he* is. I feel this emptiness … that there's someone I'm supposed to be with and sometimes his absence from my life physically hurts. Like he's just out of reach. I wonder what he's doing and why he's doing it without me." Though I've managed to get the crying under control, Jolene scoots closer and wraps an arm around me. I continue, "And then I get angry at him—or at God … maybe both of them— because here I am almost fifty and waiting and I don't understand why."

Jolene pulls back, her eyes studying mine. "You really feel him? Or … his absence?"

I nod because sometimes talking hurts too much.

"But …" and I sense her confusion as she asks, "do you know who he is?"

Now it's my turn to pull back. "Of course not."

"So … you miss someone you've never met?"

Okay, she doesn't understand. I wipe my eyes with one of the still-clean cloth napkins on the table. "And now I'm weird."

She shakes her head, and her expression turns intensely serious. "No, absolutely not. Feeling that kind of loss has never occurred to me, but it makes sense." I can tell she's thinking it through, which I appreciate. "Actually, if I'd never met Trevor, I believe I'd feel his absence."

"You would?"

"Maybe. I don't know. But we certainly have a connection I can't explain."

At that moment, Trevor comes back into the room and beelines straight for Jolene. He's barely five feet away when he says, "Are you all right?"

Wow. That is a connection. And it makes me miss *him* even more.

She looks at me questioningly, and I whisper, "Yeah, you can ask him."

Jolene grabs her fiancé's hand and pulls him down next to her. "Do you think you'd miss me if we'd never met?"

The man glances from her to me and back to her, like he's hoping one of us will tell him the right answer to that question. "Um, I don't think that's possible."

"Really? You don't think you'd have any heart indication that something important was missing in your life?"

"Those are two different questions."

I agree. "He's right."

"Yes," Jolene admits, "I suppose so." She turns back to Trevor, still holding his hand. "What I want to know is if you think you'd feel there was something missing from your life. Something important?"

He rubs his head with his other hand, then, after a moment, says, "I believe I would."

Jolene grins and they stare at each other. And that hole in my heart stretches just a little bigger.

Where's Uli?

89

It's time to go.

~ 🐾 ~

Three days later I'm back in Ohio thanks to Libby's skills as a travel agent. I walk through airport security, wondering who came to meet me. To my amazement, my dad and brother, James, are there as well as my sister-in-law, Delia, and nephew, Patrick, with his wife, Tawny. Nothing could have shown me more clearly how glad they are to have me home. We hug, then hurry to where I'm supposed to pick up Luna. It's her first flight, and I spent the entire trip worried about her and hoping she was okay. But I could hardly leave her behind for weeks that could turn into months. Besides, everyone reassured me she'd be fine.

And, to my relief, she is. Her tail wags violently against the kennel bars as she barks her greeting. As soon as she's free, she jumps on me, and I laugh as I attach a leash. Minutes later, we join Patrick and Tawny, who went to pull my suitcases from baggage claim and, just like that, we're soon on our way. That's when Tawny tells me they left their three young kids at home with my niece, Angela.

It takes over an hour to get from the Columbus airport to home, so we drive through Culver's in Marysville on the way. I'm so happy to be with family back in my neck of the woods that I don't mind the sticky heat of July that comes hand-in-hand with summers in Ohio. In fact, it feels rather nice, as I've never been fond of cold weather.

Now I'm surrounded by the love of my family as we chow on hamburgers and ice cream, and all I can think is, *I'm home. This is my home.* Colorado feels a world away. This is where I should be.

But do I have the courage to pack up my Colorado life and

move across the country? Yet, even as I ponder that question, I realize that's not the one I should be asking. The real question is, what do I have to go back to Colorado for that's worth leaving all I have here?

Chapter 12
Jolene

Not a match.

Weeks of waiting only to find out I can't help my grandchild. And now I have to call my daughter and give her the bad news. Might as well rip off the bandage.

When Vala answers, she only says, "Jolene?" but I hear the hope in her voice.

"I'm so sorry, sweetheart."

And then, silence. No, not silence, because grief isn't quiet. We share it, though, and all I can do is wish I were there to hold her. But would she even want me to? I whisper, "We're not done, so don't give up yet. Several of my siblings have gone in to be tested, as have both of my parents. Please keep hoping, Vala."

"I will. Of course I will."

"How's Livvie doing?"

"She's good. Fine." A sigh trembles through my phone. "But weak and tired. She might have to be admitted to the hospital soon."

"And then what?"

"More waiting."

Shoring up my will, I say, "If it's all right with you, I'd like to come visit. Spend some time with you and Livvie and the rest of your family."

"You don't have to do that, Jolene."

Have to? Does she think I feel obligated? The truth deflates me. Probably. She doesn't know me. She doesn't know how much I love them. But since I don't want to make her uncomfortable, I say, "My parents have asked me to visit soon. My mom and sisters want to help me shop for a wedding dress, and they're pretty sure Nashville is the only place for that."

"Well," Vala says, and I hear the smile in her voice, "they're not wrong." A brief pause and then, "When are you coming out?"

"Soon, I hope, but I'm not sure. It depends on work and when I can find a cheap flight. And a good friend is getting married at the end of August so I'd have to make it work before that or wait until September."

"Yeah, that doesn't give you much time."

"No. But I can't spend more than a week there anyway because of my job."

"You run a halfway house, right?"

She remembered. "Technically, it's for women transitioning back to normal life after prison, so yes."

"I'd love to hear more about it."

"You would?"

"Sure." She chuckles and adds, "Like you said, we're family."

And my heart skips a whole new rhythm as I tell her about Cocoon House and my work there.

"It's amazing," I tell Freddie while at her house for dinner that night. "Every time we talk, I feel us growing that much closer."

My sister looks up from mixing the ingredients together for potato salad. Everything but the hard-boiled eggs, which I'm in the process of peeling. A very frustrating process because they're new eggs and, as such, are reluctant to let the shells go. When Freddie handed me the task, she said, "Sorry, sis. I wasn't paying attention and accidentally used the eggs Sam bought last night."

Which means it's taking me forever to peel these things, and they look like they've been pounded by mallets. Oh well. The taste is the same. Since Sam and Trevor have already finished grilling the burgers and at least half of Freddie's seven kids have set the table and lined up everything else a good picnic needs on the counter, these eggs are basically the only thing we're waiting on to eat. But you just cannot hurry an egg that doesn't want to peel.

In the meantime, I've been telling my sister all about my fabulous phone call with Vala earlier. "Anyway," I conclude, "as soon as I can make it work, I'm heading back to Nashville."

Freddie stops stirring. "You are? You mean, you're going this summer?"

"Hopefully. Why?"

The men stride in carrying platters of grilled meat. It smells heavenly. Freddie says, "Sam and I have been talking about taking the kids for a week this summer, before school starts. Maybe we could coordinate our travels."

Sam adds, "We're just trying to work up the courage for that kind of a road trip."

Hmm. A road trip would save me money. And they have a big, twelve-passenger van so there would be room for me. It would be cozy with all the necessary luggage, but we could make it work.

Might as well throw the idea out there. "Well, if you had, say, an aunt with you, she could help with the kids and driving."

Freddie laughs. "She could if she's crazy."

Trevor throws an arm around me and grins. "You're in luck!"

"How about you, Trev?" Sam says. "Want to join the madness?"

"That would be great, but I have to work." Though he sounds disappointed, I'm not so sure he is. From all I know about my man—and I know quite a bit—I've never seen anything in his personality that screams, "Road trip!" As far as I can tell, he flies anywhere that would take longer than a few hours to drive.

It's something that will have to change if he plans on becoming a permanent member of the Woods clan because we love our road trips. In fact, some of our adventures are legendary. And I'd like to see Trevor become a part of that. Preferably willingly.

His expression, though, tells me I have about as much chance of talking him into a road trip as he has of convincing me to join him on a ropes course. And believe me, he has asked. I wish I could say I didn't laugh out loud the first time he suggested it.

I love how different we are. Even if some of those differences will drive me crazy someday.

Walking over to Trevor, I loop my arm through his. "Maybe you could make it work, babe. Don't you have a lot of saved-up vacation days?"

He picks up a piece of onion from the relish tray and starts noshing on it like it's an apple slice. "I do," he says, nodding. "Almost twenty, actually. But I thought I'd save them for wedding and honeymoon time."

Ah. That explains the "are you kidding?" glint in his eyes. "How long of a honeymoon are you planning?"

"Three weeks."

"Three weeks?!"

Freddie takes the at-long-last peeled eggs and starts chopping them. "He said three weeks, sis."

"But … but … but …" and then I stop because standing in a kitchen sputtering like a Model-T is not the kind of impression I want to make, even in front of those who know me best. I take a deep breath. "I can't be gone from Cocoon House for three weeks, babe. Especially considering I've already taken two and am planning a third."

And then we stare at each other for what seems like an hour,

95

and the only sounds are Freddie's knife hitting the cutting board and the kids playing in the other room. Until Sam clears his throat. "Sounds like you have a lot to talk about."

Apparently.

By the time we're sitting around picnic tables in the backyard, though, Trevor and I have put the disagreement aside for the moment. Though I admit it's rather hard to forget the suggestion of a three-week honeymoon. What would we do all that time? I glance toward my fiancé and a little thrill runs through me. Well, I know what we'd do, but we certainly don't need to put money into a trip or even leave town for that. I'd be happy enough spending a week canoodling in a remote but luxurious mountain resort with all the frills, then continuing the fun at home … while still not missing any more work.

A foot nudges me under the table, and I turn to my fourteen-year-old niece, Klinka. Though she gives off a shy demeanor, she's actually quite strong and incredibly wise for her age. But at the moment she has only one question: "Who's going to be in your wedding, Aunt Joey?"

"Well," I say, "I've given that a lot of thought. To have all of my sisters and nieces stand up with me would mean I have more people in the wedding party than in the audience."

She watches me over the cheeseburger she just took a rather delicate bite out of.

I continue, "But I'd love to have you as a junior bridesmaid and plan to get Toolah to be one of my flower girls."

"What about the rest?"

"Well, I'm sure I'll find something for all of you. But how many junior bridesmaids and flower girls can one bride have?"

"I don't know." She squeezes a glob of ketchup onto a corner of her plate and dips her cheeseburger in it before taking another bite. There's now a cute red dot at the corner of her mouth. "How many can you have?"

Taking a napkin, I wipe the ketchup off her face just like I did when she was a baby, only then it tended to be oatmeal and applesauce. She would gurgle and spit and smile at me with so much clarity it was a little eerie. Like she'd known me for years and had only been waiting for the moment she would join our family.

Instant connection. Just like the moment I saw my daughter and grandchildren. And now, I'm overcome by all the time I've missed with them. All the spills and tears, the laughs and tumbles, the messes and memories. I missed it all. It's a hole of regret I can never fill. I blink back a wash of tears and glance across the table at Trevor. He's teasing Milo, my four-year-old nephew, by trying to convince him the Incredible Hulk is green and strong because he eats a lot of broccoli.

"No," Milo says, giggling. "That's not why."

Trevor pulls back, feigning surprise. "What other reason could there possibly be?"

"It's because he's radioactive, silly."

Now Trevor really does seem astonished, but everyone else cracks up laughing. Trevor shakes his head. "Do you even know what 'radioactive' means?"

Milo says, "It makes someone turn green," like it's something he thought we should know, and Trevor might not be too bright after all. "Your *fancy* is weird, Aunt Joey."

It takes me a moment to realize "fancy" and "fiancé" are about the same word to a four-year-old. Between chuckles, I manage to croak out, "Yes, Milo. He's very weird."

And Trevor catches my eye and blows me a kiss with enough sloppy noise to turn Freddy's face slightly pink.

97

So weird.

For dessert, Freddie happily ruins my wedding-dress diet with vanilla ice cream, fresh strawberries, and homemade whipped cream served over sweet vanilla shortcake—my mama's very own recipe. Then we have a laugh-filled evening of charades and Milo's new pie-in-the-face game until, finally, it's time to wipe the Cool Whip off and say goodnight.

Soon we're in Trevor's Jeep on the way back to my temporary home at Cocoon House. But we're not even five minutes away from my sister's house when Trevor says, "So, are you going to tell me what was going on tonight?"

"What do you mean?"

He scratches his head. "Okay. Which one do you want to talk about first—the honeymoon issue or what was making you cry while you were talking to Klinka?"

I'm glad he gave me a choice. "I just don't think we need to spend the money or take the time off work to go on a three-week honeymoon."

"But don't you want it to be memorable?"

Ha. "We could stay at a Holiday Inn and it would be memorable. Or even a Super 8."

"Okay," he says, chuckling. "Point taken. But I did think it would be romantic to explore parts of the country with you."

I'd rather explore you. But I don't say it out loud. Stuff like that will just have to wait until after we're married. Instead I say, "We have our whole lives to travel together. But if I'm stressed about work, how much fun would that be?"

"Hmm. I admit I prefer an unstressed Jolene."

"Everyone does."

"All right. That's taken care of easier than I thought it would be—"

"You and me both, babe."

"—so, about those tears."

Ah. "That one's a little tougher. Though not because of you."

"Okay."

As we get closer and closer to the house, I speak of my regrets—everything I've missed because I gave away my chance to watch my little girl grow up. As I finish, I add, "It's not like you don't know all that. But, sometimes, it just hits me. I don't like that I've lost so much and there's nothing I can do about it."

Trevor reaches over and takes my hand. "We can't do anything about what you've already missed, but the future isn't set."

"You sound like you're quoting some movie."

"Even if I am, the statement is valid."

"I suppose. But how do we fix the future?"

"Jolene." We're almost a mile from Cocoon House when he pulls into a well-lit Walgreen's parking lot and stops the car. Then he turns to me. "I've been giving this a lot of thought, and I believe we need to seriously and prayerfully consider moving to Nashville."

"You do?"

"I do." He rubs a thumb across my hand like he does so often. "I think it's the one thing that will make you happy."

My heart hurts to hear him say that. I put my hand on his cheek. "You're the one thing that makes me happy."

"But you need to have a relationship with your daughter. Our relationship needs that. And that's going to be hard to do from a thousand miles away."

He's right, but I keep feeling heartbroken by all we'd have to give up. On the other hand, we'd gain so much more. My eyes search his, and we both nod. Though there's so much we don't know about what our future holds, one thing is certain: at some point it will include leaving Colorado.

99

Chapter 13
Uli

Two miles. After over a month of walking at least three times a week, I've finally worked up to two miles and, today, I ran half of that. When I arrive back at the Baker's, I'm out of breath and sweating and feel fantastic. In fact, I haven't felt this good or run this far since my mid-twenties. If I didn't need to stretch twice as long to keep my muscles from cramping, I'd feel younger too.

After fifteen minutes of those all-important stretches, I take a quick shower, slip into a simple sundress, and put on a bit of makeup, then grab a light sweater and my laptop bag and hurry out to my car. It's amazing that I can zip up the flight of stairs from my basement room to the main floor without having to stop and catch my breath once I reach the top.

I'm getting married soon, I'm losing weight and getting in shape, and today I'm meeting with a dream client. If she decides to hire me, I will be set, financially, for some time.

When I arrive at Liza Carlson's office, I'm ten minutes early. Time enough to freshen up and collect my thoughts. I'm confident. I've got this in the bag. Things are looking up for me—finally—and all I need to do is nail this interview and I'll be three-for-three: work, relationship, and health. Could it be God is, at last, smiling on me?

Liza Carlson is slightly chubby, wears big hats and too much lipstick, and is one of the sweetest potential clients I've ever met. Though clearly a serious businesswoman, she reminds me more of Mary Kay than Margaret Thatcher, but there's certainly a resemblance to both. She stands, smiles, and shakes my hand.

"Miss Odell. Thank you for meeting with me."

"It's my pleasure, Ms. Carlson."

"Liza, please."

"And I'd love it if you'd call me Uli."

"Thank you, Uli. Would you like some coffee or water?"

"Water would be great."

In just a few minutes, she has her coffee and I have a bottle of water and we're sitting around the table in her office with my portfolio spread out before us. She seems genuinely interested and knows what questions to ask. I tell her about my knowledge of Photoshop and Lightroom, the kind of camera I use, and how long it takes me to finish various types of jobs, from company logos to brochures to headshots and marketing photos.

When I'm done, she proceeds to fill me in on her various interests. Because Liza doesn't just run one company. She has her hands in real estate, computer technology, and even has several direct sales businesses in jewelry, clothes, and dietary supplements. But not makeup, ironically.

I suspect my eyes widen with each new venture. And that seems confirmed when she looks at me and laughs. "Yes, it's a lot and I stay busy, but I decided years ago that financial security was important to me. And since I've never married, the only person I could count on for that was me."

Yeah, that's exactly what I'm trying to avoid. "I wish I was as business-minded as you."

"Well, you're a right-brain creative person, and I'm all left-brain. Which is why I need you."

She then lays out the kind of work she would want me to do. It's all stuff I could put together in my sleep and the more she talks the more excited I get. I can do this. It would be perfect. I love the idea of Liza Carlson as my boss. I suspect I could learn a lot from her. And, perhaps, she could help me get more settled financially so I wouldn't have to depend on Cole as much. Not that that's a bad thing.

The interview is wrapping up when Liza says, "Do you mind if I give you a little advice?"

"No, not at all."

"Many people think you have to pick one career track and stick to it, but that's not true. In fact, it's less likely to give you the security you're looking for, especially if you're self-employed. You need to think of work like a stool—the more legs it has, the sturdier it will be."

I nod, but say, "I think that's easier for someone who's more like you."

She holds up her hands like she's giving up the argument. "Oh, it's absolutely easier for someone like me. But I encourage you to search for other sources of income nevertheless. Then, if one job has a slow month or even falls through, you have other work you can count on."

"That's a good point. Thank you. It's certainly something to consider."

Standing, she takes my hand once again and gives it a firm shake.

"You're clearly talented, Uli. I encourage you to try to be more aggressive as you market your work."

It's not until sometime later, when I'm pushing a cart past the cheese section of King Soopers, that the tone of her statement hits me. Was that her way of letting me know I shouldn't count on her hiring me?

Boy, I sure hope not.

Before returning to my temporary home, I make a quick stop at the store. While there, my single mom friend, Audrey Lennox, calls and invites me to join her and her two kids at their apartment complex pool.

"Sounds great! I'll need to change first," I say, "then I'll be over."

Less than an hour later, I'm sitting in a lounge chair letting the sun turn me a nice, crispy red. I've managed to hang on to some of the tan I brought back from Belize, but this is only the second time I've been to a pool this summer, so I make sure I don't slack off on suntan lotion. We're closer to the rays here in Colorado, which makes sunburns easier to come by. Since I have a big dinner and concert date with Cole tomorrow night I need to be careful. Showing up looking like a lobster is a good way to get teased by my fiancé.

Reaching under my chair, I pull out a bottle of diet Dew that I'm trying to keep at least somewhat in the shade, and I take a long sip. "Thanks for inviting me over," I say to Audrey. "It's been a crazy summer. I've missed hanging out with you."

"I've missed you too. And, I must say, I almost didn't recognize you." She leans back and gives me an exaggerated once-over, which makes me laugh. "How much have you lost?"

"Almost twenty pounds."

"Wow. Good for you. What's your secret?"

Ha. Like she needs diet advice. Audrey has a curvy but trim figure and certainly doesn't need to lose weight. Though, in my experience, all women think they have a weight problem. "Well," I say, "I'm doing something a little radical—eating less and exercising more."

Now it's her turn to chuckle. "Ha. That's amazing! Who knew?"

"I know, right?" Then I sigh. "To be honest, I lost about half of this thanks to a bad chicken sandwich."

"Food poisoning?"

"Awful, horrible, kill-me-now food poisoning."

"Yikes. That's no fun. But if it means losing weight—"

"Exactly. I shouldn't be glad I was that sick, but I kind of am."

103

At that moment, her kids, Jason and Kara, attack, pulling at us until we finally relent and jump in the pool. Once I get used to the cold water, we have a pretty good time playing Marco Polo and diving for coins. I've swallowed about a gallon of water when they decide to have a handstand competition.

"That's my cue," I say, and climb out of the pool. "I'd rather breathe normally for a while."

I grab my towel and dry off as Audrey joins me. "That was fun, but I know what you mean."

Draping my towel on the lounger, I plop down and start lathering on more lotion. "Yeah, I wish I had their energy."

"You did all right." She pulls a container out of her beach bag and pops the lid off. Inside is a beautiful trail mix of peanuts, cashews, raisins, sunflower seeds, and M&Ms. We both dig in like we haven't eaten all day. And as I scarf down handfuls of it I realize I haven't. I went from run to shower to interview to pool, and somehow it hadn't occurred to me to eat. That's unusual. I force myself to slow down. Just because I'm hungry is no reason to go crazy. I want to stay smart in this and not get back into bad habits.

"Hmm," I say. "I didn't realize how hungry I was."

"Would you like a sandwich? I have ham, turkey, cheese."

Audrey pushes on the arms of her chair as if to stand, but I wave her back down. "Thanks, but I'm fine." I give her a toothy grin. "If I don't eat now, I can have pizza for supper."

She smiles too but shakes her head. "I'm not sure that's the best philosophy for weight loss."

"All I know is that I want to make sustainable changes. Rewarding a low-calorie day with pizza is sustainable."

With a shrug, Audrey leans back and nibbles on a handful of trail mix. "I just want you to succeed."

"That would be nice. Especially if it makes me more ready for my wedding dress."

"True. Have you found one yet?"

"Well …"—and another handful of the snack keeps me from having to speak for a moment—"sort of. I don't love it, but it looks decent on me, and I could afford it."

She puts up a hand to block the sun in order to, apparently, see me better. "From my own experience, I can tell you this: Find a dress you adore. It's key. There's nothing you can regret more in planning your wedding than settling for the wrong dress." She pauses then adds, "Unless it's settling for the wrong man."

Oh, great. Even people who don't know seem to know. But I laugh like that's a crazy idea, and I wouldn't even consider settling. "You might be right." A few seconds pass, and I shake my head and grin. "Nope. The dress is definitely more important."

As soon as we're done giggling about that, I ask, "So what about you and men? Anything happening romance-wise? Or is it too soon?" Because it hadn't even been a year and a half since her husband died in a car accident.

"I thought it was too soon. I really did. Even if I was ready, the kids aren't." She sighs. "And then I met Richard."

That's unexpected. "Oh, yeah? Who's Richard?"

"A guy from church, but we met at work."

Audrey runs the front desk for a busy real estate company while she studies to get her license. "Was he a buyer or a seller?"

"Neither." And suddenly she seems rather shy about the whole thing. She must really like him. "He works for the Gazette as a reporter."

"A reporter? That's fun! They're really good at asking questions."

"Yeah, conversations are easy. It never feels awkward."

"And he goes to your church?"

"Uh-huh. Isn't that crazy? He's been going there for years, but we never met. And then, one day, he stops by the office to

105

get information on our annual golf classic for an article … and the next thing I know we're eating chicken parmesan at Olive Garden and telling each other about our kids and sharing our dreams for the future."

Sounds delightful. "He has kids too?"

"Four, if you can believe it. Richard lost his wife to a brain tumor almost a decade ago."

"I'm sorry to hear that."

A drop of sweat drizzles down my forehead, and I wipe it away before it gets in my eyes. It might be time for shade. The wide-brimmed straw hat I brought helps, but I can tell I'm about done with the heat. I sit up and grunt. "I feel like I'm melting."

"What time is it?"

I pull my phone out of my bag. "Almost six-thirty."

"That late? I need to get the kids in and figure out something for supper." She starts gathering her things. "Jason! Kara! Time to go in."

While I have my phone out, I check to see if I missed any calls. Nothing. But I didn't expect to hear from Liza right away. She had mentioned she was talking to a couple other people about the job. *Please, God, let me be the best candidate.* The thought of having that kind of regular income is almost intoxicating. God has to know how important this is to me.

Just because He knows, though, doesn't necessarily means He'll do anything about it. But I'm going to hope He will.

Formal dates with Cole tend to go one of two ways: either he spends the whole evening treating me like a queen or he ignores me for most of it. I never know until we get there because it depends on who we're out with. But it's Saturday night and we're going to dinner and a concert and it's just the two of us. That means most of his attention will be on me, so I put every effort into looking my best.

Since he didn't go to Tess and Brian's wedding, I wear the same pink dress I bought for that occasion. It's really the nicest thing I have that not only fits but shows off my somewhat improved figure.

Cole picks me up fifteen minutes late, no surprise. His tendency to show up when he feels like it has influenced me to fudge a little as to when we need to leave for scheduled events. So I made sure we'd have plenty of time to eat before heading to the arena.

When he sees me, he jumps out of his truck, whistles, and opens the passenger door. Guess it's going to be a Queen Uli night.

Yay.

Dinner isn't as nice as I'd hoped—Cole takes me to his favorite steak house—but the food is fine. Mostly. The broccoli I ordered as my fresh veggie option arrived swimming in butter, something I just can't handle lately. But that's the only disappointment.

Then we're off to World Arena for a Styx and REO Speedwagon concert. This is really more Cole's thing than mine, but both groups have enough songs I know to enjoy myself. In fact, I have a blast singing along with several REO hits, and Cole and I belt out "Time for Me to Fly" like we both think we're Kevin Cronin.

Then it's Styx's turn. Five songs in, though, Cole says he has to use the restroom and slips from my side. The band goes through another song, then finishes "The Best of Times" and he's still not back. So I decide to see if I can hunt him down.

I make my way through the crowd of people swaying to "Lady," and, finally, slip out into the hall. Glancing both ways, I don't see him, but I do see the signs to the restrooms and head that direction. A little farther down, a dark-haired man and a dark-skinned beauty are wrapped around each other. Cole. And Merryn.

And, once again, I'm the fool. I stand there, stunned and unable to move, until he looks my way. It's too late to hide now, especially not in a hot-pink dress. So I don't. Why should I run? Cole's not hiding. He whispers something to Merryn, who turns my way and gives me a once-over like an evil stepsister would in a Cinderella movie. Except Cole is no prince, charming or otherwise.

Merryn says something back to him before heading off in the other direction as he strolls toward me. I can't move. I can't cry. I can't feel. Anything. When he stops in front of me, neither of us speaks for a moment. Then, to my astonishment, he says,

"You're missing your favorite song."

I had told him the main Styx tune I wanted to hear tonight was "Come Sail Away" and, sure enough, the opening melody is drifting through the stadium doors. But all I know is he's broken my heart into pieces and crushed me to the ground and all he can talk about is music. What is wrong with him?

Everything. And everything is wrong with me because I believed he loved me enough to make this work despite the warnings from my friends and the facts in front of my eyes. A breath rushes out of me, which is when I realize I've been holding it in. I yank off his ring and throw it at the wall.

"Don't call me."

Then I run toward the door. Toward fresh air. Toward someplace where I can cry alone. And back toward the life of single solitude I've been running from for so long.

Chapter 14

Catie

The first time my dentist put me on laughing gas—for a root canal—was also my first experience with a drug like that. And I loved it. I laughed. I cried. I fell asleep ... but I was not aware of any drilling, which I suppose means the stuff worked. Since then, though, I've kept good care of my teeth so it was also my last flight on laughing gas.

Today I started chemo and had a similar experience. Except the dental work was easier. And shorter.

My dad and sister-in-law, Delia, take me to my first appointment as they're the only ones who don't have regular jobs. Dad is retired, of course, and Delia takes care of the house and yard and garden at the farm. Since the cancer treatment center I have to go to is over an hour away in Springfield, I appreciate their willingness to give up so much of their day to take care of me.

Of course, having my family's help and support is exactly why I came back to Ohio for this part of my journey. I was told I'd be there for hours and it's nice to know the people waiting for me consider it a privilege, not a burden. And, in fact, see it as an opportunity to get some shopping done while I'm here.

The center is nice. They usher me into a large room with about a dozen rather comfortable reclining chairs. A nurse named Dee takes my blood to check the white cell count. Once that's given the all-clear, she slides the pre-meds IV into my arm. This, I'm told, will help my body relax before it's time for the hard stuff.

A gray-haired woman at least fifteen years older than me is on my right. She seems a little more used to the process than me. "Don't worry, honey," she says. "It's not that bad."

Why would she say that? She points with her chin and I glance down. Sure enough, my knuckles are white from gripping the arms of the chair. I release them and rub my hands together. They're chilled too. What I wouldn't give to be sitting in a Panera with Dad and Delia right now, sipping a large, hot mug of coffee and enjoying a blueberry bagel and not even thinking about cancer. Or what these chemo drugs are going to do to me.

"Are you sure? It's really not bad?"

The woman nods. "Honey, I've gone through so many of these treatments I've lost count, and, as you can see, I've survived."

But surviving is not thriving. "I'm a little newer to the experience."

"First time?"

"Yes."

"What do you have?"

"Uterine. You?"

"Breast cancer. This is my second time to beat it," she says, smiling, but she sounds tired. "What's your name, honey?"

"Catie." I reach across the space between us. She takes my hand. "I'm Ruth."

"It's nice to meet you."

"And you." She leans back and closes her eyes. "Just rest, Catie. That's your only job today."

If only it were that easy. I've done my research. I have a basic idea of what to expect, and was warned that today won't be as tough as the ones ahead. It takes a day or two for the side effects to hit. But since everyone is different, I'll have to wait and see how my body reacts to the meds.

For now, though, a drug cocktail that includes Benadryl and steroids has started coursing through my veins and soon I'm floating around the room. And, just like that, I'm resting, sleeping even. At least, as much as seems possible considering the

110

situation.

Five hours later we're on our way home. Though I'm tired and lethargic, I'm also surprisingly hungry. I say as much to Delia, who's driving.

"Really?" she asks. "Is there anything in particular you want?"

"The whole time I sat there, all I could think about was a bagel and coffee from Panera. And something with bacon."

"Then Panera it is."

As we head that direction, I ask how their shopping trip went, and Dad goes into a detailed description of all the treasures filling the bags in the back. When he mentions the deal he got on chocolate caramels, I unbuckle, turn around, and start rifling through bags until I find the prize. Each bite is a little bit of heaven. As is the turkey-avocado BLT Delia brings me after a brief stop at Panera.

Funny. It had never occurred to me that chemo would make food taste better. Not that I'd ever given much thought to how chemo would make me feel. The main thing I'm hyper aware of is the coming hair loss. I've always believed my red hair was my signature feature. Without it, will any man ever find me attractive again? On the other hand, will it really make that much of a difference? My heart drops a little as it seems I'm just getting further and further from the possibility of marriage.

It will get easier over time, Catie. Take a deep breath ... and have faith.

As for my hair, as soon as it starts falling out, I'm going to shave it off. At least *that* I can have control of.

Twenty-four hours after my first treatment and I could

111

barely move. I slept on and off for two days, waking only long enough to eat toast or applesauce or orange juice, take care of a little personal business, then crawl back into bed. Poor Luna settles in at my feet the first day and spends much of the time whimpering … until I beg Tawny to take her for a walk and see if she could get my dog to play with theirs. Anything to keep her from becoming despondent.

Then, just as I'm starting to feel a bit more like myself, the pain starts. My doctor told me there'd be some pain because of how the chemo drugs stimulate the blood cells inside my bone marrow. "Some" was an understatement. It's constant and excruciating. My family members take turns sitting with me, holding my hand, and trying to distract me with funny stories and heart-felt prayers. Luna provides some comfort too, with her loud, rumbling breath and soft fur. I rest my hand on her head as I fall asleep, and it's still there when I wake up the next morning.

I'm not sure if the nausea that follows is a result of the pain or the drugs, but I am sure I wouldn't have gotten through it without anti-nausea pills. And then, just like that, everything starts to improve.

On my fourth day after treatment, my Aunt Honoria comes to visit. She's always been my favorite aunt and, as a single woman too, the one I feel most connected to. We settle into cushioned wicker chairs in the sunroom with glasses of cold strawberry lemonade and a bowl of big, green grapes and cut-up pieces of cantaloupe. It's surprisingly cool as July days go—barely hitting the mid-seventies—and with the windows open and a fan blowing, we're quite comfortable on this lovely summer day.

Honoria sets her glass down and studies me closely. "You look tired."

"I am tired."

"Hmm." She bites into a grape. "I'm worried about your Da."

I swallow down the thought that I should be hurt by that. "Dad? Why?"

"It's not easy for him, watching another of his loved ones deal with cancer."

Of course. Why hadn't I thought of that? After all he went through with my mother, this must be more difficult for him than for anyone else. "Thank you, Honoria. I should have considered how this would affect him."

"You should *not* have!" For a second, she seems about to slap my hand. "The last thing you need is something else to worry about."

Leave it to my aunt to bring up something to worry about, then command me not to worry about it. Surely she knows I can't *not* be concerned about my dad now?

"So, what's the deal with your job?" she says, changing the subject as fast as she goes from eating grapes to cantaloupe. "How much time are they giving you?"

"Six to eight weeks, but I can take more if necessary."

"And then what?"

"'And then ... what do you mean?"

"This is going to change your life, you know."

"Yes. It already has." I slurp down the last of the lemonade, then snap open a bottled water. "But it could be for the best, couldn't it?"

All she says is "Hmm" and licks cantaloupe juice off her fingers.

"In fact, I'm considering moving back to Ohio. For good."

She leans back and crosses her arms across her rather large chest. "Well, of course you are."

That makes me laugh. "Do you think that will surprise anyone?"

"Hardly." My aunt shakes her head and her shoulders at the same time. It's very endearing. "Not anyone who knows you."

113

"Really? But I love Colorado." Leaving it can't be as simple as Honoria makes it sound.

"This home is in your heart, Catie-girl. You just needed some time away to realize it."

My aunt stays through my next treatment, which doesn't take quite as long as the first. I'm a little more prepared this time for what's ahead—the exhaustion, the pain, the nausea. It won't be easier to handle, but I'm ready for it.

Ruth is there again, and we have a little more time to chat. She tells me about her kids and her grandkids and her husband; I talk about my life in Colorado and my family here. When I mention my faith, though, she nods and smiles and talks about something else. Maybe it shouldn't, but it surprises me—meeting an older, kindhearted grandmother who isn't a believer. And I wonder what it would be like to go through cancer twice without God. I'm fairly certain I wouldn't have made it through the initial diagnosis if I hadn't had God there with me.

All the way home, I can't forget about Ruth and what I have that she doesn't. It's not often that I think along those lines, tending, instead, to focus on what I'm lacking. Suddenly, I want to tell her about my relationship with God. As far as I know, next week is her last treatment.

Father, give me the courage to tell Ruth about you. Tell me what to say.

I have one week to get ready.

Later that night, I connect with Jolene and Uli on FaceTime so we can finally catch up. We had planned the online get-together on Facebook yesterday after I let them know the day of my treatment is when I feel the best.

After basic hellos, they ask how chemo is going. But I'd

rather know why Uli's face is blotchy-red and her voice is hoarse. There's pain in her eyes too. I wish I was close enough to hug her. I'll ask about that later, though. After giving them a quick rundown of the joys of chemo, I say, "And that's about it."

Only that's not about it. Having already been through this with her sister, Jolene has several specific questions about the side effects.

"No," I respond to one query, "I haven't lost any hair yet."

Jolene says, "I guess it's a bit early for that."

"A bit."

"What will you do?" Uli tucks a curl behind her ear, which is when I notice her naked ring finger. She adds, "About your hair, I mean."

With a grimace, I say, "Shave it off, I guess."

"Really?" Jolene tilts her head. "Make sure you consider all the ramifications. That's what Freddie did and she definitely struggled with it, wondering if she should have waited."

"I get that. But I'd rather have control of my baldness."

Both of my friends laugh but don't say anything else about it. They know all about my control issues.

"Enough about me," I say. "What's going on with both of you? Jolene, how are things with Vala? Did you find a kidney donor for your granddaughter yet?"

"As a matter of fact, yes!" My friend's face lights up with joy. "We found out last week that my sister Lynelle is a perfect match."

I lean closer to my camera. "That's wonderful, but will she do it? Because that's a huge sacrifice."

"Yes, the whole family knows what this means. Lynelle and her husband are talking and praying about it, but I believe she will. I hope to get down to Nashville soon and introduce everyone. They'll all fall in love with Livvie the minute they meet her, and then it won't be such a sacrifice."

115

Uli and I both promise to pray for Jolene and her family and this big decision, and what it will mean for all of them. Then it's Uli's turn to share. Should I mention the ring? Maybe there's a way to bring it up casually.

But I don't need to. Jolene must have noticed too because she gets right to the point. "So, Uli, I couldn't help but notice you're not wearing your engagement ring."

Uli rubs a hand across her eyes. She opens her mouth several times without speaking until, finally, she grumbles, "Well, you'll both be happy. Cole and I are over. For good."

Jolene and I repeat, "For good?" at the same time.

She nods. "Which is exactly what you wanted to hear."

"No," says Jolene. "We would never want to hear that you'd been hurt like this."

Uli bites her lip, like she's trying to shut herself up. And then, because I don't think it through, I ask, "What are you going to do?"

"Do?"

I say, "With your life," and immediately wish I'd been the one to bite her lip. Because as far as I can tell, this is the first time it's occurred to Uli that in addition to losing her fiancé, she's lost her future home and financial security.

And she's not ready to handle that.

Chapter 15
Uli

Leave it to Catie to cut to the chase and remind me I'm floating here, without a fiancé or a job or a place to live. Nothing. I have nothing. Certainly not anything to keep me in Colorado. Iowa is my only other option, which is just slightly more appealing than staying here. At least I have a place to live and, once school starts again, some fairly decent income as a substitute teacher. And it's all kinds of miles away from Cole.

So, I say to my friends, "I guess I'm going home."

Catie nods, but Jolene looks like she's about to cry. "I'm going to lose you both," she says. "I wish we could have had one more Accountability Monday before all of our lives changed."

Me too. "Maybe we can plan one when we all come back for your wedding, Jo."

"I'd be up for that," Catie says. "And who knows how things will be in October."

Jolene asks me, "When do you think you'll head to Iowa?"

"As soon as I can get everything together and figure out how I'll get there."

Two days later, my plans are accelerated. Forest fires that have been destroying land west of Colorado Springs for two weeks have hit close enough to the Cheyenne Mountain area to require an evacuation of homes on the town side. Including the Baker's place. It hadn't occurred to me to be worried. Or, I suppose, I was too caught up in my own drama to notice the concern everyone had about this threat.

You don't have to live in Colorado long to know that fires

117

are a very real problem in this super-dry state, especially during the summer months. It's just always been "over there," on the other side of the mountain range that many towns nestle up against. Every once in a while you get a whiff of smoke, but somehow it's always contained before it can reach the city.

But now we have to leave the area. My temporary landlords, Mel and Lynn Baker, scurry about, gathering the things they need and looking rather dazed at the idea of losing their home. I can't even imagine. It takes me about fifteen minutes to pack up my two suitcases. I'll miss this couple who so graciously gave me a temporary place to live; I'll really miss their cat, Chilly. He's become a bit of a comforter, and even sat on my lap, purring, while I wept over my broken heart the night things ended with Cole.

Who, fortunately, has not called. He must have believed me. Or doesn't care enough to try to fix things. Either way, it's never felt more over. I haven't cried since that night, though. All I feel is numb, which is better than being overwhelmed by grief. That's coming, I'm sure, but for now, I'll keep my emotions in a bubble.

The one bit of good news was that the Bakers decided to go spend time with Lynn's sister in Omaha and offered to take me that far. When I told my mom, she agreed to pick me up there. And so, just like that, I find myself on my way back to Iowa only two months after I left.

Driving with Mel and Lynn reminds me of an eighties movie. They spend most of the trip joking, telling stories, and singing show tunes. Chilly sits calmly on the backseat next to me. He might be the first cat I've known that doesn't freak out in a car. It's nice to have the company. And, at one point, he looks at me during a rather spirited rendition of *Annie*'s "Tomorrow" and, I swear, rolls his eyes.

Usually, I would join in. I'm not averse to singing loud and strong, especially not random songs from Broadway shows. But

118

the music isn't there. The only song I feel like singing is "Send in the Clowns," and that doesn't seem to jive with the atmosphere in the Baker's SUV. So I smile and answer their questions and act like everything is fine. Because if they can sing knowing they might lose anything, I can be upbeat even though I already have.

It takes just over ten hours to get to Omaha, and we arrive at the modest ranch home right around seven. Lynn introduces me to her sister, Jean, and Jean's husband, Tony, before we're herded onto the back porch where they have supper waiting: buckets of KFC and a few sides from the restaurant, along with sliced tomatoes, cottage cheese, and fresh fruit.

Jean and Tony are just as nice as Mel and Lynn and do their best to make me feel welcome. It's a bit awkward, having a family meal with a family that's not mine, but they're all so nice, I force myself to relax and enjoy the good-natured evening.

By ten everyone's yawning, even me, and Jean smiles apologetically. "We only have one spare bedroom, so you get the couch. But I've slept there several times and can promise it's comfortable." She picks up a stack of sheets, blankets, and a pillow sitting on a chair and hands it to me. "If you need anything else, there's a linen closet at the end of the hall."

"This is great," I say. "I'm just so grateful to have a place to sleep."

"No problem." The woman's red hair reminds me of Catie, and she looks about a decade younger than her sister. There's something very sixties housewife about her, but she wears it well.

Funny the things you notice about people you will probably only meet once in your life.

Not surprisingly, I barely sleep that night. Besides the fact that I always have a tough time nodding off in a strange place, my insomnia has been hitting me hard lately anyway. That doesn't surprise me either.

All of which means that as soon as the family starts stirring

119

around seven the next morning, so do I. Might as well. Once life gets moving again, there's no way I'll fall back to sleep.

Since I'm not the first one up, I have to wait for my turn to use the hall bathroom. As soon as I lock the door behind me and settle on the seat, I discover there was a reason I had cramps the night before. I'd hoped it would hold out until I got to Mom's, but at least I have a shorter drive ahead of me today. It also explains why I've been fighting stronger-than-usual mood swings and chocolate cravings for days. Though I love how much better I've been feeling about myself weight-wise, I'm not sure I have the strength or motivation to keep it up. The exercise part, maybe, but the diet might be too much for me to handle on top of everything else.

Which feels like I'm giving up. Maybe I am. Now I need to decide if I'm okay with that or if I'm ready to believe I could still have a good life. *Oh, God, make me ready.* If He cares.

Mom shows up just before one, and I'm happy to see Sandy not only with her but driving. I hug Mel and Lynn goodbye and thank them for everything. Jean also comes over for a hug, then hands me a bag of sandwiches and chips and bottled water. I try to protest, but she waves me off.

"Don't be silly," she says. "You'll get home faster if you don't have to stop for lunch."

And, just like that, we're on the road. Since Mel did most of the driving from Colorado with Lynn handling it for a few short bursts when he needed a break, I offer to take the wheel and get us home. Mom and Sandy both seem quite happy to let me. I like driving, so it's a win-win.

We stop at a 7-11 a few blocks from Jean's, where I grab a thirty-two-ounce diet Coke. It's not until I'm back in the car, plugging Mom's address into my phone's GPS, that I realize such a large beverage might have been a mistake. It would be nice to get to Cedar Rapids in one leg, but too much diet pop will make that almost impossible. Which means I'll have to stop, and Mom will get frustrated and be annoyed with me the whole way back.

Not exactly something to look forward to.

Thankfully, it doesn't take long to reach interstate 80. Once there, I turn the GPS off since I know the way now. It also doesn't take long to need a bathroom break. I ignore it as long as possible—which isn't long at all—until, to my relief, I see an exit for a rest area near Underwood.

"I hate to do this so soon," I say, "but I need to make a quick pit stop."

Mom groans and opens her mouth to, I assume, complain. Then Sandy comes to my rescue, adding, "Sounds good to me."

With a sigh, Mom says, "Yeah, it's fine." She glances at my huge beverage and adds, "But maybe you should slow down on the pop."

"Yeah, I know. But the caffeine helps me stay alert."

She purses her lips at me as I pull into a parking spot. "If you're having trouble staying awake, maybe you should let me drive."

"No, it's okay. I'll be fine." On three hours of sleep. Sure. But she doesn't need to know that. I'm also worried that if Mom's driving, we won't stop until we're home, and the only way I'll make it will be by peeing in a cup. I'd rather not.

For now, though, I jump out of the car and hurry into the rest area. I get there just in time—at least, that's how it feels. On the way back to the parking lot, I catch up with Sandy. Her eyes tell me she knows what's bothering me. She might even know everything that's bothering me. She smiles. "If you want me to drive, I-promise-to-stop-if-you-need-me-to."

And that's when I realize how much I've missed my mom's fast-talking friend. "Thanks, Sandy, but I'm good. I'd rather concentrate on driving than … other stuff."

I haven't told my mom the wedding is off yet, just

121

postponed temporarily while I work some things out. But Sandy is a smart woman, and Mom can read me quite easily so, as far as I know, they've both figured out the real story, and they're just waiting for me to admit it. Something I'm not in a hurry to do.

Once back in the car, I swallow down three ibuprofen with another gulp of diet Coke to fight the pain in my gut and hope this time the pop doesn't go through me as fast. We pull out the lunch sack Jean sent with us and eat ham salad sandwiches with too much mayo along with little bags of barbecue chips, which are not my favorite. But Sandy discovers Jean also included some of the best homemade chocolate chip cookies ever, which makes the rest of the lunch not seem so bad.

Despite two more bathroom stops, we manage to get to Cedar Rapids by six. Funny how this little condo feels as much like home as any place … which isn't really saying a lot. Because if home is where the heart is, I'm not sure where that is anymore. Yes, I love my mother, but I can't say my heart resides with her. I don't feel drawn to her and Iowa. Certainly not like I did to Cole and Colorado.

For the time being, though, I'm back to being an Iowa girl. I'm not sure what that means for the future but hopefully I can make the most of it.

All the next day, I curl up on the couch with a container of ibuprofen and a bag of M&Ms while I watch a marathon of *Murder She Wrote* on TV. Mom is also taking it easy as the long day on the road yesterday was hard on her hip, which is still healing from a bad break last spring. So we're both wrapped in afghans, and I'm wearing slippers because my mom insists on keeping the air conditioner set at arctic temperatures. It's not even that hot outside—not for July anyway.

At one point, I said, "Can't we please turn off the AC and open some windows? A good box fan would get a real nice breeze going through here … and bring in lots of fresh air."

"It's too hot," was her only response. And that's why we're dressed like it's a snowy Christmas morning rather than the middle of summer.

That's basically the way it is for the next two days—until I start feeling normal again. As soon as I do, I call Penny Bradley, the old school friend I reconnected with in April. Because I'm bored out of my skull and even helping her and her husband, Jason, around their farm or babysitting her three children sounds better than one more day as a couch icicle.

She sounds happy to hear from me. "Uli! I saw on Facebook you were back. What's going on?"

Since I'm in my bedroom with the door shut, I can talk freely and tell her why I'm back in Iowa and, possibly, here for good. Then I admit I haven't told my mom about my failed relationship. I've hinted at it, but I'm just not ready for The Talk quite yet.

"Well, she probably already knows," Penny says, oh-so-helpfully. "You're obviously not talking about your wedding, which would be a significant clue."

"I know. And my truth is probably better than her imagination."

"Most likely."

Ugh. "I should just get it over with."

"Rip it off, Uli. It's the only way."

She's right. Tonight. I'll take care of it tonight. But, for now, "So, is there anything fun going on? Any church activities? Softball games? Cookouts?"

"Softball is over for the season, but there's a carry-in picnic after services on Sunday, and the church has organized a day trip

123

to Adventureland next week."

"Really? I haven't been to Adventureland since we were in high school. Remember? Tenth grade, right? So many good memories."

Penny laughs. "I remember you flirting with every boy in the park. And that scream-laugh you did when we went on the Tornado."

"Oh, the Tornado! Is that old thing still there? Best rollercoaster ever!"

"Yeah, it's still there."

For a second I try to remember the last time I was even at an amusement park, let alone rode on a rollercoaster. It would be fun. And pricey.

But I say, "You have to admit we did pretty okay with the boys there. Like when we ordered small ice cream cones and that kid piled it so high it fell over. Ha. Wow, I miss having guys notice me like that."

My problem, though, was not being able to get beyond flirting. All the boys I met when I was young, and I only dated a couple of times. Cole was my first serious relationship. What a sad commentary on the life of a romantic.

"Well," I say, "I'd love to go but ... how much is it? I have very little income right now." Yeah. Try zero income.

After a short pause, Penny says, "You know, I think there are a couple of free tickets. If you can cover your own food and drinks, you should be able to get in free."

"Really? That would be great ... but I don't want to use it if someone else needs it."

"Don't worry. We've worked things out so everyone who wants to go will be able to."

"It sounds like fun. And I could help out with the kids, if needed." It sure would be nice to get out of the house for a day. "Okay, count me in!"

124

Penny says, "I might take you up on the kid thing so Jason and I can do a ride or two together." There's another break, and then, "And will we see you at church Sunday?"

"Absolutely!"

Because, at this moment anyway, church is about the only thing I have.

Chapter 16
Jolene

Well, what do you know. I've fallen in love with the first wedding dress I tried on.

"Mama is going to kill you, you know," Freddie says behind me.

I twirl around, viewing it from different angles. "Not when she sees the price tag." I face my sister and her oldest daughter, who are both grinning. "So stop making threats and take a picture to send her."

Freddie does as she's told, and Klinka says, "You look so pretty, Aunt Joey."

"Thank you, sweetie," I walk over and tug on one of her braids. "You're looking pretty adorable yourself."

A phone dings and Freddie checks it. "She sent prayer hands, a kissy face, and something that looks like a baby rattle."

"What?" I peer over Freddie's shoulder. Mama has just recently been introduced to the land of emojis, and she's taken to using random ones that usually have a meaning only she understands. It's like her own form of hieroglyphics. "I'm going to interpret that as a thumbs-up. Did you tell her the price?"

"Oh right." Freddie texts the amount, then, moments later, her phone dings again. She takes a quick look and cracks up as she turns it toward me. Mama sent the poop emoji because she thinks it's happy-faced chocolate and we—her beloved children—have decided not to tell her otherwise until it stops being funny.

It's still funny. Especially when she pairs it with another kissy face. She really likes that kissy face. A third message pops up, this time from my dad's phone, though we've begun to suspect it's probably from Mama too. As far as I know, Dad has never texted and will never text. Why our mother switches between phones is anyone's guess.

The latest message has applauding hands and a face with dollar signs instead of eyes. Freddie and I look at each other and shrug at the same time.

My sister says, "I think that means she approves."

"Sounds good to me." I turn my back to her. "Now help me get this off so we can go find Klinka the sweetest junior bridesmaid dress in the history of junior bridesmaids."

Klinka laughs. "And shoes. Don't forget the shoes."

"How could I?" In that moment, my niece stops being a little girl to me. She's growing into a young woman, a lovely one, inside and out. I smile at Freddie as I pull on my shorts and blouse and slide on a thick headband to tame my wild hair. "You're going to need to keep an eye on this one."

"Don't I know it." Freddie hugs Klinka close to her side and shakes her a little. "My baby girl is growing up!"

My niece tries to pull away, but though she's now almost as tall as Freddie, she's not quite strong enough to break free of her mom's iron grip. "Well, I like that," Klinka says. "Most of the time you're telling me to stop acting like a kid!"

Freddie gives me a shocked expression. "I have never said that!" She pauses, shrugs … "Well, maybe once or twice."

"Don't believe her, Aunt Joey. She likes to downplay things."

"Klinka, my love," I say. "I've known your mother her whole life, and she's just as ornery now as she was when she was a kid."

"Ha! I knew it." Klinka giggles and tries once again to pull away from her mom. Instead, Freddie just hugs her tighter until the girl groans and says, "Mom, I can't breathe."

Freddie loosens her grip a bit. "I just don't want you to forget how much your mama loves you, baby girl."

127

Mothers and daughters. It's a beautiful thing to see that special bond. Oh, how much I've missed.

But enough contemplation. I say, "Come on. Somewhere in this shopping center a pizza is calling my name."

I can't believe I'm going to do this. My heart breaks a little more every time I consider the choice I've made. But after hours and hours of prayer and long talks with Trevor and my parents, I know it's right. It's time.

Yet I also know the thought of leaving Cocoon House is shattering my spirit in a deep way. Nashville is calling, though, and what's waiting for me there will surely mend the brokenness. And I'm fortunate enough to have a fiancé who agrees it's where we should be. He's planning to put in his notice at work soon, then will stay at the training center where he's a therapeutic recreation specialist through September—long enough for them to find a replacement.

Now I'm sitting in the living room of the home I've run for six years, watching the women I've come to love like family. The women who've faced so many hardships and continue to amaze me with their growth and courage. Especially Benita Jensen. She's the one I'm most concerned about. I want more than anything to find some way to reunite her with her son before I leave. But doing that without her ex-boyfriend—who's also the boy's father—finding out won't be easy.

Good thing I like a challenge.

I've already told the board, as well as SueAnn, who basically runs the place, and our counselor, Tina, my plans ... and why. They were, of course, very supportive and encouraging. Though I recommended SueAnn take over as the head of the home, she flat-out turned me down. "I like being in the kitchen," she told me. "I like the relationships I have with the girls there."

Since I couldn't argue with that, I immediately began making calls and asking around, trying to find just the right person to take my place. I couldn't hand this home over to just anyone. Then one of my contacts at Taylor University recommended Marty Cortés, a social worker who ran a similar kind of home in Indiana until her husband's work relocated him to Colorado Springs. My contact let me know Marty was eager to find a ministry here.

She's coming to meet with me in thirty minutes, which is enough time to tell our residents the news. Because I want them to have a say in my replacement as well. They've been enjoying a relaxing afternoon inside, mostly due to the arrival of the rain we've been praying for since the first signs of fire four weeks ago.

"Girls," I say, getting their attention, "could you all come here for a minute?"

They set aside their games and books, and our newest resident, Candy, turns off the TV. Once I have their attention, I take a deep breath. "First of all, I want to apologize for being gone so much these last few months. A lot has been going on in my life, and I'm not just talking about my engagement to Trevor."

Everyone grins and a few applaud until I continue. "Yes, it's a wonderful thing, but it's relatively minor compared to the rest. You see ... I discovered in May that I have a daughter and two grandchildren."

They're clearly shocked, and Benita says, "You didn't know?"

"No." *Okay, Jolene, you can do this. You need to do this.* "The thing is, when I was young I had an abortion. Actually, I had two. I won't go into details, but I went to Nashville to face what I'd done and find some level of peace and, hopefully, forgiveness, and instead I learned one of my children—a daughter—survived

129

the procedure."

Jillie, Benita's close friend, asks, "How's that possible? Kids can really live through an abortion?"

I nod. "Yeah. In fact, it happens more than you might think."

Several start asking questions, but a few seem rather disconcerted. I know at least two of my girls have had abortions and continue to struggle with that choice. I make a mental note to talk with them one-on-one later. But for now, I hold up a hand to calm things down. "The point is, I have a family ... in Tennessee."

It's like I hit the mute button. Six pairs of eyes stare at me, some with mouths open, others already with a glint of tears. My own eyes sting so I blink a few times, which sends a tear or two trickling down my cheek. "Because of that, I've decided to move back home to be close to them."

No one speaks for a moment, then Benita says, "How soon are you leaving?"

"My official last day will be the eighth of August, but I'll be around to help out with things until the end of September."

"So you'll be here when I graduate out of the program?"

"I wouldn't miss it for the world."

Benita expels the breath she's been holding in. But another resident, Davia, says, "What about the rest of us? How can you just walk away so easily?"

"There won't be anything easy about this." I expected several of the girls would be hurt, even angry, and tried to prepare myself. "It breaks my heart to leave. That was the hardest part of this decision—I didn't have an easy choice. Whether I stay here or move there, I will end up being too far away from people I love."

Slowly, I look into the eyes of each of the women there. "You need to know I will make sure the person who replaces me is the absolute best woman to help each of you get through the program effectively. In fact, our top candidate is coming over this afternoon, and I would deeply appreciate it if you gave her a chance. And treat her better than you ever treated me."

Several of the women laugh, remembering most of them weren't exactly pleasant when they first moved into Cocoon House. I say, "Try not to have certain expectations, and please don't determine to immediately dislike her. I think, if you are open to a new person, she'll soon make you forget all about me." Realizing what I just said, I add, "But don't forget me!"

A few more chuckles ... and the doorbell rings so I excuse myself and hurry to answer it. The woman at the door is dressed like a gypsy, all the way from her painted-leather-sandaled feet to the multi-colored scarf stylishly twisted around her head.

I hold out my hand. "Are you Marty Cortés?"

"Yes." She takes my hand and gives it a firm shake. "You must be Miss Woods."

"Jolene, please." I stand aside and motion her past me. "Our residents are waiting to meet you."

She puts a hand over her heart. "Wow. Throwing me right into the fire?"

"They're wonderful women ... and I want them to feel like they're a part of the process."

"Actually, I think that's a fantastic idea."

The front door is only a short walk from the archway leading into the living room. "I'll just do a brief introduction, then we can talk more in my office."

Marty nods as we join the girls. My residents are relatively nice—well, they're not out-and-out rude anyway. All I tell Marty as I introduce them is each woman's name and how long she's been at Cocoon House. We leave it up to each resident how much she wants the others to know about her past. Marty will get that information from me and their files if she takes the job.

131

By the time Marty shakes my hand goodbye over two hours later, I'm as confident as I can be that she's the person God sent for the job. She even loves the idea of our Grr-l Stuff Saturday fundraisers and plans to keep them going. I have so much peace about her, in fact, that it makes me finally feel like moving away is the right thing to do.

Because how can I really know? It seems that either decision would glorify God and isn't that the goal? So unless He sends a neon sign flashing an arrow in the direction He's sending me, what else can I do but keep moving forward … and keep praying He'll redirect me if necessary? Having Trevor's support doesn't hurt, and my parents, of course, are delighted.

My sister Freddie and her kids, however—that's another story. Not so much that they don't want me to move closer to my daughter, and they certainly understand how important it is to me, but they don't want me to leave. Of course, I'm miserable at the thought I won't be close enough anymore to enjoy our weekly meals together, and the children—my seven beloved nieces and nephews—will continue to grow, and I will no longer be a part of their lives. On the other hand, I'll now be able to develop stronger relationships with my Tennessee nieces and nephews.

Another bright spot is that if everything works out with Marty, I'll be able to road trip with Freddie and her brood to Nashville in two weeks. And who knows?

Maybe I can convince them to move east too.

Chapter 17
Uli

"Please don't hate me."

"What? Why would I hate you?" It's Wednesday night, and I was getting ready for bed early when Penny called. I have to be at the church at eight for our Adventureland adventure. "Did you try to arrange a blind date or something?"

"No, but … we can't go tomorrow."

I sit down on the edge of my bed. "Why not?"

"Jason's dad had another heart attack."

"Oh, no! Is he okay?"

"Well, they think he's going to be fine, but we just can't enjoy an amusement park while worrying about him."

"I get that." I do. And who I'll hang out with at the park doesn't matter. "You know I'll pray for him and your family. How did the kids take it?"

She groans. "They weren't happy. We promised we'd go another day as soon as Grandpa is better. We also promised Dairy Queen. Ice cream has a way of calming them down."

"Ha. Okay, well, why don't I just wait and go later with you?"

"Absolutely not! You go tomorrow when you have a free ticket. You'll have more fun with that group anyway."

I doubt that. I'm not even sure who else is going. Though we talked about it at church on Sunday, all I know is it's enough people to take a bus. Since I don't want Penny to worry about me, I say, "I think I'd have more fun with you and your family, but okay."

"Good!" She takes a deep breath. "That's a relief. And it might even be better this way—you'll *have* to make new friends if you're not stuck with me and my crew."

133

"Maybe you're right." I'm an extrovert. Making friends isn't usually a problem. "I really appreciate you letting me know, though."

"Of course!" Then, in the background, a child cries. "I'd better go, but I will definitely pray you have a wonderful time, Uli."

"Thank you. I'm sure I will."

After we hang up, I sit quietly for a moment. I'm really not that sure. Hopeful, but definitely not sure.

The church bus to Adventureland is almost full, mostly with families. And I immediately feel like I don't fit in—a feeling I fight by being friendly and asking a lot of questions. But I'm like one onion ring in a container of fries. Not only does it seem I'm the only single person over the age of sixteen, but they all know each other. I'm the stranger. It's funny how people can be super polite, and you still feel like an outcast.

We're not even at the park, and I already regret coming. It seems I'll either end up spending the day wandering around by myself, or I'll hoist my company on whoever smiles at me first. This is the single life. My almost two years with Cole and my close friendships with Catie and Jolene had made this side of it easy to forget. Now it all comes rushing back.

If only I'd brought a novel with me. I could find a comfortable chair somewhere near a place with free pop refills and spend the day reading. If your nose is in a book, it looks like you're alone on purpose.

A sense of dread shivers through me, but I tamp it down. *It will be fine, Uli. Just calm down.* For all I know, someone will invite me into their party, and I'll have a wonderful time.

If only. Five minutes after entering the park, my fellow adventurers split up into small groups and disappear in every direction. And I'm standing there in my jean shorts and dark blue tank top with a bright pink headband to prevent a scalp burn and what little cash I have in a Ziploc bag in my pocket (in case I go on a water ride) and suntan lotion on my face … abandoned and pathetic and trying not to cry.

It's all I can do not to call Cole right then and beg him to take me back. I don't … because I left my phone on the bus. Why would I want to bother with a phone while I'm running around an amusement park?

But now what do I do? Should I go on rides? I take a few steps down Main Street. It's small and quaint and not that busy for early August—probably due to the sweaty Iowa weather— and the whole place smells like french fries and funnel cakes.

The map and schedule they handed me at the gate indicates there are a few shows throughout the day. Well, that would be okay. Watching a performance is a perfectly acceptable thing to do by yourself. Who would even notice? Add that to a lunch of something deep fried and fattening plus a few rides, and it's not a terrible day.

But I'm glad I didn't have to pay for it.

I've been standing outside the Raging River ride for ten minutes now, trying to decide if it's worth waiting in line for. Do I want to get soaked? Do I want to ride alone? Do I want to stand in line for half an hour or more? On the other hand, I love whitewater rapids rides like this.

So far, I've sailed from one side of the park to the other on the Sky Ride twice and took flight on the Storm Chaser, a giant swing ride. That was exhilarating … and it's not so noticeable when someone goes alone. And I drank root beer and ate nachos while watching the magic show at Sheriff Sam's Saloon. Now here I am at the Raging River, which involves hopping into a big, round, raft-like boat that seats six. Would they just put me with other riders? They wouldn't send me off on a raft alone, right?

Well, I might as well move into the line. If I change my mind, I can always leave. A family of six follows me in. Everything's moving along fairly quickly, and then the two boys in the group behind me start goofing off. One pushes the other, and the pushee shoves back, knocking his brother into me so hard I almost lose my balance. The mom grabs my arm to keep me from falling, then turns on her kids like an angry bear.

"This is why I keep telling you to settle down! You almost knocked her over!"

The boy who fell into me looks rather sheepish. The other does not. He has an expression that says he'd push his brother again if he had the chance, and it's my fault for not getting out of the way. Seeing such stubborn orneriness almost makes me laugh out loud. But I bite my lip instead, then say,

"It's fine. No harm done."

"I appreciate that," Mama Bear says, "but I still want them to apologize." She turns to her boys, hands on hips and eyebrow arched. "Well? What do you say?"

The one who might actually feel bad says, "Sorry, ma'am." The other shrugs, mumbles "Whatever," and seems done with his apology. At another glare from Mom, though, he adds, "Sorry."

Mama Bear growls and waits a few seconds before stating, "No ice cream."

"But Mom!"

She repeats it, slower. "No … ice cream."

The boy crosses his arms and grunts. It's like a little bear family. Ornery Cub glances at Papa Bear, who's carrying one girl

136

and holding hands with the other, and says, "Dad!"

"Listen to your mother," says Papa.

It kind of feels like I'm watching an episode of *The Berenstein Bears*.

Mama eventually gets tired of glaring at her sons and turns back to me. "I am sorry."

"It's okay. I hardly expect to leave an amusement park unscathed."

She smiles. "Well, that's one way of looking at it."

After a slightly awkward silence, she asks, "Are you from around here?"

"Cedar Rapids."

"Oh, nice. I love Cedar Rapids. We live in Iowa City."

I give her an up-nod because I'm not really sure where to go from that. Then, for reasons I can't explain, I say, "I just moved back home after living in Colorado for almost a decade."

"Really? Why would anyone leave Colorado? It's so beautiful there. And I'd give anything to escape this Iowa humidity."

Hmm. Why *would* I leave? Because my friends have scattered? Because I'm unemployed and financially strapped and need my mother's help? Because I ended my engagement when my fiancé cheated on me? So many great answers to that question. But I go with,

"My mom broke her hip and needs me." Which is a great answer—I'm not lying and I sound like a wonderful daughter who rushes to her mother's aid in a time of need.

"Wow, that's wonderful. Not many people would make that kind of sacrifice. And your husband didn't mind moving?"

"My husband?" I try not to laugh and fail miserably. "I'm not married."

"Oh, I thought—" and she glances at some random guy standing sort of near me. I'd be more offended if he wasn't cute and, as far as I can tell, younger than me.

137

"Ha. No." I lean closer to her and whisper, "I wish."

She turns slightly pink and says, "Sorry about that."

"No worries."

Mama Bear holds out her hand. "I'm Julie."

"Uli." I shake her hand and laugh again. "That rhymes."

"It does. Though I gotta admit I've never heard that name before."

"Ah, yes, well, my mother chose it for that very reason." I shrug. "She saw it on some news report and liked it. Even though it was a man's name."

"No, really?"

"That's my mom for ya."

By now, we're almost to the front. We must be close to our turn because her kids have stopped swinging from the line bars like little monkeys. The group in front of me hops into their raft. Since each one only seats six, I let the Berensteins go ahead of me, waving goodbye as they float away. I have to wait for two more rafts before a group of four comes along that I can ride with.

As I'm rocking back and forth and getting splashed, it hits me that the reason I kept the conversation going with Julie was that I just wanted to talk to someone besides the guy I ordered my lunch of chicken tenders and onion rings from.

How sad is that?

The rest of the afternoon saunters by. A few more rides—including twice on the Tornado because I love wooden rollercoasters—plus an hour enjoying the Adventureland Circus, and it's almost time to meet the group back at the entrance.

Once more across the park on the Sky Ride, which I find quite peaceful, should get me where I need to be right on time.

As my chair—which looks more like a slatted park bench for two than the usual gondola—slowly makes its way toward the front of the park, the ride stops for a bit longer than usual halfway across. Since all I can see are trees and rollercoasters and other sky riders, I'm not sure what's going on. But we eventually get going again.

When we finally get to the base, I jump off. I'm about five minutes late, but I really have to pee. Besides, what's the chance they'll leave right when they said they'd meet? Surely other people would be running late too. And, of course, they'll do a head count to make sure they don't leave anyone behind.

A small voice suggests I not take the chance, but I drank a lot of pop today. I find a bathroom on the way out, take care of business, then scurry toward our meeting place. I don't see my group or, for that matter, anyone I recognize. Am I the first one here? Ha. I knew it. I check my watch. Yep. I'm barely ten minutes late. I can't imagine they gathered thirty-plus people and loaded them up in a bus that fast. Even if they did, they'd soon realize one person was missing.

Wouldn't they?

I wait another five minutes. Then, with dread growing like a lump in my throat, I slowly make my way toward where our bus is parked.

Was parked. The space is empty.

They left without me. And took my phone with them. If only I'd listened to that little voice that told me it might be a good thing to have on-hand, just in case. But I didn't want to have to deal with it on rides.

So, here I am, alone again. Still. Standing in the middle of a parking lot less than an hour before the place closes. Well, I need to call someone. I'd phone Penny and ask her to get in touch with someone on the bus, but I don't have her number memorized. Who memorizes phone numbers anymore? It will have to be Mom, I suppose, who will love having to leave home this late to drive four hours roundtrip.

Okay, first I'll find a phone; then I'll deal with what this means for Mom. And what waiting in a dark parking lot until midnight will mean for me.

No. Wait. First I'll pray. Because I'm feeling a little freaked out right now. The sun has pretty much gone down with just a dim reflection of burnt orange coloring the sky. I spent most of what little money I had with me on food. I'm alone, vulnerable, stranded. And forgotten. They drove away and didn't even notice I wasn't there. Does anyone remember I came with them? Will they realize I'm missing before they get to Cedar Rapids? And if they do, will they come back for me?

It doesn't matter. I can't count on that. I need to find my own way home. So I say that much-needed prayer and ask God for guidance and protection. Though my heart is filled with doubt that He loves me enough to take care of my little problem, I keep praying until I feel there's not much else to say.

Squaring my shoulders and convincing myself I have nothing to fear, I scan the parking lot for people who look friendly. It's inconceivable that I'd ask someone who doesn't own a phone because who doesn't have a phone nowadays? That's why we don't memorize numbers. All I need to do is find someone who wouldn't mind me using theirs.

Plenty of people are exiting by now, yet I keep coming up with reasons not to ask anyone. Then, to my amazement, Mama Bear appears at the gate like an angel. She and Papa are both carrying sleepy children while each pulls one of the other kids by the hand. I can ask her! What was her real name? Rhymes with mine. Right.

"Julie!"

She stops mid-stride and, praise the Lord, smiles when she sees me. "Oh, hi! Uli, right?"

"Yes. Oh, thank goodness. Is there any chance I could use your phone? My bus left without me, and my phone's on the bus. Can you believe it?!"

She shakes her head. "What? They left without you? Why?"

"I have no idea." Because I'm not going to tell her they forgot me. "But if I can call my mom, hopefully she can come pick me up."

One of their little girls moans, and Papa says, "We should get the kids to the van."

Julie nods and motions for me to follow. "Of course you can use my phone, but what will you do while you wait for your mom? It will take her, what, at least an hour or so to get here?"

"About two, actually. But what other option do I have? I don't have phone numbers for anyone on the bus. And I know first names but not last."

By now she and Papa are loading their kids. Once they're all buckled in and, as far as I can tell, immediately asleep, she gets out her phone and starts to hand it to me. Then stops. "Hang on a second."

Julie goes around to the other side of the van and speaks quietly with her husband. A few minutes later, she's back. "If we took you with us as far as Iowa City, could your mom come down to I-80 and pick you up there? Less of a drive for her, and you wouldn't have to wait in a parking lot for two hours."

To my embarrassment, a wash of tears fills my eyes. "Um … are you serious?"

"Yes, of course. It wouldn't be a problem."

And just like that, I'm genuinely crying. "That would be wonderful. I really wasn't looking forward to hanging out here alone."

She puts a hand on my arm and smiles. "Who would? And we're happy to help."

After handing me her phone, she gets in her van and I call my mom.

Wow. God answered that prayer. And fast. Maybe He really does listen.

141

Chapter 18
Catie

It's my second check-up with my Ohio oncologist, Dr. Zoya Shelley, and I've been looking forward to it for two weeks. Not so much because I love meeting with the doctor, but because of what I want to talk to her about.

After we've taken care of all of the official cancer business, I finally get my chance.

"There's something I wanted to ask you."

"Of course." She finishes putting my file away, then gives me her full attention. "What do you need?"

I clear my throat and cross my fingers. "My family is going to the beach in a couple of weeks and I was wondering if that's something I could do."

"When specifically?"

"Leaving on August fifteen and getting back on the twenty-fourth. Which means I'd miss my sixth treatment."

"Flying?"

"Driving."

"Okay." She steeples her fingers in front of her face. "You really shouldn't miss that treatment, but I could see if there's a quality center there that you could go to. If there is, I believe a vacation would be a good idea."

"Really?" I take a deep breath so as not to seem too excited. And fail completely when I add, "That would be wonderful!"

"You would need to take extra medication just to be safe, and you must protect yourself from sunlight—wear hats, long sleeves, and use a high SPF sunblock on any exposed skin."

And I nod obediently but hope she writes everything down because I'm too distracted and excited to make a mental reminder. I get to spend a week on a beach with my family!

Won't that be a blast? So much fun, in fact, I might even forget I'm sick.

On Saturday, my family packs up a picnic, plenty of camp chairs and blankets, and lots of suntan lotion to carpool down to Indian Lake for an all-day outdoor music festival a local Christian radio station puts on. Well, that's the plan, anyway, but it takes us forever to wrangle three enthusiastic children—including a five-year-old who thinks it's perfectly reasonable to wear Frosty the Snowman leggings and a Donald Duck t-shirt for a day of swimming and running around a beach.

Tawny chases little Bryn around the house for thirty minutes with a blue-flowered one-piece swimsuit, but the child only laughs and dances away. Until finally Tawny stomps her foot and commands, "Bryn Louise Delaney! Either put on your swimsuit or stay home!"

It must have worked because five minutes later we're piled into Dad's car and Patrick's van and are on our way. We arrive early enough to find a decent spot in the grass—not too close to the stage but not too far back either. My brother and his son set up the beach cabana for shade while the rest of us get out the chairs and the food while also taking turns on kid duty. Three children under the age of six are, in a word, a handful.

We're about to eat when there's a shout. My niece, Angela, walks toward us, grinning and hand-in-hand with an attractive young man with dark, wavy hair who's a head taller than she is. Delia had mentioned her daughter was dating but I hadn't met him yet. In fact, this is the first time I've seen my very busy niece since I got back to Ohio.

She skips over and gives me a hug. "Hi, Aunt Catie!" Then

she runs her hand over my recently shaved, scarf-covered head. "You look so cute."

"Really?" I touch the multicolored silk, still not quite used to it. "I don't look too much like a Bohemian artist?"

Angela tilts her head with a thoughtful expression as she studies my overall appearance. "Maybe a little. But I like it."

"Well, I could always take up painting."

We laugh as Tawny joins us. "Why not? You've always had a good eye for color."

It's not the worst idea.

"In fact," Angela says, "I just heard they're offering beginner and advanced classes at that new art supply store in downtown Bellefontaine."

Hmm. Bellefontaine is a slightly bigger town about twenty minutes from the farm. It's certainly worth looking into.

But, "Enough about me," I say. "Who's your friend?"

Angela smiles up at the boy next to her. "This is Ian Michaelson. He's taking marketing classes at OSU-Lima too. We just … hit it off."

Obviously. They both spend more time gazing adoringly at each other than looking anywhere else.

That's when Angela's big brother, Patrick, sneaks up behind her and musses her hair. "Well, look at this," he says. "Little Angie finally has a boyfriend."

Angela elbows him in the ribs and growls, "Knock it off" at the same time his wife and mother both say, "Patrick!"

For a brief second, I see the little boy who used to beg me to push him on the swing and grumble when I stopped. He grunts and rolls his eyes. "I'm just joking."

Tawny puts an arm around him. "Honey, not everyone appreciates your sense of humor like I do."

"And by 'not everyone,'" Angela quips, "she means no one."

Patrick takes a step toward her like he's about to give chase.

Angela squeaks like a frightened mouse, but as she makes a quick move behind Ian, Delia announces, "Lunch is ready!"

The girl sticks out her tongue playfully, and Patrick teases, "Saved by chicken salad, little sis."

But the two continue to bug each other as we load up our plates with chicken salad on croissants, chips, and juicy watermelon slices that are so fresh the scent is overwhelmingly wonderful. Behind the joking between the siblings, though, something isn't quite right with Angela. She gives as good as she gets, yet I can't help but feel she's not happy about it.

The food is delicious, no surprise—Delia could open her own restaurant if she wanted to—especially the chicken salad. It's filled with cashews and cut-up grapes and just enough mayo. I'm telling Delia how good it is when Angela, who gradually became rather quiet, says, "Excuse me. I'll be right back."

She squeezes her boyfriend's hand, then heads toward the rows of vendors and art exhibits filling a grassy area near the stage. Something's definitely going on, so I get up and follow her.

"Hey, wait up," I say as she hurries away. Angela turns to me as I add, "I'll go with you."

"I thought I'd get a lemon shake-up."

"Sounds good."

The food truck with a big lemon on its roof is hard to miss. Since there's a bit of a line, we have to wait. I take my niece's arm and say, "Okay, what's going on?"

"Nothing."

"Oh, there's definitely something. But you don't want to talk about it?"

With a deep sigh, she says, "All right. You have an older brother."

"I do."

"Is yours as annoying as mine?'

We take a step forward. "Absolutely." At her surprised look,

I continue, "Brothers consider annoying their sisters to be part of the job description. They can't help themselves."

"I just ..."—another step—"wish he'd treat me like an adult once in a while."

Studying her face, I finally get it. "Especially in front of your boyfriend."

"Yes! Ian probably thinks I act like a child now, even though I'm never that way at school."

"Hmm." It's our turn so I order two large shake-ups and pay the woman taking the orders. While we wait, I say, "As far as I can tell, the main thing that boy is thinking about is how wonderful you are."

An older man finishes shaking up our lemonade, then hands one tall plastic cup to Angela and another to me. Slipping the straw out of its wrapper, I enjoy my first sip. Mmm. So refreshing. So perfect for a hot summer day.

As we slowly make our way back to the picnic area, I say, "Sweetie, it's a fact of life that being around your family will always make you feel younger than you are, and sometimes those feelings turn into childish actions. I don't know why, but it happens to me every time I come home. It's better now. But that doesn't mean there aren't days when I want to push your dad down and pull his hair ... what little he has left."

Angela laughs and links her arm through mine. "Well," she says, "as long as it's natural."

We haven't made it back yet when my niece whispers, "By the way, what do you think of Ian?"

"He seems very nice."

"Nice!" She pulls away a little. "Aunt Catie, didn't you tell me once that saying a guy is nice is like saying he's boring and predictable?"

Did I? Hmm. It does sound like something I might say. I laugh. "Well, sweetie, in case you haven't noticed, I'm not the

146

best person to give dating advice." With a sigh, I add, "And right now, nice sounds absolutely delightful."

Angela stops and faces me, taking my lemonade-free hand with hers. "I don't know why you're still single, Aunt Catie. I think you're wonderful ... and all the men you've met must be idiots."

Which only makes me love her more, something I didn't think was possible. In a whisper I say, "Marriage isn't everything, Angie."

She nods. "I get that. I really do. But is it okay if I pray God brings you someone who's actually worthy of you? Someone who'll take care of you?"

"You are so sweet." I pull her into a hug. "But we have to trust God to take care of me. Maybe it would be better if you prayed His will would be done in my life."

Angie takes a deep breath and tightens her hold on me. "I can do that. And I'll pray His will includes an amazing husband who will treat you like you're the most fantastic woman who ever walked the earth—because you are—and give you more love than you ever dreamed possible."

Apparently, my niece didn't inherit that practical gene that seems so prevalent among us Delaneys. James and I especially have always had trouble believing good things can happen. Losing your mother when you're young can have that kind of an impact on a person. I've made some progress, but James, as far as I can tell, is doing much better. He married a good woman and had two smart and well-adjusted children, for starters. Something I can now see I was afraid of when I was younger. Not so much afraid of having, but something I was afraid of losing.

As soon as lunch is done and cleaned up, we settle in. There's music all afternoon—some average and some stirringly beautiful. I'm glad we have the beach cabana because the shade it provides plus the breeze floating off the lake are the only two

147

things that keep us from getting heatstroke. It's so hot, I consider dipping my feet in the lake water. But the thought of having wet, sandy feet sounds so much worse. It's not like a little lukewarm lake water would help that much anyway.

In between the second and third musicians, Tawny asks if I want to walk around a bit. The event includes numerous vendor tables with all kinds of wares, and Tawny has been itching to check it out all afternoon. Delia jumps up to join us. I'd invite Angela, but she and Ian took their chairs closer to the stage not long after we finished eating.

I'm impressed by the quality and variety of homemade products. Though I've put myself on a budget, I feel a bit like splurging, so I purchase a lovely corner bookshelf made out of an old door, some sandalwood and peppermint essential oils that were recommended for people going through chemo, and a big bag of kettle corn for everyone to share. Since it's now nighttime and hours since we ate, we also stop at a Mexican food stand for tacos and burritos along with chips and salsa.

Tawny buys food for her kids, and I grab a couple extra tacos for Dad, but when I suggest we also get something for James and Patrick, I'm told by their wives they can take care of themselves. And, sure enough, when we get back to our chairs the three men, my dad included, are devouring brats and leftover chips from lunch. Since we have a cooler half filled with Cokes, Sprites, and bottled water, it would seem we're set to sit back and enjoy the rest of the concert.

What is it about outdoor events in the summer? It always takes me back to my high school years when you had several friends to run around with, giggling and eating popcorn and cotton candy, and one cute boy to flirt with or, at least, to hope you'd see wander by so you could follow him around. And always that tingle of hope that he'd follow you and, perhaps, try to hold your hand.

148

I miss that. Now, any time I see a man my age I have to assume he's married since he probably is. Though I suppose there are a few single men in the area, I've yet to meet any. I sure would like to. It would be nice just to have a conversation with a Guy With Potential again.

Which reminds me of my last significant chat with a single man—Wes in the back of the van while on a ministry trip in May. He smelled so good. I close my eyes and let the music of this night and the memory of that one wash over me. If only I could combine the two and have someone close to me right now. And, again, it's like I can almost feel his presence, whoever *he* is. What's he doing right now? Does he miss me too? Is he even remotely curious as to who—or where—I am?

Or maybe there is no one. Maybe he isn't out there. What a sad thought.

No. This isn't the night for that. So I'm just going to sit here with my eyes closed. And believe I have this feeling because God is preparing my heart for something—someone—truly fantastic, like Angela said. I'll cling to that instead of feeling sorry for myself.

It's a far better way to enjoy an evening.

Chapter 19
Jolene

It doesn't take long for almost everyone involved with Cocoon House to agree that Marty Cortés is the right person for the job. For the final part of the interview process, we have a big meal at the House with Marty, her husband, Jesse, and all the board members and their spouses as well as, of course, the staff and residents, including some who already finished the program. I'm particularly happy to see Sara, who was pivotal in starting our Grr-l Stuff yard sales and still helps out when she can.

After a fine, catered meal donated by one of our board members, I stand to make the announcement. I want this to be a significant and sanctioned event. Clinking on my water glass, I gain the attention of the two dozen people gathered around the tables we've set up in the large dining room. It only takes a few moments for the chatter to die down and all eyes to turn toward me.

I clear my throat. "Tonight is one of those evenings where I find myself torn between great joy and great sadness. I planned to spend the rest of my life working at Cocoon House but, as we all know, God's ways are not our ways. He had something else in mind for me." Everyone smiles and turns toward the other end of the table where Trevor sits, beaming. I wish he were close enough to hold my hand, but I feel his strength from fifteen feet away. And so I continue,

"As soon as I realized God was calling me to Tennessee, we—" and I nod to SueAnn and Tina—"began praying for Him to bring the person He would have take over my work here. Should any of us be surprised that He did exactly that?"

A few people laugh, several nod encouragingly, but most have tears in their eyes. I look at Marty. "And so, without further

150

ado, Marty Cortés, I would like to take this opportunity to officially offer you the position of managing director of Cocoon House." And I hold out my hand.

She stands and shakes it, thanking me and everyone else there. Then I sit and she takes my place at the head of the table, literally and figuratively. "It is an honor to be here and to accept this position. Sometimes you can see God's hand all over your life. Sometimes, He even pushes you." Marty turns her back to the room, then glances at us over her shoulder. "Do you see handprints?" Everyone laughs and she faces us again with a smile. "Just checking. But it is clear He called me here, and I'm happy to pick up where Jolene leaves off." Her eyes, shining with strength and determination, meet mine. "I won't let you down."

You'd better not. But I grin back and say, "We have every faith in you."

The evening ends with a time of prayer—first for me as I prepare for a new chapter in my life, then for Marty as she settles in as director, and, finally, for the ministry of Cocoon House. But when Benita and Jillie come to the front of the room and get everyone's attention, I discover the night isn't over yet.

Benita says, "We know Miss Woods plans to stick around until September before she runs off with her hunky fiancé and forgets all about us." People laugh as warmth crawls up my neck. To deflect my embarrassment, I say,

"It would be impossible for me to forget any of you." I wiggle a shame-on-you finger at the girls and add, "Especially after this."

They grin back at me and Jillie continues where Benita left off. "Well, we wanted to make sure, so we got a little help from Ralph and SueAnn and several of the people here … and found some stuff to help you remember us."

Together, my girls slip into the hall, and then, in a moment, a few come back. Benita leads the way, carrying some lovely red begonias in a white marble planter. She places the obviously heavy gift on the table in front of me and says, "This is to represent the life you showed us we could have. We hope you'll find a place for it at your new home."

That's when the tears start.

Next, Jillie comes forward and holds out a fine bottle of champagne. "This is to celebrate answered prayer."

As I take the bottle, my heart is overflowing. The tears are falling in earnest now. I don't even try to stop them.

Davia follows Jillie carrying a small blue box. Her face is a little red as she pushes it toward me. "It's a necklace."

The other girls nudge her and say, "Come on, Davia."

"No," she says, "it's too cheesy."

Jillie grunts. "Just say it."

"Fine." Davia takes a breath and mumbles, "This is so you always have us close to your heart."

Grinning, I open the box. Inside is a large but thin silver pendant on a delicate chain. The front has the words "to the moon and back," and the names of all the women who've been through the program have been engraved on the back. I clutch it to my heart, trying in vain to wipe the new wave of tears from my eyes. "I'll wear it all the time. Thank you."

Finally, the rest of my girls enter carrying a mid-century modern desk chair with thick cushions covered with a deep blue and red plaid material. If I could have designed the perfect chair for my future office, it would look just like this, and I tell the girls so.

One by one, they each come up and hug me, and they're followed by similar goodbyes from most of the board members. As for SueAnn, Tina, and our current residents, we'll have a more official goodbye party in September.

It's late by the time I walk Trevor out to his Jeep. We hardly had a chance to talk at all, but I tell him again how grateful I am that he was there.

"Where else would I be?" He says it sincerely, and yet there's something in his tone. I stop and he turns to face me.

I ask, "What is it? What's wrong?"

He shrugs. "I'm just very proud of you."

"Thanks." But that's not it.

He kisses my cheek. Something is definitely off. I'm just too tired to work through whatever it is that's bothering him. This needs to be done when I'm more rested and less emotional. As I'm about to ask when he wants to get together next, he says,

"Why don't you come over tomorrow night?"

That surprises me since we've made it a rule not to hang out at his place alone. But it would be nice to talk things over in private. "All right. I'll make dinner."

"Sounds good."

I laugh. "It won't be long until I'm making you dinner every night. Are you ready for that?"

"Ha. Don't kid yourself. You know I'll do most of the cooking."

"Actually, I don't *know* that, but I am hopeful."

Trevor gets in his Jeep and rolls down the window. "If you handle dinner," he says, "I'll take care of dessert."

"It's a deal." I hold out a hand so we can shake on it, which he does … then he drives away. I'm standing there, trying to remember the last time he didn't kiss me goodnight.

Something is *not* right.

I decide on chicken cacciatore for supper at Trevor's. Pasta is always a winner. Since I don't know what Trevor has on-hand, I just buy everything needed before driving over to his place.

When I knock, there's no answer. I pull out my phone to call him, and the door opens. He's wearing old jean shorts and a plain white button-down—one he's had forever, but at least it's clean.

He looks great, of course. Simple and casual and delightfully kissable. I'm wearing a classy new sundress and strappy sandals, and he somehow manages to look better in stuff he pulled out of the back of his closet.

After I get my first kiss of the night, I hand him the heavier bag of groceries, but my fiancé is such a gentleman, he takes both and carries them into his tiny galley kitchen. How much am I going to love being married to this man?

Trevor removes the items from the bags, setting the fresh vegetables on a cutting board and putting the rest of it by the stove. "What's for dinner?"

"Chicken cacciatore," I say, "with garlic bread and Caesar salad."

"Yum."

"And for dessert?"

One side of his mouth curves up somewhat self-consciously as he points to a box on the counter. "I went all out."

I step closer. Frosted lemon cookies from the grocery store. They look tasty, but I'm surprised he didn't bake something like he usually does. Not that I'm going to turn down good cookies, no matter where they came from.

A half hour later I'm straining the spaghetti when there's a knock on the door. The expression on Trevor's face surprises me. Scared. Excited. Maybe both. He says,

"Excuse me," and goes to the door, which isn't far in this small apartment. A man with skin as dark as Trevor's but with a full head of hair stands on the other side. Trevor smiles, says, "Daniel," and pulls the man into the room and into a hug. I set the pasta aside and move toward them. The way they're both now watching me indicates something significant is about to happen.

"Jolene," Trevor says. "This is Daniel … my brother."

Which is a strange thing for him to say considering he never told me he had a brother. A little sister named Belinda, desperate parents with more hope than resources, and a million cousins … but what a way to spring a brother on a girl.

Okay. I hold out my hand. "It's a pleasure to meet you." Then I turn to my fiancé. The small beads of sweat on his forehead tell me he knows he has some explaining to do. But I say, "Supper is getting cold." I smile at my future brother-in-law. "Are you hungry?"

Daniel grins back at me. "Starving, actually." Striding toward the table, he adds, "Something smells fantastic." He has a strong accent, but I can't place it. French, maybe, but a little old-school English too. And there's a musical quality to it, which I rather like. He's good-looking, like my Trevor, except for a wicked scar that draws a jagged line from his left eyebrow down his eye and stops right under his chin. It doesn't seem to have affected his vision, though. And I can't help but notice that Daniel's scar is similar to the one across Trevor's chest and arm.

All this time I've patiently waited for my man to be ready to tell me whatever it is he hasn't told me yet. Tonight I'll let them eat. Then it's time to talk.

Supper is nice, pleasant even. Quiet but friendly and easygoing, Daniel seems content to let Trevor and me do most of the talking. Yet I sense a deep strength within him, like a steel core. These two brothers have a lot in common.

We finish the meal and clean up. While the guys take care of the dishes, I refill our glasses with tea, put the lemon cookies on a plate, and set it all on the coffee table in the living room. Soon, the men join me. We talk about basic things at first—wedding plans, our upcoming move to Nashville, how Trevor and I met. Then I ask Daniel about himself. That's when the flavor of the evening changes.

155

Trevor says, "Daniel works in … law enforcement."

"Oh, wow." I noticed Trevor's hesitation and it tweaks my curiosity. I ask Daniel, "What do you do in law enforcement?"

Daniel sits back and rolls his shoulders like they hurt. "I help free child soldiers in Africa."

Just like that. He says it as casually as someone might tell you they finished the dishes. But the brothers exchange a look, and that's when I put it all together—Africa, the secrecy, those awful scars.

I turn to Trevor, who's sitting on the couch next to me, and put my hand on his. "That's it, isn't it? That's what you've kept from me. You were a child soldier."

"No, yes, well—" he glances at Daniel—"not for long. Daniel got me out."

This is unbelievable. "And your scar?"

"Well," Daniel says, "it wasn't easy. Once a kid's in the army, they like to keep you there."

Great. He's as bad at giving details as his brother. I stare at Daniel for several seconds, hoping for more. Finally I ask, "What about your scar?"

"Oh, that." He waves his hand like someone scratched him with a pencil. "They didn't like my tendency to, what is the word?" Daniel looks at Trevor, who offers, "Rebel?"

"Yes," Daniel affirms, "rebel."

And, once again, he seems to be done. I'm about to pull my hair out when Trevor says, "It's really not that interesting, Jolene."

Yeah, right. I say, "I'd still like to hear it."

Daniel stands and leans against the small fireplace mantel as he speaks. "All right. I was taken when I was ten and served in the army for five years. Then I met up with a man from our village who told me Trevor had been grabbed the week before. When I tried to escape, they gave me this." He traces the scar

156

with his left hand. "The second time, they poured boiling water on me." And he holds up his right hand, where I now see the pink, tight skin of a third-degree burn. "But on the third time, they don't catch me."

"Dear God," I say. "You were just a child."

"True," he says, "but Trevor was only nine. They wouldn't do to him what they did to me. I found him and got him out."

"And not just me," Trevor adds. "He freed six other children that day. Plus hundreds more since then."

"Hundreds?"

Daniel shrugs. "I could get the exact number if you're curious."

I am, but I tell him that's not necessary. It's an amazing story ... and I'm still trying to get over the fact that Trevor didn't tell me, the woman he claims to love. How could he keep something that significant from me? I ask Daniel, "So, what are you doing here?"

Now he's the one who seems surprised. "Trevor said you need my help."

"What? I do?"

They both laugh and Daniel says, "You are right, brother. She's very funny."

Trevor puts his arm around me. I stiffen, but he shakes his head with a laugh. "He's joking. Daniel is my best man. I invited him to come spend my last two months of bachelorhood with me."

"It was good timing, actually." Finally sitting again, Daniel grabs a cookie and chews off half of it in one bite. "My captain said I needed a vacation."

They both chuckle, but I don't find it too funny. I grab the glasses and cookie plate and take the dishes into the kitchen, wondering all the while if I know my fiancé at all.

157

Chapter 20
Uli

"And they just left you there?"

Then, to my amazement, Penny laughs. In my face.

"Gee, thanks for the support."

"Oh, Uli, I am sorry. That must have been upsetting."

You have no idea. Because married women don't get it. Even when they try.

I found Penny in the church café before Sunday school, not surprising. She's stirring cream and sugar into a Styrofoam cup filled with coffee. We're surrounded with people, and I didn't want to seem upset when I told Penny what happened on Thursday. It just hadn't occurred to me she'd take it so lightly.

"Well, yeah," I say, trying to keep my voice low. "I was two hours from home without a ride or a phone."

"Yikes. What did you do?"

I shrug. It doesn't matter. "I made it home." Obviously.

She takes a sip, says "ouch," then blows a few times on the steaming drink before asking, "Did you at least have fun?"

Though a part of me wants to tell her exactly what kind of a day I had, a little voice whispers, "Don't bother." Because it might just make me seem pathetic. She might not want to hang out with me if all I do is whine. "It was fun," I say, then quickly add, "How's Jason's dad?"

"Much better." And she tells me about her weekend as we start down the hall toward our Sunday school room. She's a nice, good woman and fun to hang out with on occasion … but I need to stop thinking of Penny as my close friend in Cedar Rapids. Our situations are too different. If I'm going to have friends here like I did in Colorado, I'll have to expand my social circle.

That might mean changing churches and finding one with a

good singles group. Or maybe I'll meet people at the school when I start subbing again. The point is, I'm going to have to be more proactive about it.

A few days later, I finally get the call I've been waiting for. The business call, anyway, from Liza Carlson. She's surprised when I mention I'm in Iowa, but since it was a mostly work-from-home job, I didn't think it would make a difference where I live.

And it doesn't make a difference as she's decided to go with someone else. A lump of dread drops in my throat. Will I ever get good news?

But she does say, "I'd like to keep you in mind for some projects, though, when my regular designer's plate is too full. Would you be interested?"

"Yes, of course. I'd be happy to help out with anything." She thanks me, wishes me luck, and the call ends.

Well, I'll never hear from her again.

Turns out, there's a large, Christian singles group in Cedar Rapids, though it's connected through a social website rather than through a church. I join as soon as I find it and sign up for a potluck and game night on Friday. That morning, I make my go-to potluck dish, an orange Jell-o salad, and put it in the fridge, then go for a run. Though I stopped caring about my diet around the same time I ended my engagement, I'm still exercising regularly. Which means I haven't lost more weight, but I haven't gained any back either.

By the time I get home from the two-mile run, I'm dripping with sweat. I can't wait until fall temperatures drop enough to energize me so I can go farther and last longer. But I did it anyway, and I have the sweat to prove it. And I can now reward myself with a delightfully cool shower.

Once I'm cleaned up and relatively put together, I leave my room dressed in khaki capris and a loose, orange button-up blouse over a tank top. Stopping at the hall mirror, I put in my earrings and check my hair. Mom, who's once again ensconced in her favorite chair in the living room, says, "Are you going out?"

"Yes." I walk over to her. "Singles potluck and game night."

She sighs and shakes her head. Well, that means something. Something I'm probably happier not knowing, so I ask, "What are you up to tonight?"

"The girls are coming over for bridge."

How much do I want to sigh and shake my head? So much. But I don't. Though I do wish I knew why her game night is acceptable while mine is sigh-worthy.

I say, "That's nice," while going into the kitchen to get the Jell-o salad. I pull it out and check to make sure it's set, only to discover there's a corner missing. Great.

"Mom." I carry it into the living room. "Is there a reason part of my salad is gone?"

"Salad? What salad?"

"The orange Jell-o salad I put in the fridge."

"You call that a salad?"

Take a breath, Uli. "Yes, I call it a salad. What would you call it?"

She looks up at me from the blanket she's crocheting. "Tasted more like a dessert."

"Well … whatever. Why did you eat some of it?"

"Why not?"

"Because I made it for the potluck tonight."

160

"Oh. Oops." And she goes back to her blanket. "I'm sure no one will care."

"That's not the … oh, never mind." Because it's not worth arguing over. And, for all I know, no one will care. It is a singles potluck, which, in my experience, means most of the items will be store-bought anyway. What's the chance anyone will even notice?

I go back in the kitchen and snap a plastic lid on the dish. Before I leave, I kiss Mom on the cheek and say, "I'll probably get back around eleven."

She blows a kiss sort of my way, tells me to have fun, and turns on the TV. Which is odd. It's already after six. Shouldn't she be getting ready for company?

Oh, well. I'm sure she knows what she's doing.

It only takes me about fifteen minutes to find the church that's hosting the game night. Following the directions on the website's event page, I park in the back and enter through the center door as instructed. By the time I start up the stairs, the chatter and hubbub of a get-together guides me to the right room. Over twenty people had signed up to be here, but I'd say there are at least thirty milling around. That's good. Gives me a better chance of connecting with at least one person. I hope.

A dark-haired woman with thick glasses and a big smile hurries toward me. "Hello! And welcome!"

I smile back. "Hi, I'm Uli."

"I'm Kelly. It's nice to meet you."

"You too."

She grabs my arm gently and leads me to a table near the door. "First, we need you to sign in and get a nametag." Indicating my dish, she asks, "And is this a main dish or …"

I'm about to say "salad" but hesitate. *Thanks, Mom.* "It's … Jell-o."

"Great! I'll get a spoon and set it out."

Before I can say thank you, she hurries off. So I turn to another smiling woman—this one older and with gray hair—manning the sign-in table. She says, "Hello! What's your name?"

"Uli Odell."

She goes down the list, finds my name, crosses it out, and then hands me a peel-off tag with my name already printed on it. And spelled correctly. They didn't even do the "O'Dell" spelling that drives me crazy. Mostly because it reminds me too much of kids singing "The Uli in the dell" when I was in grade school. Only they would draw out the "oo" in Uli so it sounded more like "ew." Gotta love the creativity of children.

I thank the woman at the table but don't ask her name since there are people waiting behind me. Then I turn and face the room. Time to mingle. Figuring out where to start is always a tough decision. Fortunately, I'm no novice when it comes to singles mixers. I have a pretty good idea how these things work. I know, for instance, that you befriend the women first. To do otherwise not only screams "Desperate!" but does not exactly endear one to the females. No one likes a new girl coming in and immediately trying to get her hooks in one of the guys.

Good thing I have no interest in hooking anyone. I'm here to make friends. Kelly is standing near the food table talking with two other women, so I mosey that way. She smiles, says hello again, and asks, "Remind me how to pronounce your name?"

"Oo-lee, but it's spelled U-l-i."

"That's so pretty!"

"Thanks."

"This," she says pointing first at one woman, then the other, "is Meg and Tara."

"Nice to meet you."

Tara says, "Are you new here?"

"Sort of." Then I shrug. "I actually grew up in Cedar Rapids, but I've lived in Colorado for over a decade."

162

"Really?" Kelly scratches her nose. "What brought you back to Iowa?"

I'm about to answer when a tall but hefty guy calls out for our attention. For some reason, he reminds me of a henchman in a spy movie, like *The Bourne Identity*. Once the room quiets, he says, "Thank you all for coming ... and for all the great food. Because I know that's the main reason we're here." He pats his belly and we all chuckle. Okay, maybe not a henchman. After the laughter dies down, he continues, "Before we get going, though, I'd like to say a blessing on the meal and fellowship."

Everyone bows their heads as he prays. When he's done, he says, "Let's eat!" and a few people move to make a line. Turning to Kelly, I ask, "So, who was that?"

"Oh, that's Len. He's kind of in charge."

"Kind of?"

"The online group has several administrators who approve and sponsor events. He's the one for tonight."

"Oh." I move to get in line. When I turn to say something to Kelly, she's gone. But it's a small room so it only takes me a few seconds to find her on the other side of it, talking to a different group that is, again, mostly women. I'd say there's at least three girls to every guy. Good thing I'm not looking for a date.

I'm in line with Meg and Tara, though, and they talk to me as we choose between a couple buckets of fried chicken, three crock pots of meatballs, at least a dozen salads, and more chips than a Super Bowl party. Kelly put my dish with the desserts. I guess Mom was right.

Since they seem friendly and inviting, I follow Meg and Tara to a table. Over our meal, I learn Tara is originally from Korea and works as a nurse for a general practitioner, and Meg is an office manager with two children. Three other women sit with us, but it takes me about twenty seconds to forget their names.

After everyone's done eating, we clear off the tables for

163

games. One group of four immediately starts a round of Euchre, another dozen people go for Apples to Apples, and a third group dumps a case of dominoes on the table for Mexican Train. Since it's one of my favorites, that's the one I go for.

Over the years I've come to realize I can tell a lot about people by the games they like to play. It's better than a Myers-Briggs test. Euchre players—serious, focused, and a bit cutthroat. Apples to Apples is for those who are easy-going and like things simple with just a touch of creativity. And Mexican Train people? Noisy and a little goofy with short attention spans. That's my crew.

Tara joins the Mexican Train table I'm at while Kelly and Meg both go with Apples to Apples. Since only eight people can play off one hub and twelve people want to participate, we split into two games of six, each group at its own table. We end up with four women and two men in our group. One of the guys, Steve, is actually kind of cute and has a good sense of humor. He's easy to flirt with, and I don't even try not to.

At one point, he nudges me because it's my turn. That causes my hand to bump my row of dominoes, knocking several over. I turn on him with a half smile, half glare. "Very nice."

"Thank you," he replies. "I'm just trying to help."

"Hmm … I think you're trying to get a glimpse of my strategy."

"Now why would I do that?" he asks with the innocence of an elementary student who spilled his milk. "You're losing."

I gasp. It's a stage gasp—completely fake—and makes him chuckle. Then I slap a hand over my heart and, with my best Southern accent, say, "How dare you, sir! I'm hardly losing."

He scrunches his face at me. "I've won two rounds so far … and you, princess?"

Since he's obviously joking, I elbow him in the arm, and he has the wisdom to wince and look at least slightly injured. I say,

164

"I'm just warming up."

But when he leans over and whispers, "So am I," a wave of heat rushes my face, and all I can do is hope he didn't notice. He keeps nudging me throughout the game, though. And I don't mind at all.

We're on the double eights round when one of the women—Chondra, I believe—mentions a singles retreat over Labor Day weekend. They all talk about it like it's something everyone goes to. Well, that sounds like fun. So I ask for more details.

I discover it's at a conference retreat center on a lake in Wisconsin. It only takes about four hours to get there, and the price is surprisingly reasonable. With school about to start, I'll have money from subbing, which would help pay for it. I ask Chondra for more information. She gives me her card and writes the name of the conference—The Northern Midwest Labor Day Singles Retreat—so I can look it up later.

It's about nine-thirty and, for me, the night's just getting started when Len stands and announces we need to clear out of the room by ten. I turn to Tara.

"By ten? Is he serious?"

Tara lifts her hands helplessly. "I think that's the deal they have with the church."

"Well, that stinks."

"I agree," Steve says with a grin. "The night's still young … and so are we!"

Cheesy, but cute. I smile back, and he adds, "Maybe we could find some place that stays open later and hang out there."

Though most of the group seems quite ready to call it a night, several of us decide to meet at a nearby Perkins. I have no idea who actually intends to join us there, but we make sure everyone knows the plan. As we're leaving, Steve nudges me one more time and says, "See you soon?"

I nod. And really, if it's just him and me, that's okay too.

He distracted me enough that I almost forgot my dish, so I run over to grab it from the table. It's still over half full, which is disappointing. Especially since the August heat won't do it any favors while I'm at the restaurant. Hopefully, it will still be edible once it's refrigerated again. Mom would like that.

As soon as I get in my car, I plug the restaurant's address into my phone's GPS. It's only a few minutes away. When I get there, I wait in my car with an eye on the door until I see Len, Tara, and Steve stroll up and head inside. Well, that's a decent group. My main goal, besides having a fun evening, is to not get home before my mom's bridge buddies leave. Making my way into the restaurant, I discover they already have a table and I end up sitting next to Tara and across from Steve.

No one's really hungry, but we can't exactly hang out in a restaurant without ordering anything. Everyone gets something to drink. Since management seems to have set the air conditioning at just-below-freezing, I ask for a hot chocolate. Then Tara and I decide being chilled is worth it and order the chocolate chip sundae to share while the guys each ask for a slice of pie. Once the waitress leaves, the conversation is stilted, at best. It would seem the other three don't know each other that well either. At least I'm not the odd girl out.

While we wait for our order, we share bits of basic information—where are you from, do you have family in the area, what do you do—in between moments of silence. It's not too bad, though. But it's funny that we ended up with an even number of men and women. And no matter what we each might claim, we're all wondering if there's any potential here. Which means that underlying every word, smile, gesture, and glance, there lurks that question. "Could you be the one?" We know it and feel it and it doesn't make the awkward moments any less awkward.

166

You don't have to be in singles groups for long before you start to see the hidden meaning behind every conversation. Thinking this way reminds me of my cynical side. But why shouldn't we want to know if the person sitting across from us has what we're looking for or is completely messed up? Especially if you're someone who's afraid of making another big relationship mistake. And I've watched enough *48 Hours* to know it's a good idea to step into any new relationship with wisdom and a great deal of caution.

By the time our desserts arrive, I've learned a good deal about the people sitting at the table with me. Steve works at a bank and is the only one at the table who's been married before, while Len is an associate pastor. When Steve mentions he has two adult children, I almost fall off my seat. He's clearly older than he looks. And he looks nice. Not as attractive as Cole but cute in a friendlier, I-won't-cheat-on-you kind of way.

If there's one thing I learned from Cole it's that looks aren't everything.

The desserts are tasty, but the most memorable moment of the evening is when Steve and I discover we both love the sci-fi movie *Galaxy Quest* and start quoting our favorite lines to each other. By the time we crack up over "It exploded," Len and Tara are laughing too—though it might be more at Steve and me than the actual movie quotes.

"Well," Len says, "maybe we should have a *Galaxy Quest* movie night."

Steve and I both say yes at the same time, and he adds, "We could do it at my dad's farm—I have a projector so we can show it on the side of the barn."

I say, "That would be cool," and Len and Tara agree.

"We could make it a cookout too," Steve says. "I'll take care of the meat if everyone else brings the rest. And chairs because I'm not sure Dad will have enough."

So he's generous and hospitable and has a solid relationship with his dad. Good qualities.

Before we call it a night, the cookout/movie gathering has been planned and a date set. As we head toward our cars, Steve and I hold back a little. That's when I get a whiff of his scent. It's nice. Fresh and clean, like cucumber soap. I take a step closer. He says,

"It was great meeting you."

"Yeah, you too."

I linger by my car, fiddling with my keys, hoping for … I have no idea what. But then he says, "Well, maybe I'll see you around" and I say, "That would be great," and he walks away, and I drive home.

Whether it was a love connection or not, I had a good night, and I like the ribbon of hope that wraps around my heart. Though I have to remind myself I need to feel hopeful about life getting better, not about some guy I might never see again.

Oh, who am I kidding? I'm totally hopeful about the guy.

Chapter 21
Catie

It's just as beautiful as they promised. I'm standing on the beach near Nag's Head on the Outer Banks, drinking in the salt spray and soft breezes coming across the ocean while my family splashes around in the water. Except for my dad, who's next to me.

We drove seven hours yesterday and another seven today, but we made it. I'm actually at a beach for the second time in one summer.

After getting the key to the house we rented and unloading our luggage, we took the short hike down to the water to check it out. It's after five, so most of the tourists have left and there's just us and the sand and the seagulls. If we all weren't so hungry, we'd stay longer.

But it's our first night. There will be plenty of time for ocean-gazing during the week. At the moment we need to eat, then go grocery shopping.

Three hours later, we're back at our gorgeous, three-story home-away-from-home. We put the groceries away, then everyone wanders off to their rooms to unpack. The house even has an elevator, which makes things easier on my dad ... and me.

Not too surprisingly, the children fell asleep in the car on the way back from the store. Which means the adults can take a deep breath and settle onto the comfy couches and chairs in the living room for some kid-free conversation. We're so beat, though, that all we do is chat quietly for a bit before calling it a night ourselves. But it's enough. I enjoy these quiet moments with my family.

And that's pretty much how the week goes. Time at the beach, time at the pool, bike riding and wild horse watching,

169

good food and quiet conversations, a little shopping, a little sightseeing, a lot of family time.

I followed the doctor's orders and went in for my chemo treatment on Monday, but each time is a little easier and this one knocked me down for only two days. Good thing the beach is a place of healing for me. Sitting on a camp chair under our canopy with my feet dug into the sand seems to send energy through me from the tips of my toes to the top of my head.

It's funny, though, because it makes me realize I've never seen my cancer as a deadly disease. The number of my days is in God's hands, and nothing indicates He's done with me yet. I suppose most sick people feel that way, so only time will tell. But, surprisingly, I'm not afraid.

As we head home after a week of sun and sand, I feel stronger than I have in months. I'm ready for a new chapter in my life.

Whatever that might be.

Birthdays have never been a big deal to me. It's just an excuse to eat too much of whatever your heart desires and get your pick of dessert and have people who claim they love you sing loudly and embarrass you in front of strangers. If you're lucky.

For my fiftieth birthday party, apparently I'm very lucky. My family took me to our favorite local Mexican restaurant next to Indian Lake. It's fun to dress up for the evening, and Angela has helped me find several ways to wear all my new head scarves that, she said, make me look cool, even a little artsy. Then she teased me about buying a few caftans. Well, I did take my first art class last night and really enjoyed it, so why not? Maybe it's time to create a whole new Catie.

Against my protests, Patrick and Tawny left their children with a babysitter. "I want to spend the evening celebrating and talking with you," Tawny said, "not chasing three kids around a restaurant." I understand her sentiment, but it doesn't feel right not having them around. To compensate, we'll save dessert and presents for when we get back to the farm.

Not that we had much choice on that. Bella, who recently turned six, has had something planned for my birthday since her mom told her it was coming up. No one knows what she has in store, but I'm sure it will be delightful. Plus, she and her sister insisted on helping their grandma make the cake. It's possible the at-home party will be more fun than the dinner out.

Cuter, anyway.

We're almost finished with dinner when an older gentleman with gray hair comes over and says hi to my brother. After they've taken care of the requisite how-are-you? dialog, James tells us the man is Peter Wilson. "Peter," he says, "is an entrepreneur who's been helping a lot of small businesses in the area. And he's on a hundred boards around here."

We all say hello as James introduces us one at a time. When he gets to me, Peter says, "Oh, you're the sister! James has mentioned you a few times. You work in … pharmaceuticals, right?"

I nod. "Yes. Well, for now."

My whole family looks at me like they're surprised. As if the topic of me quitting my job and moving to Ohio permanently hasn't come up several times. Did they think I wasn't serious about that? I guess so. Trying not to sigh in frustration, I smile at Peter. "It might be time for me to move back home."

"Is that right?" He opens his phone case and pulls out a business card, which he hands to me. "When you're ready to start job hunting, let me know. I might have a few ideas."

171

I take it and thank him. "You can expect to hear from me. Probably soon."

"Sounds great." Peter talks with James for a few more minutes before he leaves.

Once he's gone, Dad says, "Catie-girl, do you really think you're ready to give up your life in Colorado?"

"Well, I don't think of it so much as giving up something there as gaining something here. Yes, I'll miss what I had in Colorado Springs, but I miss all of you even more when I'm there."

Delia reaches over and takes my hand. "I fully support this decision."

"So do I," Tawny chimes in. "And the kids would love to have you nearby."

The men agree. Their surprise, it would seem, came from not wanting to get their hopes up that I'd make this decision. But it feels right, and I'm excited to see what kind of job opportunities Peter has in mind. I'll call my employer in Colorado first thing tomorrow and give them the news. They'll want to start looking for my replacement right away if they haven't already.

Once we get back to the farmhouse, we find three surprisingly wired children. Angela and her boyfriend, Ian, are also there and seem to have been conspiring with the little ones. They couldn't make dinner because of college commitments but apparently relieved the babysitter when they showed up early. And it looks like the kids kept them busy. A makeshift stage has been set up in the living room complete with lights and music. Bella takes charge of the evening, insisting everyone take a seat to prepare for The Show.

We settle down ... and wait, talking and laughing as we anticipate what the girls have planned. Five minutes later, Bella enters the room. She's wearing a yellow Belle princess dress and red cowboy boots and has feathers sticking out of her dark, curly

172

hair. But before we can get too excited about what's to come, she beckons to Angela and whispers, "Come here."

Angela grins and does as she's told. I catch Tawny's eye. "What are they up to?"

She just shakes her head. "I have no idea, but she's been singing into her hairbrush for days."

We all laugh … and then Angela steps back into the room.

"Ladies and gentlemen," she announces, "it's time for the Bella and Bryn Show!"

Everyone cheers and claps as the girls skip in, followed closely by their little brother, Will. Bryn is wearing a blue Cinderella dress and bright pink boa. And she's barefoot. Will has on a pull-up and that's it, which I've learned is about the most we can hope for when we're home. That boy does not like clothes. Bella is clearly in charge; Bryn stands behind her, pulling on her dress as she twists back and forth while Will runs around the room, chasing the cat and trying to stay out of his mom's reach. My, but that's a lot of cuteness in one room.

"Thank you, thank you, thank you," Bella says. "For our show … this is for Aunt Catie … 'cause it's … it's her birthday … and she's really nice." She claps her hands and everyone applauds with her. Then she says, "We love you, Aunt … oh, wait," and runs out of the room. She comes back carrying a plastic princess tiara, which she sets on my scarf-wrapped head. I smile and give her a hug. And, just as quickly, she runs back to Angela and whispers in her ear. Angela nods and goes over to laptop attached to speakers, which is the source of our background music.

After a few seconds, the opening melody of "Let It Go" trickles through the room. Bella folds her hands in front of her and begins to sing along. Bryn occasionally joins in. They—Bryn especially—don't know all the words, but they certainly know the chorus, which they sing with all the gusto that's appropriate for

173

two little princesses. Will just says "let it go" over and over at first, then insists they sing the "thummer thong" instead. I have no idea what that means. But every time he says "thong," we crack up … which of course only encourages him to keep saying it.

The musical portion of the show ends, and the girls head off toward the kitchen. As they're leaving, Bella shouts, "Grandma!" so Delia gets up and follows them. Angela goes along.

"James," Delia yells from the kitchen, "get the lights!"

He does and, a minute later, they all march back in with Delia leading the way, carrying a chocolate sheet cake with so many candles it looks like it's been set ablaze. That makes me laugh. "One candle per decade would have been plenty."

"Now, what fun is that?" Delia says. Then she starts singing the birthday song and everyone joins in. When they finish, I blow out the candles as Tawny snaps photos with her phone. My dad sets out three different kinds of ice cream, and we all dig in. I request cookies 'n' cream with my cake, then eat it slowly because it's just so good.

I'm barely halfway through it when they start handing me presents. The children give me coloring books and no, they're not the kind created specifically for adults. Tawny shrugs when I look her way and says, "They really just want you to color with them," which makes me like the kids and the books even more.

My dad gives me a card with a gift card to the local coffee shop. In fact, I mostly get gift cards, including one to Maurice's from Delia and Tawny with a promise to go on a shopping excursion for new fall clothes. I wonder if they sell caftans.

The evening ends with hugs and kisses and all the love a girl could ask for.

Best birthday ever.

174

~ ❦ ~

Maybe I should wait, but I just can't. So I call Peter Wilson the next day and hope eagerness is a quality he admires. He answers right away.

"Peter Wilson."

"Hello, Mr. Wilson, this is Catie Delaney, James's sister. We met last night?"

"Yes, of course. How can I help you?"

"Well, I'd like to start putting out feelers for a job. I need to take care of things in Colorado, of course, but it doesn't seem too soon to get the process going."

"When do you think you would be able to start work?"

"I'm looking at the end of October, early November." Because I could go back to the Springs next month to put my house on the market, sell the stuff I don't need and pack the rest, take care of whatever needs to be done at work, and spend a few weeks with my friends before Jolene's wedding, which she's asked me to be a bridesmaid in.

All in all, it will be a busy fall if I add finishing my chemo treatments plus finding a new home here. As much as I love being at Dad's, I need my own place. That's what I'm used to. Angela moved into her own apartment last year leaving her room at the farmhouse available for me, but that means there are still nine people living there. And four dogs, including Luna, plus a few cats, though most of them are kept outside. It can get loud, and this single girl who's lived alone since college needs her downtime.

But first, I need a job.

Peter says, "Actually, I'm glad you called. I've had several people mention recently that they're looking for candidates for various positions. Chances are you'd qualify for at least one of them. Besides pharmaceuticals, what else have you done?"

175

I give him a brief rundown of my résumé, which includes mostly sales and office management. He asks a few questions, then says, "I think I do know of some possibilities. Could you email me your CV so I can pass it on to a few people? The address is on my card."

"Yes, of course. And thank you!"

"It's not a problem. We're always on the lookout for good candidates to help improve our area. And from what I know about your family, you would be an asset to the community."

"I really appreciate that."

Once the call has ended, I set down my phone and take a deep breath. This just might work out after all. Someday soon Ohio will be my home. Yet as happy as that thought makes me, saying goodbye to Colorado and the life I had there won't be easy. Will I be able to develop good friendships here? Where will I meet people? I'm not sure I want to do the singles-group thing anymore but where else would I make friends? Since I don't like bars and rarely go dancing, church is the best place for that. The art classes, perhaps. Or maybe I'll connect with people at whatever company God places me in.

This is a small-town community. It's not a big city with tons of single people like the Springs. I might have a tough time finding friends.

Oh, but why am I worrying about that? First things first. Take care of leaving Colorado and settling in here. Then I can start pursuing a social life.

At least, that's the plan. And hopefully it's one that follows God's will. But it sure would be nice if His plans overlapped with mine … in one area anyway.

Chapter 22
Jolene

Driving across Kansas on interstate 70 might actually be more boring than every algebra class I ever took. If it weren't for the fact that I'm surrounded by my loud and crazy family, I would gladly exchange this interminable drive for eight hours straight of Mr. Heinrich droning on about binomial coefficients and quadratic formulas.

Wow. I'm totally impressed with myself for remembering those terms. I don't know what they are, but I imagine Mr. Heinrich might even crack a smile to find out something got through. I might have to make sure to bring this unexpected bit of knowledge up in conversation sometime. Not that I need to prove how intelligent I am or anything.

Anyway, we're about two hundred and fifty miles into the over four hundred we have to cover before crossing into Missouri. I've been driving for almost three hours and believe I should get some kind of special accolade or, at least, chocolate for taking the wheel during what's arguably the most monotonous leg of our two-day road trip. Thankfully, we're almost to Salina, where we plan to stop for lunch. We've been on the road for over seven hours now, and the kids have been telling us they're hungry for two. And yes, we fed them breakfast and they've been snacking ever since. But Freddie discovered there's a Popeye's chicken in Salina, so we decided to push through.

At last our exit comes into view and soon I'm pulling into Popeye's parking lot. Freddie and I unload the kids and head into the restaurant while Sam drives the van over to a Shell station to fill up the tank. Herding the children through the bathroom and ordering for everyone is actually a little easier now that we have Klinka helping more with corralling than needing to be corralled.

The next oldest, Oscar, is about as ADD as they come, and as soon as Sam gets back, Freddie hands Oscar over to him while she grabs four-year-old Milo before he can plow through a group of elderly women waiting in line. They seem to have noticed how close he got to running them down because they comment on how cute he is with a tiny bit of fear in their eyes.

Lillie, who's ten, and Charlie, nine, are fine as long we keep an eye on them. Which leaves Klinka to hang on to seven-year-old Junie and I'm in charge of Toolah, who just turned five. All this madness makes me wonder how they can handle them all without me. But of course they can because that's what parents do.

As soon as we're loaded up with chicken and Cajun rice, green beans, mac and cheese, and plenty of biscuits, we pull two tables together and settle in for lunch. Because you don't try to eat this kind of a meal with this many kids in a van. Besides, some of us need a break from the road. And I don't just mean those who are ten or under.

Now that the little ones are busy eating, Freddie leans across the table toward me and whispers, "So, are you going to tell me what's going on?"

I roll my head and shoulders, still trying to work out the kinks from all that driving, while I consider the best way to answer that question. It doesn't seem like the ideal time to delve into Trevor's past with Freddie, especially with the kids around. Plus, I'm sure I'll have to go over it again with my mom and two other sisters at some point.

On the other hand, telling a story more than once has never bothered me before. And, honestly, I have to say something before I explode. "Did I ever tell you about the big scar on Trevor's chest?"

She leans back and pulls Milo—who's on her lap—closer. He shrieks, "Mama, too tight!" and she hands him to Sam.

178

"He has a scar?" Then she whispers, "When did you see his chest?"

I raise my eyebrows and huff out a breath. "Good grief, Freddie, I didn't rip off his clothes if that's what you're getting at." I give her a half-smile and add, "Though the thought has crossed my mind."

Now it's her turn to raise an eyebrow. But just one—something I can't do. She simply says "Jolene," so I continue.

"Believe it or not, there are perfectly innocent ways to see a man without a shirt."

"For instance?" She pauses, then, "Because I know you, Jolene, and you don't do a lot of swimming."

I glance around the restaurant, looking for an answer. Oh, well. Honesty is best, so I say, "We were in a hot tub."

Really, my sister never needs to talk because her face tells me everything she's thinking. And right now she's thinking hot tubs and innocence don't go together.

"Okay, before you jump to a wrong conclusion, we hadn't started dating yet and we were with friends at a singles retreat. So I repeat: perfectly innocent. We might have even talked about Christian stuff."

Which makes her laugh. I wave my hand between us. "But that's not the point. Can we talk about the scar?"

By now, the kids are mostly done eating and there's an air of anticipation, like runners just before the starting pistol goes off. We really should get back on the road. Freddie asks Sam if he's ready to drive, and he nods. After tossing out the trash and taking care of one more bathroom break, we all climb into the van. Freddie and I crawl into the back with the two little ones so we can talk. With the children all preoccupied with movies or games or sleeping and Sam focused on the baseball game he found on the radio, we should be able to talk without interruption … or any little ears listening in.

179

"So," Freddie says, "what about this scar? Is it bad?"

"Yeah. It crosses his chest and continues onto his arm. But when I asked about it, he said it was an accident."

"But it wasn't?"

"Well," and I take a deep breath, "two nights ago I met his brother from Cameroon."

Freddie gasps. "Did you know he had a brother?"

"No, but that's nothing. Both boys were stolen as children and served as soldiers."

Toolah, who's asleep with her head on my lap, sighs and snuggles closer as Freddie stares out the window. All she says is, "Wow." Then she turns to me. "Soldiers? For the government?"

"I don't know."

"Well, what else did he tell you?"

"Nothing. I left."

"Wait a second." She touches my arm. "He told you this and you left? Why?"

Really? "Because it's a significant part of his life, and he waited forever to tell me."

"Yeah, I get that." She shifts a sleeping Milo so he's sitting a little more comfortably in his car seat. "But I don't understand why you walked away. Have you talked to him since then?"

"Um … no. I'm not ready."

"Hmm." And then she gives me that look that lets me know I'm about to get a talking to. She huffs out her breath. "You need to talk to him about this."

"I will. Of course I will."

"No, not 'will.' You're not just dating Trevor; you're going to marry him. You can't think of this in terms of what's easiest for you but what's best for him … and your relationship." She glances up toward Sam and a small smile curves her lips. "And trust me, when it comes to a marriage, you have to deal with things. You can't wait until you 'feel like it.' And you definitely can*not* just walk away and leave him wondering where he stands. Your man should always know where he stands without having to ask or wait for you to feel like telling him."

"But shouldn't I think things through first? Shouldn't I wait until I calm down so I'm not getting into this while I'm angry?"

"Why are you angry?"

"Wouldn't you be?"

"That's not an answer."

Fine. The reason is—what is the reason? "He kept this from me!"

"And you've kept things from him."

"That's different." I take a drink from the orange-flavored vitamin water I've been sipping on all day. But it's not different. I know that and, according to Freddie's face, she does too. She says,

"Jolene, your years as a single woman have made you strong and independent. These are great qualities and, I imagine, some of the reasons Trevor loves you. But there has to be a shift in how you deal with things when you promise to share your life with someone. It's not just you anymore."

Wow. My sister is right. Not that it surprises me. She knows a lot about marriage … and I don't. What I do know is that I am in many ways still acting like a single woman with a boyfriend instead of an engaged one who is only two months away from vowing to spend the rest of her life with this man.

As soon as I have a private moment, I need to call Trevor and talk things out.

"A private moment." In hindsight, it's pretty laughable. When you spend about twenty hours driving over eleven hundred miles with nine other people, it's just not going to happen. Even when we stop for the night at a hotel near St. Louis, I'm too tired to do anything but collapse on the bed I'm sharing with Klinka. Lillie, Junie, and Toolah are in the other double bed while the boys are all in an adjoining room with their parents.

The next day, we're able to finish the trip in just over five hours. Finally, we pull into my parents' driveway and the children exit the van like a heat wave of energy, cheering and screaming, "Mimsy!" and "Papa!" as they race toward the door.

I chuckle and say, "What are they more excited about? Seeing Mama and Dad or getting out of the van?"

"Ha." Freddie shrugs. "It's a toss-up."

The adults let the kids attack first. Once all the hellos and "Guess what's" and "I lost/found/etc." were exhausted, Mama turns to hug Freddie and me. Then she leans back and studies my face. "Okay," she says, "what's going on?"

Seriously. I just got here. How does she always do that? I put a hand on her shoulder. "Mama, can you maybe … possibly accept the fact that the events of my life mean there's almost always something going on?"

"Yes," she says, turning toward the kitchen. "If you can accept that I will always want to know about it. Now, come help me finish supper."

Freddie and I follow her while the men wrangle the kids. Or, at least, try to. Once there, I wonder what on earth she needs help with. She has a beautifully done turkey on the island, mashed potatoes on the stove, and a corn casserole in the oven. It's like Thanksgiving in August. Maybe I *shouldn't* have the seamstress take in my wedding dress.

But Mama puts my sister and me to work getting a few salads out of the fridge and setting the table. In minutes, everything's ready and we call the gang to the dining room. Blessings are given and dishes are passed around and we dig in.

182

It's all delicious, but my mind is on other things. Calling Trevor. Calling Vala. And trying to figure out what on earth I'm going to say to both of them.

Then, later that night, as I'm checking my phone to make sure it's charged enough, it rings. Only it's not Vala or Trevor. It's SueAnn. When I answer, she's nothing less than frantic. And she gets right to the point.

"Jolene, have you heard from Benita? We can't find her. Anywhere. Please tell me she called you."

Before responding, I check my phone. No, nothing at all from Colorado. And that's what I tell SueAnn. "Is there a reason to worry? Maybe she's visiting a friend or got called in—"

SueAnn doesn't let me finish. "Diego was here."

"What?!"

"Last night. He wouldn't leave until she talked to him, and this morning she was gone. And Marty's in Indiana at her cousin's funeral. I don't know what to do!"

As I try to calm SueAnn down, I scroll through my options. There's definitely a reason to be concerned ... terrified even. Especially if Diego discovers she's been hiding a son from him for more than eight years. Something needs to be done right away.

"SueAnn, you need to call the police."

"I have. They don't consider it an emergency."

No, they wouldn't. *Dear God, please protect her.* "Okay," I say, "let's not freak out yet. God has Benita in the palm of His hand. In the meantime, I'm going to make a few calls."

Actually, just one call.

Chapter 23

Oli

Taloosa Lake, located in southwest Wisconsin, is, in a word, unremarkable. Though it's everything a lake should be—blue, surrounded by foliage and, I assume, wild life, and kind of round—I get the feeling its best moments are at sunrise and sunset. I'll have to test that theory, preferably with my camera. The sunset one, anyway, since I don't do daybreak unless I'm forced.

It's the Friday before Labor Day, and I spent the afternoon traveling with four people to The Northern Midwest Singles Retreat. We cut it pretty close since we couldn't leave until everyone got off work, but since they all took half a day, we manage to get there before dinner. The registration desk is easy to find, and we quickly check in.

They give us nametag lanyards and packets telling us everything that will happen over the weekend, then a bubbly girl named Valerie leads Tara and me to the room we'll share in Eagle Lodge. It's the cheapest … for a reason. Everything in the room looks like it's been part of the décor since they built it in the 1950s—from the paisley bedspreads and matching curtains to the wood paneling. But it's clean, we have our own bathroom, and it's close to the lodge where we'll eat and attend meetings. So at least there's that.

The five of us—and yes, by some miracle, Steve came along—agreed to meet back at our van after we were settled in but before heading to the dining area. Tara and I join them last, which leads Steve and the other guy in our group, Todd, to give us a hard time about primping. Maybe they're just joking, but it's annoying, especially since we watched them walking toward the parking lot from barely a block behind them. But since I have a tendency to get testy about things that aren't worth getting testy about, I push down my annoyance and laugh along.

"Well, let's get going," Todd says, then glances at me and adds, "before someone decides her hair needs a few more curls."

Sheesh. And before I can stop myself, I say, "If it bothers you that much, feel free to go on without me next time." Oh, great. Now they think I'm Miss Touchy-Sensitive. I really need to learn how to not always say the first thing that comes to my mind before making sure I won't regret it later. But then, with a nod at Todd's slightly pudgy frame, I add, "Though we know you're just worried there won't be any meatloaf left."

Steve says, "There's meatloaf?" with such an exuberant, hopeful expression that it instantly eases the tension. Is that what he meant to do? A glance at his face tells me yes.

"The registration packet includes a menu for the weekend." Wow. What a fascinating conversationalist he must think I am.

But he doesn't seem to mind, wagging his rather impressive eyebrows and whispering, "I do like meatloaf." He has such an irrepressible yet grown-up way about him; it's rather endearing.

All of which leads me to think happy thoughts about Steve again. *Stop it, Uli. Even if you were ready for a new relationship—and you're definitely not!—you need to relax and focus on building friendships this weekend.*

At least one-hundred and fifty singles crowd the cafeteria, alongside a Greek Orthodox church group holding their own conference. In Todd's defense, it does seem we're the last to arrive. But in mine, there's plenty of meatloaf for everyone. And scalloped potatoes. And at least two vegetable dishes I'm not sure about. I go for the one that looks like it doesn't have any onions. We move through the buffet lines quickly, then find seats at a table with one woman sitting alone. Steve asks if we can join her and she nods. She has short, wavy brown hair and sad eyes and tells us her name is Jill.

185

It doesn't take long to get to know each other. Jill is a divorced mother of three who found out only a month ago that her cancer was in remission. Why is there so much of that horrible disease around me? The way Jill talks tells me it's been a rough road, though that doesn't surprise me. And I think of Catie and her pain and how none of the stuff in my life that I tell myself is a nuisance or a struggle or a heart-breaking reality even begins to compare. But I've spent my life finding it difficult to put myself in someone else's shoes when I'm so busy complaining about my own—they're not pretty enough; they're too tight; I can't afford them.

Todd asks Jill, "Where are your kids this weekend?"

"They're at my mom's." Jill moves her fork through her potatoes like I do when I'm looking for onions. "She helps me out whenever she can."

"That's great," Chondra, the fifth person in our Ohio group, says. "We all need that kind of support."

Jill simply nods, which tells me she'd say far more if she wasn't speaking with strangers. She puts her fork down without taking a bite. "Did you all come together?"

"Yeah," Steve says. "We met through an online social group in Cedar Rapids. What about you?"

"I came with a friend, but she has a headache from the drive and decided to go to bed early."

We all commiserate, especially those of us who understand the downside of car travel. Chondra says, "I'm not sure I'll be up late either," and Tara agrees.

"The important thing," Jill says, "is that we all made it safely. And, hopefully, Karen will be fine in the morning."

There's a brief lull in the conversation as, one by one, we finish our meal and reach for the slices of cheesecake in the middle of the table. The one in front of me looks like a turtle version, which I love, but when Steve, who's sitting on my right,

186

asks if I'll trade for his raspberry one, I agree. It's cheesecake, after all, and you really can't go wrong with cheesecake. And the smile he gives me makes it definitely worth it.

A few bites in, I turn to Jill, who's on the other side of me. "How are you doing? I have a friend going through chemo right now."

"Oh, I'm so sorry," she says, putting a hand on mine. "I'm doing okay. It's been a long road, but God gave me strength and brought me through it. He is so good ... and I'm blessed."

He's good? Maybe her definition is different from mine. Going through the nightmare of cancer while trying to raise three children does not sound like the blessing of a good God. I've struggled to see any good in my own situation for years, even though I have my health and only have myself to take care of. I'm trying to think of an appropriate response that doesn't make me sound like I'm the sole guest at a pity party when a microphone comes on and a male voice says,

"Hello, everyone, and welcome to the Northern Midwest Singles Retreat!"

He says it with such enthusiasm that everyone cheers. Though I'm not quite ready to declare it cheer-worthy, I go with the crowd and clap my hands. But I'm not going to shout, "Hooray!" We'll see how the weekend goes first.

The man—older, with gray hair and a friendly smile—tells us he's Ed Speers, the director of the retreat. Then he introduces the other main speaker, a raven-haired beauty named Sophia who's probably never worn sweatpants or eaten a Cheeto in her life. But she has energy for days, and if her initial brief "hello" message is any indication, we might just end up with a cheer-worthy weekend. At least, that's what I think until she concludes,

"Most importantly, we'll talk about what a good Father we have, even in our singleness!"

Well, "we" can talk all she wants, but she's going to have a hard time convincing me that hard times and loneliness are evidence of fatherly goodness. Because I had a father who was good and would never hurt me.

Until the day he died and broke my heart.

I don't make it to breakfast Saturday morning. The combination of the strange bed, a bad pillow, a nasty bout of insomnia, and too many thoughts about my dad and Cole and even Steve kept me awake half the night. The last time I checked the clock it was almost four. I must have passed out due to exhaustion. Fortunately, Tara is so quiet while getting ready that I don't even hear her leave. I don't hear anything, actually, until Tara nudges me and says,

"Uli? Sorry to wake you, but the first session starts in forty-five minutes … if that's something you want to go to."

"Okay," I mumble. "Thanks." And, with a groan, I crawl out of bed and make my way to the shower. By the time I'm out, Tara's gone again, and I just can't seem to hurry to get ready. I want to look cute, so I choose capri-length jeggings with a fun tunic blouse and contrasting scarf. My stomach growls a little while I'm putting on make-up, but I came prepared for that. As I finish getting ready, I munch on one of the chocolate chip granola bars I brought. That does the trick. Wouldn't want a chatty belly in a quiet room full of single men. Well, not full. Once again, I'm at a singles event dominated by women.

When I finally get to the meeting room, I'm over fifteen minutes late. They're still singing, though, so it's easy to slip in. The room is set up with about a dozen round tables, each seating eight, as far as I can tell. Everyone's standing in worship, which makes it harder to find my group but easier to blend in. At last I spot Steve—because he's the tallest, I'm sure. It takes only a few seconds to realize their table is full. Not that I expected anyone to save me a seat, but it would have been nice. Then I see Jill, and she waves me over.

"Hi," I whisper, not wanting to interrupt a lovely version of "Your Love Never Fails." But Jill simply smiles, points to the chair next to her, and says, "This seat's available." I thank her and put my stuff down on the table. When I turn back toward the stage, the song is almost over, but I join in with gusto anyway.

Maybe if I sing it loud enough I'll start to believe it.

Once the worship time is done, Ed encourages us all to participate in an ice breaker. Each person has a "Getting to Know You" bingo card at their seat. The first participant to get ten signatures wins. I find five people to answer the easy options—Allergic to Cats, Been Overseas, Only Child, stuff like that—right away, then seem to keep running into people who can only sign the ones that have already been claimed.

Depending on which is available, I either take the space saying "Been in a Musical" or "Has a Tattoo." The latter is thanks to a memorable spring break while I was a freshman in college.

It's fun meeting people, though, even if I don't win. I'm laughing about those college indiscretions with a group from Chicago when someone taps me on the shoulder. I turn around and find myself staring at a rather nice, manly chest in a pale red and white checkered button-up shirt. I raise my eyes up, up … until I'm looking into Steve's hazel ones. He grins and says,

"Can I have your autograph?"

With a chuckle, I respond, "I'll trade you."

As we switch cards, he says, "Sorry we don't have an extra seat at our table. I tried."

"Thanks." I sign his musical square while he takes care of the scuba diving one on mine. My eyebrows pop up. "You've been

189

scuba diving?"

"Yeah, a few times. I used to live in San Diego."

What? "Why on earth would you move to Iowa?"

"When your boss says, 'Move,' you move."

Oh, right. I sometimes forget the downside of a regular job. Before we can say more, though, Ed calls everyone back to their seats. He goes over a few announcements, reminds us of the various excursions this afternoon, then calls Sophia up to share the morning message.

It's no surprise when she continues on with her topic of seeing God as a good father. This isn't new information, though. How many times have I heard—or sung—about what a good, good Father He is? But it's all words. I don't want to be told God loves me; I want to see it.

I want to see it in how He takes care of me so completely I never have to worry or be afraid. I don't want to wonder if He hears this prayer or that one and then try to determine why the answer to this was no and that was yes. Why must my relationship with Him be a constant guessing game as to what He's trying to tell me or what I'm supposed to learn or what He expects from me?

Because I don't know what He expects … and I sometimes wonder if anyone does.

The session ends without any questions answered. But it feels good to at least know what my questions are. Maybe that will make finding the answers a little easier.

Jill joins my Iowa gang for lunch, then we all head off for our chosen excursions. I signed up for the canoe trip when I first registered. Now, as I watch Steve lope off with the hiking group, I wish I would have waited. But he did ask for my phone number and, as he walks away, turns back to me and says,

"Text me when you know where you're going for supper." It's one of the few meals not included with the retreat.

I say, "You too!" and wave goodbye.

The canoe trip is, well, your basic, uneventful canoe trip. I'm paired up with an older woman who lets me know she has no experience. I ask her to take the front spot so I can steer in the back. It's a two-hour journey from one end of the lake to the other. No one falls in, which might have added some excitement to the day. But we're on a lake so, thankfully, everyone is safe from the possibility of getting swept out to sea.

When I get back to the room, Tara's not there, which means the shower is all mine. It's not that I need one, but I would like to smell freshly clean for supper and the evening session. I'm finishing up my make-up when Steve texts and tells me a group is going out to a local pizza place and to meet them in the parking lot in thirty minutes. I take a deep breath, relief pulsing through me. They didn't—he didn't—forget about me.

What's sad is I really thought they would.

The second session ends with no more answers than the first. This time, though, I'm sitting with my group, including Steve. Jill's there too, nodding and smiling and even crying at one point. She gets it. Not only that, but she has a relationship with God that goes beyond my understanding. It's like she really does feel and see and know and hear Him. God is a reality to her, not just some invisible being who makes choices without telling you and keeps everything a secret until you're about to go mad.

At the end of her message, Sophia calls everyone in need of prayer to the front of the room. Jill is one of the first to head that way. A woman with a kind face walks over and puts an arm around Jill. As they stand there, heads bent together, jealousy courses through me. I wish I had the strength and courage to join them. But fear keeps me back. Fear tells me I'll have to share something I don't want to share or hear something I definitely don't want to hear. And they'll expect me to seek forgiveness, something I don't deserve. So I sit and watch and try not to let anything show on my face.

Still, this is a far more emotionally exhausting weekend than I signed up for. Singles retreats are for talking about dating and relationships with the opposite sex and working through those issues. How does God being a good father fit into it?

But deep down I know how, and it scares me. That's a question I'm not ready to answer yet.

The rest of the evening is more fun and games and dancing, once everyone comes down from the emotional high Sophia sent us on. I'm not so sure about the dancing part of it … until Steve walks up and asks me to join him. For a tall man, he doesn't do too bad, only stepping on my toes a couple of times. I don't mind, though, since each time he does, he pulls me into a bear hug apology. And then he grins … and I really like his grin.

After that somewhat slow dance, they start "The Cupid Shuffle." when Tara comes over. "You guys should see the moon over the lake," she tells us. "It's spectacular!"

Well, I do love a spectacular moon. I tap Steve's arm. "I'll meet you all there. I have to get my camera."

Several minutes later, I find a good number of people standing at the edge of the lake, along with a few brave souls who wandered out onto the rickety old dock. The view is, as Tara said, spectacular. And I almost didn't bring my camera this weekend. I take dozens of photos, some with people, some without, from a variety of angles. Several of Steve and that alluring little grin.

When I finally lower my camera and look around, the area is practically deserted. But Jill is still there, sitting on the grass with her knees tucked under her chin. I take a few candid shots of her that I expect will be some of my favorites, then put my camera back in its bag before plopping down next to her. There's silence for a moment. Finally, she says, "I almost missed this."

"Missed what?"

"This weekend. This moon. This … everything."

Since she's clearly not done, I wait.

"The thing is," and she glances over at me, "I wasn't supposed to survive this cancer. The doctors kept saying there was a chance, but I kept getting sicker and sicker. I almost gave up."

"Why didn't you?"

"Because God is good."

I shake my head. "I don't see the connection."

"Hmm." She studies my face for a moment. "What's your relationship with God like, Uli?"

Good question. Easy answer. "Strained."

"Why?"

"Lack of communication."

"From Him … or you?"

"Well, I suppose it's mutual."

"Okay." She scratches her head. "What about your relationships with men?"

That makes me laugh. "It's a long story."

"But your relationship with God isn't?"

Now it's my turn to study her. "What do you mean?"

"I mean that women—myself included—spend a lot more time thinking about and worrying about and trying to dissect our relationships with men while expecting our relationship with God to, well, require a lot less maintenance. So we neglect Him unless we need Him, then wonder why He never speaks to us."

193

Hmm, good point. I gaze out over the lake—where the moon continues to shed rays sparkling across the surface—and ponder Jill's words. Would trying to spend time with Him really make a difference? Would He maybe, possibly, respond? The thought overwhelms me, and I want to say more … when a mosquito lands on my arm, and I swat it away. And, apparently, the word is out because the next thing I know I'm in a haze of the itchy monsters along with too many gnats and flies to count. Time to go inside.

As we hurry toward our rooms, I thank Jill for giving me something to think about. One more day left of the conference, and I'm already on the verge of breaking. Everything's about to change.

Oh, I hope so. And, for once, I'm not hoping that change has something to do with a man. It's God I want to know and figure out and understand. How can I possibly go on if I don't?

Chapter 24
Catie

Looking him up was my first mistake. I met Matt when I was a junior and he was a freshman at Ohio State. Both of us business majors, he'd taken some courses during high school, which is how we both ended up in the same business ethics class. Angela's relationship with Ian reminded me and, out of curiosity, I decided to search for him on Facebook.

He was easy to find. There aren't many men named Matt Roveunak from Michigan. And, wouldn't you know, he still lives there, and he's on Facebook. I scroll through his page on my phone and … suddenly the boy I remember is looking back at me. In a photo taken a few years ago, he's staring at the camera with a half-smile and those blue eyes I couldn't turn away from. The memories of a lost love hit so hard a few tears fill my eyes. One of his hands rests on the table beside him, just as lean and strong as it was thirty years ago when he kissed my fingers and told me I was pretty and that my hair reminded him of Red Hots.

I liked him so much. And he liked me too … for about one semester. But the ethics class ended and he didn't write or call while we were on Christmas break. When I returned to campus, I didn't see him for two more weeks, even though I went to many of the places I thought he might be. Just as I started wondering if Matt had dropped out, I ran into him on the way to class one afternoon. He was holding hands with a pretty blonde. He said, "Hey, Catie! Good to see you," and kept walking.

And that was that.

Now as I stare at this picture of a man whose face I remember so dearly, sitting next to a blonde who may or may not be the same one he dated in college, I understand why it didn't work out. His "stunning wife," as he describes her, is far more

195

attractive than I have ever been. And though I know looks aren't everything, they definitely count for something. Because why would a man choose someone who's average when there are so many lovely women around?

With a sigh, I lean back in my chair at the treatment center. Why did I look that up here of all places? Well, the drugs will kick in soon, and then I can forget.

"It gets better."

I turn to the man sitting next to me. He's a bit scruffy and desperately thin, but he has a nice smile. He adds, "The drugs, I mean."

"Oh, I know. I just seem to be more emotional lately."

"Ah." He takes a deep breath. "That gets better too."

"No, actually, it's okay." When he gives me a puzzled expression, I say, "I'm a woman. I don't mind being emotional. In fact, sometimes it's the only thing that gets me through."

"So ... being high-strung gets you through?"

High-strung? Am I? But when I glance over I can tell by the spark in his deep blue eyes that he's teasing me. "Very funny," I say, "but didn't anyone ever teach you not to pick on defenseless women?"

"You don't seem like the defenseless type."

"Really?" I'm lying here, strapped to a chair as a machine pumps me full of drugs, sapping my energy and making me want to do nothing more than sleep. That seems pretty defenseless. And, of course, he saw me crying. "You have no idea."

"Maybe not, but you seem strong. I suppose it's the freckles." He smiles again, softer this time.

"Okay, I'll take it." I turn slightly in my chair so I can see him better. "I'm Catie Delaney."

He stretches a hand toward me. "Jake Fleming." His grip is strong.

"Nice to meet you." Honestly, I'm a little disappointed when

196

he lets go. Resting my head back against the chair, I close my eyes, thinking that's it for our conversation. Then he says,

"Tell me about yourself, Catie Delaney."

When I open my eyes, he's watching me and seems genuinely interested. All right. So I tell him about my life in Colorado and my family here and how easy it was to decide to leave the mountains for the hills of Ohio. Yes, we talk about work a little, but, somehow, that's no longer the most exciting part of my life. Then I ask him to share his story, and he does.

His family owns a large farm, which he helps out at, but his real passion is music. He has a small shop in Urbana where he mostly tunes and repairs guitars. And then, before it even occurs to me to ask, he tells me about his faith. It's strong and part of his family legacy. I try to hide my surprise because he doesn't look like your typical church-goer, but I must have failed. He says, "What's that face?" and points right at my nose.

"What face? I only have one."

Jake shakes his head. "Yeah, but that expression tells me you think I look more like a street rat than a holy roller. Looks can be deceiving, you know."

Yes, I know. And I should know better. "You have a point. In my defense, I was going to say 'beach bum,' but okay."

He laughs. "All right. I'll take beach bum. That has a nicer ring to it. And I do love the beach."

With a sigh, I say, "Me too."

"So, what are we doing land-locked in Ohio?"

"Mmm." And I close my eyes again, trying to picture the waves at the Outer Banks or feel the soft sand under my feet on Ambergris Caye. "Maybe we should run away."

He doesn't say anything for a moment and, finally, I look over, wondering if he fell asleep. But he shrugs and whispers, "Maybe we should."

My heart leaps just a little before I push the hope down. I've been through this too many times. A soft word, welcoming eyes, a friendly smile … only to find out it meant nothing or, worse, I was just a filler until someone better came along. My little, broken heart has become quite cynical over the years. And now, it hits me upside the head several times until, eventually, I give up any thoughts of romance and tell Jake, "Well, the beach is overrated."

Before he can respond, I yawn and say, "I think I'll see if I can get a little sleep in."

Then I turn away and squeeze my eyes shut and listen for any sounds coming from the chair next to me.

He doesn't say a word.

But even though Jake and I don't speak again that day, I think about him for the next week, wondering if I'll see him again.

It's interesting the people God has introduced into my life through chemo. First Ruth, who listened closely as I told her about my faith. It went far better than I anticipated, and I like to believe, if nothing else, that I planted a seed and can trust God to keep working on her heart.

And now Jake. Talking with him during the treatment made the day a little easier to take. And then I pulled away. Like I always do. Incapable of loving someone and of being loved, at least not in a romantic way. So why do I still ache for it? How can I tell God He's enough, and I'm satisfied with Him alone, yet yearn for something a little more … earthy at the same time? He has to understand, right? This was all His idea—this love and marriage thing—not mine.

A week after meeting Jake, I arrive at the treatment center and, though I fight it, the first thing I do is scan the room. It's quickly apparent he's not there. I blow out a breath of disappointment. But perhaps it's just as well. I can't go getting ideas about another guy who's not interested.

Walking across the room, I take an empty chair and settle in.

Soon I'm as relaxed as a person getting chemo can be. But just as I'm about to doze off, a voice says, "How about now?"

My eyes pop open and he's standing right there, watching me. I say, "How about now ... what?"

"Oh." He eases down onto the chair next to me. "I thought a week of humid Ohio weather would make you change your mind about the beach."

That makes me smile. "I did think about it."

"And?"

"And I've heard worse ideas, but I'm not a runaway kind of girl."

"Hmm. You don't trust me."

"I don't know you."

He gazes into my eyes for so long I start to wonder if he can read my mind. Then he says, "I think you do."

No. This is too fast. I need to lighten the mood and steer things away from how intense he gets, like he's making up for lost time. So I laugh. It's not a real laugh, but it will do. "I think it's best if we both stay out of the sun, for the time being at least."

"Okay." He pauses again, and I realize how much he listens to everything I say and always gives careful thought to his responses. And I'm reminded again how deceptive appearances can be. He looks even more gaunt than he did a week ago. Is someone taking care of him? It's an important question, so I ask it.

Jake tilts his head, humor lighting his eyes. "Aw, then you do care."

"I care that someone is helping you."

"And I appreciate that. My mom and sisters and big brother take turns watching out for me."

"Oh, good. I'm glad." Because I am.

Dee comes over and gets my medicine cocktail going, then

does the same for Jake. She jokes with us about both wearing the same color shirt—bright blue—and then notes that our eyes are also a remarkably similar shade of blue, before moving on to her next patient.

A few minutes go by. I can't sleep, so I just lie here, listening to him breathe. Then he asks, "Are you seeing anyone?"

Now I'm unshakably awake. "Um, no." I want to give a reason for why I'm not in a relationship, but everything I come up with sounds too pathetic. Instead, I say, "It's not a good time for dating," which makes it sound like I typically date a lot but decided to hold back until this cancer thing was over. Before he can respond, I ask, "Are you?"

He shakes his head. "Not at the moment. But I'd like to."

"Anyone in particular?" and then I stop breathing while I wait for his response.

"Yes, actually." There's that silence again. I don't want to look at him, but I'm not strong enough to hold out for long. When I finally do, he says, "Catie, have you ever heard someone say 'when you know, you know'?"

I nod. "Several of my married friends have told me that. But it sounds like wishful thinking."

"It does. But at the moment, wishful thinking is my favorite kind."

Every once in a while he says something that reminds me he's a musician. I ask, "Do you ever write your own songs?" Partly because I'm genuinely curious and partly because I know what he's getting at. And he knows I know. And it scares me to feel this connected to someone this fast.

Then, just like when we first met, he stretches his hand across the space between our two chairs. I reach over and grab him, clinging to his hand like it's a buoy in a raging sea. "Someday," he says, "you'll know, and you won't be so scared. That's going to be a good day."

200

"Promise?"

"Yeah." He squeezes my hand. "I promise."

A week later, Jake doesn't show up for his treatment while I'm there. Why didn't I ask for his schedule or, even, his number? Why didn't he ask for mine? When he's not there again the following week, I take a deep breath and ask the nurse, Dee.

"Oh," she says, her voice sad but resigned. "He didn't make it."

"What?" *Please, please let it be that he didn't make his appointment.*

But Dee responds, "Jake's cancer was just too far advanced. He passed away a little over a week ago."

And that's when I realize how much I'd fallen for him. Whether our bond was romantic or not, we helped each other and found strength in each other in only a few short hours. It doesn't take long for two souls to connect. I cry a lot that night.

Next time someone asks me to run away to the beach with him, I'm going to say yes. But even as I grieve the loss, that short, brief relationship meant something. More importantly, it gave me hope. It has been so long since I've truly believed romantic love was still possible for me, and suddenly my heart is full and strong and ready. More ready than ever. Though I wonder what could have been if I'd met Jake sooner or if we'd had more time, I'm grateful.

Two weeks later I'm back in Colorado Springs, packing up my recently sold house and looking forward to celebrating my best friend's wedding.

Chapter 25
Jolene

Less than twenty-four hours after SueAnn's call, I'm back in the Springs. I was able to catch an early morning flight, so it's not even lunchtime when I arrive. Trevor meets me at the airport, grabbing my suitcase and marching toward the car at a pace I can barely keep up with.

"Any news?"

"We know where Diego lives. Daniel's there now."

I halt mid-stride. "What's he doing there?"

"Watching. Waiting."

I'm so out of breath I can't ask any more questions. We finally reach his Jeep and Trevor throws my bag in the back. Then he turns and puts both hands on my shoulders. "It's going to be okay, Jo."

He says it with so much confidence I can only nod. But I wish we knew a little more about the kind of people we're dealing with. All I know is what Benita has told me—that Diego is a thief, a drug dealer, and just an overall lowlife who takes what he wants and expects everyone to do as he says. And he has a gang of equally nasty lowlifes eager to follow him. Back to prison, I hope.

As soon as Trevor has us on the parkway headed toward downtown, he calls his brother. Daniel answers right away, and Trevor puts the call on speaker.

"There's nothing going on here," Daniel says. "They might be holed up somewhere else."

"Or not at all." Trevor gives me a quick glance before turning back to the road so I continue, "They might not think anyone's looking for her. I'm sure they're familiar enough with the workload of local police to know it's not a priority."

"Good point," Trevor says, then, to Daniel, "We need to start asking around."

"All right. There's a shady-looking pub down the street a bit. I'll text you the name and meet you there."

Trevor says, "We're ten minutes away," and hangs up.

"When we get there," he tells me in his no-argument voice, "I need you to stay in the car."

But he knows that voice doesn't work on me. "I am definitely not staying—"

"In the car with your phone ready to dial nine-one-one."

"No."

"Jolene."

"No … and I realize you're worried about me, but this is my job. This is what I do—I deal with tough people in tough situations." I try to cool things off with a smile and my hand on his arm. "If I have you and Daniel and the Lord on my side, what could possibly go wrong?"

He rolls his eyes and takes a deep breath. "Well, don't say that."

"Famous last words?"

"I certainly hope not."

I slide my hand down and grip his fingers. In a few minutes we're outside Chessy's Bar in Knob Hill, one of the seedier areas of Colorado Springs. Daniel is standing near the door, talking to an elderly man whose bent frame rests against a broken and rusted bicycle rack. He has a cigarette between his yellowed fingers, and the ground beneath him is covered in cigarette butts. As we get closer, it's clear he's coughing more than speaking.

Daniel says, "Her name is Benita Jensen. Does that sound familiar?"

The man shakes his head and coughs again. "I don't get a lot of names."

"That's okay." I click on my phone and pull up a photo of

203

Benita. "This is her. Have you seen her recently?"

"Nah. But her old man was here last night."

I step closer. "Her old man? You mean Diego?"

He coughs and nods and I say, "How do you know he's her old man?"

"She used to follow him around, back before he got nicked."

Trevor asks, "But you haven't seen him since?"

The old guy drops his cigarette on the ground and crushes it, coughing so hard he can't speak and, again, just shakes his head. Then he shrugs and shuffles away.

"I'm gonna check things out inside," Daniel says. "It should be mostly empty at this time of day."

As he strides through the door, Trevor turns to me. "Any other ideas?"

"I'm worried about her son."

"Where is he?"

"In Pueblo." And it hits me. I jerk my eyes to my fiancé's. "I have the address at the office. Let me call SueAnn."

Trevor hands me the keys. I walk back to the Jeep, dialing Cocoon House, while Trevor hurries into the bar to get his brother. Five minutes later, I have the address pulled up on my phone, and the three of us are on our way to Pueblo.

I decide to sit in the back so Trevor and Daniel can strategize. It's fascinating to watch them together and brings to stunning light a side of my fiancé I haven't seen before. As much as I hate to sound like a cliché, I've never been more attracted to him. But then, who wouldn't be? This is a man who will fight for what's right … and knows how. And he's joined by a brother who's just as strong and capable. I couldn't ask for a better team to help me rescue Benita and her son. If I had any doubts before that God directs events to see His purposes fulfilled, I don't anymore.

We find Benita's mother's house easily enough and park

204

down the block. It's a modest, one-story bungalow across the street from a small park in a family-friendly neighborhood. It couldn't look less threatening, yet I suspect there's something truly dire going on inside.

Trevor turns to me, his gaze intense. "We're going to check things out. Just stay here long enough for us to know what the situation is. You can do that much, right?" But there's uncertainty in his voice.

It's not that I want to worry him, but I don't like being told not to do my job. Benita is my responsibility. "I'll wait a couple minutes. That's the most I can promise."

He holds my hands for a moment, clutching them tightly as if he doesn't want to let go, then nods. He and Daniel get out of the Jeep and walk toward the house. But instead of going to the front door, they split up, each going around a different side. As soon as they're out of sight, I open the door and step out onto the pavement. Some things need to be tackled head on. With a silent apology to my fiancé—and the hope that at least two minutes have passed as promised—I walk straight up to the front door and knock.

There's a bit of shuffling inside, then the click-slide of a chain lock being put in place. The door opens just enough to show the face of someone I can only assume is Benita's mother. "Mrs. Jensen? My name is Jolene Woods. I run Cocoon House. Is Benita here?"

Another click … a different kind … and the door shuts. Seconds later, the lock slide-clicks and the portal is thrown wide. Diego stands there grinning, a gun in one hand and Benita's wrist in the other. She's surprisingly calm. If it wasn't for the weapon the situation would seem almost domestic. At least the gun is pointed at the floor. I take that as a good sign and step inside.

The home is simple, cozy, and clean with old furnishings and a large crucifix prominently displayed on one wall. A delightful

205

scent of onions and cilantro wafts toward me from the kitchen. But my gaze is focused on the short but powerfully built man standing in front of me.

"Hello, Diego … Benita." I turn to the older woman. "You are Benita's mother, right?"

She nods and starts to close the door behind me. But I slide my foot back just enough so it doesn't shut all the way. She glances up at me and I smile, hoping it's enough to convince her not to press the issue. Since she doesn't say anything and quickly moves away from the door, it must have worked. Without missing a beat, I say,

"We were worried about you, Benita." I use my stern, Cocoon House director voice. "Though you're almost finished with the program, you need to let someone know when you're going to be gone overnight."

"I'm so sorry, Miss Woods. I should have called." Her voice is steady as she looks toward the couch where her mother now sits next to a young boy. He's about as cute as they come, with thick, wavy hair and his mother's big, russet-colored eyes. Then Benita turns back to me, her own beautiful eyes pleading. Diego has yet to say anything, but he's taking it all in with an intensity that reminds me of a wildcat when it's about to pounce.

With an it's-going-to-be-okay smile for Benita, I walk over to the couch, putting myself between the gun and the boy, and hold out my hand. "I'm Miss Woods. You must be Luis."

He gives me the slightest hint of a nod as he shakes my hand. "Yes, Miss Woods."

Then I turn back to Diego. "What seems to be the problem?"

"There's no problem." And he's still grinning. "We're just a family enjoying some time together."

"Um-hmm. That would be a lot easier to believe if you weren't holding a gun."

For a moment he stares at me as if trying to come up with a good answer. "It's for their protection."

"From …?"

A sound at the back of the house draws his attention that way as, out of the corner of my eye, I see a shadow pass by the front window. Diego turns and glares at me, his eyes narrowed to slits. "Who else came with you?"

I shrug … and there's another bang, only louder. Diego swears, his grip on the weapon tightening. He looks from me to Benita and back. *Oh, please, God, have him take me.* In that instant, he seems to make up his mind. Dropping Benita's wrist, he grabs my hand and pushes me in front of him. "Come on, *Miss Woods*," he growls. "Let's go say hi."

It's a small house, and we don't have far to go, passing through a modest kitchen into a mud room with a door to the backyard. Diego pauses, listening … and something scuffles across the living room floor. His gaze darts to me, the gun falters, and a familiar voice yells, "Jolene!" I drop to the floor and throw my arms over my head. Two bodies slam into Diego, knocking him to the ground as the gun drops and skitters across the kitchen tile. In a few seconds, Diego's hands are zip-tied behind his back—because, apparently, someone has zip-ties—and I've called nine-one-one.

With the police on their way and Diego's gun disarmed, the men walk him onto the porch while I comfort Benita and her family. Though the low rumble of Trevor's and Daniel's voices reach the living room, I can't quite make out the words.

Once Diego is in custody, Trevor, Daniel, Benita, and I pile into the Jeep for the drive to the police station. I lean forward from my place in the back seat and ask,

"What were you two saying to Diego while you were on the porch?"

The two exchange a glance, then Trevor says, "We were

207

letting him know Benita was under our protection now."

"That's it?"

Another glance and Daniel adds, "We might have said something about our childhood and some of the weapons we're … familiar with."

"You did?"

Trevor's eyes meet mine in the rearview mirror. "You bet we did."

What a man.

It takes hours to complete the interviews and paperwork. Once finished, we drive back to Benita's mother's home. I just didn't have the heart to separate Benita from her son after the events of the day, and the young woman promised she'd have her mom return her to Cocoon House the next morning.

To our delight, Mrs. Jensen insists we join them for a carne asada feast. Since none of us has eaten all day and it smells so good, we are powerless to resist.

It would also seem Daniel finds Benita a bit hard to resist as there are sparks flying between the two of them throughout the meal. How wonderful it would be for God to bring a good man to Benita. And if Daniel is anything like his brother, they don't get much better.

When we finally get to Trevor's apartment in Colorado Springs, he invites me in. I'm too on edge to say no or even think about sleep. Daniel immediately wishes us a good night, then saunters off to his room, while Trevor and I snuggle on the couch. I rest my head on his chest and breathe in his curry-spice scent. He says,

"I wish you hadn't done that."

"I know."

"And I'm glad you did."

I pull back and smile into his eyes. "I know." Leaning forward, I press my lips to his quickly, then put my head back down.

"You are the bravest woman I know," he says, holding me tighter. "But you could have been hurt."

"Any one of us could have been hurt."

"But you're my main concern—you're my only concern."

Pushing myself away, I sit up, crossing my legs in front of me. "That's something we need to talk about."

He sits up too, facing me. "What is?"

"You have made me your priority, time after time, and I don't know that I've ever told you how grateful I am."

With a shrug, he says, "I love you. You don't have to say anything."

"Yes, I do." I grab his hands and cling to them, staring at his fingers. "I've taken you for granted. I've always taken you for granted." Tears fill my eyes as I add, "You are leaving your job and your home and moving across the country for me. And you need to know how thankful I am … and how much I adore you."

He's silent for a moment, then, "Jolene, I—"

"No, hang on. There's one more thing." I bite my lip, so in love with this man words don't seem adequate. "I need to apologize for not saying anything sooner and for walking away after I found out about Daniel and what you both went through as children. I made something that wasn't about me … about me." I nudge closer to him. "I want you to tell me everything about that and your family and anything else you've kept hidden."

"There's not much to tell," he says with a shy grin. "But I'll answer any of your questions."

"Actually, that's not true. Because you have stories you haven't told me yet, and I want to hear them all."

209

"We have plenty of time for that." He pulls me back down into his arms. "But tonight I'm tired and just want to sleep with you."

I jolt back, searching his face, and he laughs. "Real sleep, Jo. We're both exhausted … and my brother is in the next room."

"Oh." I snuggle in close.

That I can do.

Once everything is settled with Benita, I catch the cheapest flight I can find back to Nashville. My wedding is less than two months away and I'm desperate to spend time with my daughter and grandchildren before I get married. Besides, my sister and mother are there, waiting to help me nail down a few more wedding details. Though I'll have to admit to them that daisies or lilies, red velvet or lemon, piano or violins—or both—are the last things on my mind. I'm not worried about the ceremony—it will all come together as it should. And, really, as long as I'm Trevor's wife at the end of it, nothing else matters.

My relationship with my daughter, however, is a far different story.

A few days after I get back to Tennessee, I drive my mom's red sedan down to Bell Buckle to meet Vala for lunch, mostly to talk about the upcoming kidney transplant. I still haven't had the chance to introduce everyone, but I'm not sure how to bring that up. Maybe that's why I'm more nervous this time than I was when I first journeyed to the quaint Southern town not that long ago. Though being with Trevor certainly helped. He really knows how to strengthen my confidence.

It rains the whole way, but I somehow manage to arrive ten minutes early at the little café where Trevor and I ate just a few months ago. It still smells like barbecue and, this time, pizza. Thanks to the extra time, I hurry to the bathroom to freshen up, then find a table in a quiet corner. The waitress takes my order for one of their famous hand-squeezed lemonades. I almost order one for Vala too, but I'm not sure if she's on a special diet … or even if she likes lemonade.

Finally, Vala comes through the door, looking just as beautiful as the last time I saw her. I stand as she takes a seat, then slide onto the booth bench across from her. She asks,

"How was your drive?"

"It was fine. Stormy but I didn't have any trouble."

The waitress comes over and Vala does, in fact, order a lemonade. Then she says to me, "Well, they're saying this is perfect tornado weather, so please be careful on your way home."

"Thanks. I will."

Neither of us says anything as we look over the menu. The waitress returns and Vala orders a BLT while I go for the pulled chicken chef salad. We both ask for the cucumbers and tomatoes on the side. It's hard to resist when Vala assures me they'll be fresh from the garden this time of year.

We sit quietly after the waitress leaves, sipping our lemonade. Finally Vala says,

"The kids would like to meet you—and the rest of the family."

I swallow, hard. "They would? Do they know who I am?"

"Yes," she says and looks at me steadily. "I told them everything, including the fact that I forgave you. And that I expect them to do the same."

"Oh. How did they respond?"

"Well …" and she smiles, "they want to meet you."

And, just like that, all my prayers have been answered.

Chapter 26
Uli

Jolene's wedding is only two weeks away, and I'm back in the Springs. And I don't know if I'm going to move to Cedar Rapids permanently or try to make a go of it here again. I wish I did. But every time I think of living in Colorado, a sense of dread trickles through me. That should be proof enough that I need to leave, but something holds me here. And, as much as I hate to admit it, that something is Cole.

The singles retreat I went to a month ago still haunts me. It made me think about God in a different way, and now I need to go from "thinking about" to understanding. I'm confused about my relationship with Him. What does He want from me? Though there are several ways to answer that question, I don't know how to discern which one is right. But I asked my new friend, Jill, for advice, and she suggested I pray for wisdom.

Well, it's a start anyway.

At the moment, though, I'm scurrying into Mimi's Café where I'm meeting my Accountability Monday friends for the first time in months. The last time we were all together was at Tess and Brian's wedding, and I'm happy to see my newlywed friend sitting at a booth with Jolene. They're laughing about something. I'm so overwhelmed with joy, I race up to the table and throw open my arms. Both jump up, and we're in the middle of a group hug when Catie says, "Hey, what about me?" Then the four of us are clinging tightly to each other, laughing and crying and talking all at once about who knows what.

All too soon we pull apart and take a seat. I study them closely. Each woman looks even more lovely in her own unique way than I remember. Catie has a soft orange, deep blue, and aqua scarf tied around her head with a fun knot just behind her right ear. And she's wearing her make-up in a different way. Add that to her colorful dress and dangly earrings and it's a new, adorable Catie. Or maybe it has nothing to do with her appearance but is something coming from inside. Because there's an aura about her I've never seen before.

Jolene has changed too, though not as drastically. Her hair is longer, and she might be down a few pounds. But she sure seems relaxed for someone only two weeks from a wedding. Then there's Tess, who is glowing to such a degree that her announcement, "I'm pregnant!" comes as a surprise to no one. As far as I can tell it's a honeymoon baby—due in April.

While we wait for dinner to arrive, Tess tells us about their new home and the colors they painted the walls and how long it took them to unpack. When she says they didn't finish with the last box until they'd been there a week, like that's excessive, I almost laugh. I won't mention the suitcase at Mom's that still has a few things from the retreat I need to put away.

To hear Tess talk about Brian as her husband is strange. Just over a year ago, the four of us sat in an Applebee's while she told us all about the new Guy With Potential, or GWP as we usually call them. Tess thought she was bringing news that could lead to a relationship for Catie, Jolene, or me. None of us would have imagined it turning out the way it did, especially Tess. At the time, she was fully committed to missionary work and the single life. Now she's married and settled and a mother-to-be.

Anyway, she finishes her update not long before our waitress shows up with heaping platters of deliciousness. The aroma of cheddar cheese and bacon almost makes me sigh with delight, and I dig right into my chicken mac and cheese, pushing down the little voice that thinks I should return to healthier eating habits. But I've kept up with the regular exercise and haven't gained any weight back. For now, that's enough.

Once that first rush of enjoying our food while it's hot

passes, Tess says, "So, Jolene, how are your wedding plans coming along?"

Jolene swallows a bite of grilled salmon and smiles. "Unless I've forgotten something, we're good to go."

"That's pretty impressive," I say. "And you don't seem 'bridezilla' at all."

"Nope. I made a deal with Trevor: he would move to Nashville with me if I promised not to become a perfection monster over the wedding."

"Well," Tess says, "if I were you I'd agree to anything to be near my child. And it sounds like you got the good end of that deal."

"In more ways than one." Jolene practically jumps out of her seat when she adds, "And, by the way, the kidney transplant surgery was a success. Lynelle and Olivia are both doing great and should be able to attend the wedding."

"That's wonderful news," I say. "I can't wait to meet them."

"And then you're moving away." Catie shakes her head and sighs. "I can't believe you're going to live in Tennessee."

"You're leaving too!" Jolene says. "And we all know Uli will end up in Iowa eventually." She smiles at me, but I simply nod. She's probably right. There's not much left for me here.

Jolene continues, "Soon Tess will be the only one of our group left in Colorado. We'll have to stay accountable online." Then, to Catie, "Have you found a place yet?"

"No … yes … maybe." Catie laughs. "Okay, I've looked at several and there's one I'm leaning toward—it's a small but really lovely cottage near the lake with an amazing backyard. Luna would be so happy there. And I made enough off the sale of my house here to afford it."

Tess asks, "Then what's the hesitation?"

Catie sets down her mushroom cheeseburger and stares out the window next to our booth for a second. She seems lost in thought—or in a memory—and I get the feeling I'm not the only one who doesn't want to interrupt. Finally she says,

"I met someone and, I don't know, but it's making me think differently about things."

No one expected that, I'm sure, and I don't hold back a gasp. No wonder she's glowing. But then she holds up her hand. "It's not what you think. I mean … it is. At least, it was."

Jolene says, "was?" as if she's afraid to hear an answer.

Again, that faraway look. Catie says, "I met him during chemo—just a couple times. We really … clicked."

I wait as long as humanly possible, then, "And …?"

As if that breaks her out of a spell, she gives me a soft smile. "And … he didn't make it. He passed away a few weeks later."

That doesn't make sense, not in light of her expression. I have to ask. "Then why are you smiling?"

"No reason." She shrugs, and laughs. "Okay, that's not true. Because it was … beautiful. I know it was short and simple and never went beyond talking about life and holding hands, but it was beautiful. Like a gift from God." Seeing our expressions, she bites her lip. "I guess that sounds pretty cheesy."

"Cheesy, sure," I say, "but also sad. Don't you miss him? Aren't you the least bit upset that you didn't get more time?"

She gives it some thought, then nods. "Yes to all of that. But it's not about me. Jake was tired and in pain, but he knew God and God took him home. I'm glad he's at peace." A few tears drip down her face, and she blots them with her napkin. "For a few weeks, though, I felt precious to someone. That's what I'll remember."

Jolene reaches across the table and covers Catie's hand with her own. "I think it's cool. And it proves to you that you *are* worthy of love. Something we all know but that I think you've doubted in the past." She leans back. "Sorry … probably not love, per se, in such a short time."

"Well," Catie says, "he asked me if I was familiar with the saying, 'when you know, you know.'" She lifts her shoulders shyly. "He said he knew."

Wow. In only a few hours she developed a deeper connection than I had in almost three years with Cole. They bonded emotionally and spiritually; Cole and I only bonded physically. No wonder Catie seems content. She's able to take what God gave her and not ask for more. Something I have yet to be able to do.

As I look around the table at my three friends, it occurs to me that the events of the past year have allowed each one to find contentment in God alone. And I suspect they could lose everything—love, family, job, home—and still, like Catie, see their lives as an extraordinary gift from Him. They're all moving on, stepping forward, trusting Him to prepare them for anything that lies ahead.

But here I sit, always wanting more. Never satisfied. Wanting … expecting God to prove His love with my happiness. That's my definition of a "good God." It's not the definition any of my friends would use, though.

Where is my heart? With men? With myself? Or with God?

We've about finished eating, and Jolene has launched into an extraordinary story of how God used her and Trevor and someone named Daniel to save one of her girls, but all I can think is,

How can I move from where I am to where they are?

Jolene and Trevor chose to have their wedding outside on a hill near a small church in Woodland Park, which is just up the pass next to Pikes Peak. The weather is chilly and cloudy and

216

smells like rain—very unlike Colorado—but the location is absolutely gorgeous. In fact, I'd say there's a tumultuousness in the air that adds a spark of peril to the day.

Our bridesmaids' dresses are sleeveless, which means we're freezing all during the photos and the ceremony. Every chance I get, I throw on the thick cable-knit sweater I brought and pray my nose and cheeks aren't red and chapped in the pictures. If they are, hopefully the photographer knows how to clear that stuff out ... and does. Or I'll do it for him.

But none of that matters. Jolene is a stunning bride. Even if her dress wasn't perfection, which it is, there's so much joy bouncing off her she seems almost giddy. I suspect part of that is having her daughter, Vala, and her family there. Jolene beams at the lovely young woman as she passes her and gets an answering smile in return. It's such a remarkable picture of love and forgiveness, I almost start crying before the minister gets to "Dearly beloved."

Trevor is gorgeous, of course, especially as he watches Jolene practically float down the aisle. His brother standing next to him is just as handsome, even with the scar marring the side of his face. The first time I saw Daniel, he was holding the hand of a woman with dark hair and russet eyes who reminds me a little of Salma Hayek. They're clearly smitten with each other, so once the reception is underway, I hunt down SueAnn to ask her about it.

"Oh," the older woman says, "that's Benita. She graduated from Cocoon House last month."

"How did she meet Daniel?"

"That's pretty romantic, actually." She leans toward me. "Daniel helped Trevor and Jolene rescue Benita from her thug ex-boyfriend."

"Oh, right! I think Jolene told us about that. What an amazing story."

SueAnn nods with a far-off smile that tells me she watches a

217

lot of Hallmark movies. "Yeah, well, I guess they hit it off."

I guess so.

The celebration is about over when I glance up right in the middle of a conga line during "Dancing Queen" and see Cole striding toward me. It's so exactly what I've been hoping for since I got back in town two weeks ago that my heart barely skips a beat. Actually, it skips several, but it doesn't stop altogether, which I consider a win. Even though I doubted I'd see him, I've rehearsed what I would say if I did many times. Yet here he is, and all I can squeak out is, "What are you doing here?"

"We need to talk," and he takes my hand and starts pulling me out of the reception hall. I can barely keep up. Everyone is watching, including my friends, and my main goal is maintaining a respectable level of composure. Hard to do when you're in heels and a floor-length dress and someone is dragging you across the room, but I try.

And all the while I'm freaking out at seeing Cole and wondering if this means he still wants to be with me … just as I'm getting past the whole thing. And underneath that is a feeling of dread that I'll mess up all over again and hurt the relationship with God I've been working on. Am I capable of making Him my priority over a man?

"Cole, slow down!" I say in my loudest whisper. "You're hurting me."

Once we're in the entryway, he turns down a hall, then leads me into a small meeting room and shuts the door behind us. He turns around and looks me straight on.

"Have you had enough?"

"Enough?" I'm dumbfounded. "Enough what?"

"Enough being angry at me for one mistake. I tried to give you your space, Uli, but this is getting ridiculous."

"One mistake? I caught you with her twice! Which tells me there were plenty of times when I didn't catch you."

Cole lets me go and runs a hand through his hair, as thick and black as when we first met. To my dismay, he looks almost exactly like he did when I fell for him—handsome and confident. *That's not fair.*

"But that's all changed now," he says. "It's over with Merryn."

Right. "You told me—promised me that before."

He grunts. Annoyed or frustrated ... probably both.

"Cole," I say, "why do you even care? You don't love me."

That makes him jerk back and shake his head. "Of course I love you."

"Do you? Really? Because I'm not even sure you know what love is." I put my hand on one side of his face, aching to get through to him, aching for him to see what I finally see—that it really is over and has been for some time. "Cole, love is sacrifice. It's commitment and always putting the other person's needs ahead of your own. It's—"

And I stop, staring at him. I'm such a hypocrite. When have I showed someone that kind of love? Have I ever had that heart for any human being, let alone God? Did I offer Him any part of me without expecting something else in return? Or have I always—always expected Him to meet my needs first and then, only then, would I seek Him?

My hand drops to my side, and I back away. "Please forgive me," I whisper.

"Forgive you? For what?"

"No, I didn't mean you." But my mind is racing with all kinds of thoughts, none of which involve Cole.

He says, "Are you seeing someone else? Is that the problem?"

It takes me a second to realize what he's asking. I shake my head. "Of course not."

The expression in his eyes lets me know he doesn't believe

219

me. "Why of course not? You must be meeting men in Iowa. And you're telling me you aren't dating any of them?"

Men? I shake my head. Yes, there are men in Iowa ... and I think of Steve. Cute, funny, always-up-for-a-good-time Steve. Who flirts with me every moment we're together ... and I hear nothing from him in between. I don't have a clue where I stand with him. And it doesn't matter. I can live a happy life without a man.

Because God *is* good. The truth washes over me like a fountain. Even with my broken heart, God is good. Even with cancer, He's good. Even if I never marry ... and Catie never marries ... or neither of us has children or someone we love gets sick and dies, He's good. I can't look for proof of His goodness; it doesn't work that way. I have to start with the foundation that He is good ... and then trust that everything else makes sense within that framework. And because He's good, He reminds me of the verse telling us all we have to do is ask for wisdom and He will give it generously. So I can ask Him to show me His goodness even in the worst situation.

I turn to Cole and cover his hands with mine. "I forgive you, Cole. And I love you ... but not as much as God loves you. Someday, I hope and pray you'll see the truth of that."

All he says is, "You've changed."

"Yes."

He nods. "It looks good on you."

Peace usually does.

Epiphanies don't always bring closure, but they certainly help. I have a lot to ponder over the next week as I prepare to leave Colorado behind me for good. During that time, I spend as

220

much of it as possible with Catie, who's doing the same. We decide to help each other out by taking turns—me at her house and her at my storage locker—sorting all of our stuff into take, sell, giveaway, or toss piles. Audrey comes over and helps one afternoon too, a further reminder of all the friends I will miss here.

At one point, I tell Catie what I'm in the process of learning about the goodness of God, starting with events in Iowa and the Labor Day singles retreat. When I'm done, she nods and says, "I never thought about it that way, but it's true. We really can't measure His goodness according to our happiness." Then she tells me about an actual mountaintop experience she had where God showed her that He had to be first in her life, above all else.

"I think that was the beginning." She sits down on a recently packed box and takes a breath, and I wonder how much this is taking out of her. She seems better but not one-hundred percent by any stretch. She continues, "Since then, I keep trying to put God first. It's not easy, but I know I never could have handled Jake's death a year ago. Everything God allows to happen in our lives prepares us for whatever's yet to come … good or bad."

Oh, how I'm going to miss this woman. I take her hand. "Please promise we'll always stay in touch."

She nods and squeezes my fingers. "Maybe next year I can join you over Labor Day weekend … if you go back."

"That sounds like an excellent idea."

Because time moves so quickly, I'm soon back at my mom's condo in Iowa, missing my friends but grateful to have a home. I'm still substitute teaching whenever I can. In the meantime, I've decided to pursue several different career options, but I'm leaning

221

toward one in particular—one that utilizes my artistic skills while also giving me an opportunity to minister to single moms like Audrey and Jill.

Whatever I end up doing, though, I now trust God's hand is in it. And I'm not sure if I'll ever date again, but I trust Him with that too.

One late October day I'm walking through downtown Cedar Rapids, admiring the perfect fall weather and checking out the various stores after stopping at a printer to pick up new business cards. As I pass the flower shop, a display catches my eye. A large ceramic vase dominates the space, filled with strikingly brilliant sunflowers. In that moment, I remember a day so long ago when my dad made me promise I'd follow my dream, whatever it might be. Contentment ripples through me because it's no longer about my dream.

It's about His.

Epilogue
Catie

It's an amazing thing, watching God at work in people's lives. Six months ago, I stood with my friends as Trevor and Jolene pledged their lives to each other. Since then, so much has happened.

Jolene and Trevor, along with his brother, Daniel, and Daniel's fiancée, Benita, have been setting up a ministry in Nashville—a home for children rescued from sex trafficking. I pray for them daily, knowing the kind of work they're doing not only requires strength and compassion, which they all have in abundance, but courage and resolve and an ability to never let anything stop them. So they choose to put their lives in danger for what's right … and I choose to believe those lives are safe in God's hands.

Then there's Uli. Her changed life is more gradual, but I've watched her become a stronger, happier woman. She told me just last week that she'd had a chance to speak to a group of college women about purity and seeking God's will as far as relationships go, and they've already asked her to come back.

"How strange would it be," she asked during our video chat, "if God called me to talk to people about everything I thought I wanted to forget?"

And we both laughed because that seemed exactly the kind of thing God would do.

Tess and Brian, meanwhile, welcomed their son a month ago. Born too early, he's struggled ever since and has yet to leave the hospital. I suspect Tess's updates only hint at their heartache and for this, too, I'm praying.

As for me, I finished chemo and radiation, and my doctor gave me an all-clear at my last check-up. Luna and I now live in a charming little cottage near the lake, and only five minutes from my dad's farm. One of the biggest surprises, though, is my new job—executive director at an animal shelter. My salary is enough to live on and that's about it, but I've never had this much fun at my work. Add that to all the time I spend with family, and my life is full. I rarely even think about falling in love anymore.

Rarely.

Though I've sworn off singles events for the most part, I occasionally check one out. Tonight, I decide to join a group meeting for dinner at a restaurant about an hour from me. It took several back roads to get here, but the place is known for its home-style cooking, so I anticipate it will be worth the journey. As far as dinner is concerned anyway.

I know maybe a handful of the people there and meet a few more. With twenty-plus people sitting around a large table, though, I can't talk to them all. And yet …

Throughout the evening, my eyes keep going back to a tall man with a great haircut and a perfect five-o'clock shadow. Not the kind of man I'm usually attracted to, but he's nicely put together and vaguely familiar. And it doesn't hurt that every time I glance toward him, he seems to be watching me. Or maybe that's just my imagination. It's fooled me before.

About halfway through dinner our eyes meet again, though not in that romantic, across-a-crowded-room kind of way since he just took a bite out of an obscenely large hamburger. As soon as he's cleared it, though, he asks my name. I tell him it's Catie, and he introduces himself as Kevin. Someone mentioned earlier that he's a patrol officer. I would ask more about that but the moment passes and, suddenly, I'm the one being questioned. My move from Colorado has already come up and, as usual, the big question is to wonder why I left. And, again, I mention my desire to be near my family.

He nods and wipes mustard off his chin. "I take it you're

close to your family."

"Yes. Aren't you?"

A shadow crosses his eyes, then he shrugs. "We get along." The words don't match the look and tell me nothing. I resist the urge to blow a puff of air into my recently grown-back bangs and squirt some lime into my diet Coke instead. It goes everywhere and almost hits Kevin in the eye.

The willowy blonde sitting next to me says something like, "Family is so great!" while tucking razor-straight hair behind her ear. My hair, meanwhile, has been growing back thick and wild and a little more auburn than red. I'd tuck it behind my ear, but it would just bounce right back. The blonde's name is Joan, but for some reason I want to call her Tiffany.

Kevin turns his attention toward her. "Your family lives around here too?"

She nibbles delicately on her baked potato and laughs. "Heavens, no. That's what makes them so great."

One of Kevin's eyebrows arches like a fish jumping out of a net. "Oh …" He stretches out the word as if giving Tiff-Joan a chance to re-think her comment. "I take it you don't get along."

"Distance makes the heart grow fonder."

"It's absence," I say, and Kevin sends his other brow leaping as he glances my way.

Tiff-Joan looks at me like I'm the waitress interrupting her conversation to refill her water glass. "Excuse me?"

"The saying is 'Absence makes the heart grow fonder.' Not distance."

"What's the difference?"

"Well, one is correct and one isn't."

Kevin makes a noise that sounds like a cat coughing up a hairball. When I look his direction he actually winks at me. I can't remember the last time someone winked at me, and I have no idea how to respond.

"Anyway," Tiff-Joan says with a shrug, "it's basically the same thing."

When Kevin winks again, it occurs to me he might have something in his eye. Maybe the lime squirt hit him after all. I turn back to Tiff-Joan. "I don't know about that. Absence doesn't require distance."

"But distance implies absence." This comes from Tony, an accountant sitting across from Tiff-Joan. I didn't even know he was listening. Glancing around, I realize about half the table has reached the typical eleven-minute lapse in conversation and seem relieved to have the option of participating in ours. Such as it is.

It doesn't take long to notice how much of what Kevin says is tongue-in-cheek. He's clever, which is always appealing. I really just want to talk to him alone. But we are now trapped in the middle of a discussion on absence vs. distance. Not that I'm paying much attention. I'm too distracted by the effort it takes to not make eye contact with Kevin. Is he doing the same? That would be nice.

What can I say? He makes me feel like the Molly Ringwald character in a John Hughes movie.

And that's about it. The moment passes into the cesspool of small talk, never to return. As we all file out of the restaurant, I take a chance and hold out my hand toward Kevin. "It was really nice meeting you." *If you want my phone number, all you have to do is ask.*

He takes my hand in a firm grip, gives it two quick pumps and lets go. "You too."

Using every ounce of willpower at my disposal, I manage not to groan in frustration. Instead, I give him what I hope is my most genuine—and inviting—smile. "Well, have a safe drive home."

"Actually," he says, "I'm on-call tonight."

"Oh, late shift, huh?"

226

"Something like that."

I nod, and that seems the end of it.

But then, out of nowhere, *Oh, just kiss me already.* Yes, I really think that. I would never say it out loud, but I think it. Being single for a long time has this strange effect: it makes you want to throw off all pretense and just be honest. *I like you. I don't want to spend the next six months liking your Facebook posts and hoping to run into you again. I want to move forward. Now.*

But we live in a polite society, and there are rules. So I say goodnight, and we walk off to our separate cars and go our separate ways. Knowing I might never see him again. Knowing I'm okay with that. Knowing I have to be.

These thoughts occupy my mind as I maneuver along the back roads toward home. More than anything, I want to turn my car around and hunt him down. I'm not in love. I'm in hope. It's very invigorating, despite the doubt crowding my mind that anything will come of it. As the darkness of a moonless night follows me home, it's all I can do to remember to pay attention to the small amount of road illuminated ahead of me. A Billy Squier song about lonely nights erupts from the radio, and I sing along, letting the frustration out through my voice.

As the song ends, I start to cry. A common misperception claims that often women burst into tears for no reason. It's not true. We're actually crying for every reason. The reason the tears begin to fall latches onto the reason we cried last week … then last month … and reminds us how much we love our family and hate our loneliness and how we don't want to feel like this, but it's still better to feel something than nothing. And every song I hear on the radio reminds me of all the other reasons to blubber like the last girl to be rejected on *The Bachelor*.

So here I am, soggy-faced, on one of those dark roads just a few miles from home, when I see her. She stands proud but uncertain on the shoulder, staring into my headlights. Her brown

227

eyes glisten as I realize, too late, she's going to cross the road, and I can't avoid her. Punching my foot on the brake, I hold my breath. The tires screech as my SUV slams into her dead center. It's not a hard hit, but she flies through the air anyway and into the ditch. I come to a stop, stunned, as smoke seeps slowly from beneath the hood. Something rattles in the engine, and it dies. Peering into the darkness to my right, I see the deer stumble to her feet, take a few faltering steps, then bound away into the woods.

After waiting a moment, I try to start the SUV. It stutters like a drunken poet but doesn't catch. I fumble through my purse for my phone, find it, and dial nine-one-one while using my other hand to flip on the hazard lights. As I tell the operator my situation, my chest throbs from the jerk of the seatbelt and there's a similar pain in my right knee. Other than that, I feel fine if a little stupid. What a cliché, hitting a deer on an Ohio back road. I shouldn't have let Billy distract me so. Or Kevin. They tag-teamed me.

I try to take a deep lungful of air but it's too painful, so I lean my head back and hope someone shows up soon. The night sits on the car like a sumo wrestler, its black silence broken only by the click-flash of the hazard lights and my slow shallow breaths. Everything I've ever feared about dark, isolated country roads taps me on the shoulder. I lock the doors. I mumble a quick prayer of desperation. My hand clasps my phone, but who should I call? Though I don't want to bother my family this late at night, it would be nice if someone knew I was here, trapped by my imagination, watching the wind blow through trees and tease the new spring leaves as they twist and twirl along the side of the road. Someone who could pray for me.

Rustle. Swish.

Oh, please, let it be the wind.

Closing my eyes, I try to imagine what it would be like to

have a man in my life, especially during moments like this. Despite how far I've come, it would just be nice.

I must have dozed off because a crack from outside jerks me awake. I check my watch. Thirty minutes have passed since I placed the nine-one-one call. Just how long will it take for someone to show up? Well, I don't want to drain my phone battery, but maybe I can find something to read online. I'm scrolling through possibilities when car lights break the darkness in my rearview mirror. Finally a sign that I'm not the only person left in the world or, at the very least, Logan County.

As the vehicle draws closer, the lights perched on top tell me it's my rescuer, and I let out the breath I didn't realize I was holding in. The police strobes aren't flashing, which I appreciate. The policeman gets out of his car and strolls toward me. His walk is familiar. In seconds I know why, because I'm staring into Kevin's deep blue eyes.

Yes, that Kevin.

This only happens in the movies. In real life, you don't find yourself sitting in your car, wishing you weren't alone, only to have the man you wish you were alone with tap on your window, offering to rescue you. I blink a couple of times and try to power down the glass, only to remember my car is dead in the road. I open the door.

"Well," he says, "this is unexpected."

I don't know how to reply and just nod like a nitwit.

"What happened?"

"Oh. I hit a deer."

He glances toward the woods, then back at me. "Are you okay?"

"I think so."

"Where's the deer?"

"She took off."

"Hit and run, huh?"

229

I can't help but smile. "Well, technically, I hit her but, yeah, then she ran. I'm afraid I didn't get her plates."

Kevin laughs, but I'm not looking at him as I shimmy out of the car, so I don't know if he winks or not. He says, "Maybe we can put together a line-up" in his gruff Sam Elliott voice, like he has to at least consider the possibility. *You are adorable.*

The air is as crisp as an iced mocha, and a hint of fresh-cut grass comes from a nearby farmhouse. An ambulance pulls up behind us, its flashing lights giving the night an even eerier quality. Kevin waves to the driver. "We'll check you out," he begins, then clears his throat, "and make sure you're not hurt. Then we'll fill out the accident report." He points at me. "Catie, right?"

"Yes, Catie Delaney."

Kevin takes a deep breath and stares at me like I said I was a Muppet in disguise. "Delaney?"

"Yes. Do I know you?"

He scratches his temple, his eyes wide. "You had cancer." It's not a question.

"Well, I did. I'm better now." And completely bewildered. "How did you know?"

"Oh, sorry." He holds out his hand, and I shake it. "I'm Kevin Fleming." And I'm still trying to figure out what's going on when he continues, "I'm Jake Fleming's brother."

Now it's my turn to stare. Jake Fleming? The man I fell for after spending only two days with him? I sway a little, and Kevin grabs my arm.

"Jake Fleming's brother?" He nods and another thought hits me. "And he told you about me?"

Kevin runs one hand through his hair as he turns and leans against my SUV. "He wanted me to look you up."

"Really? Why?"

"Well, he promised if I did, I would know."

230

No, that can't be right. *When you know, you know.* That's what Jake had said. He'd been talking about us, right? So why would he tell Kevin to find me?

I have plenty of questions, but the first one has to be, "Why didn't you?"

"Why didn't I what?"

"Why didn't you look me up?" I say it in a whisper, leaning beside him, surrounded by the sounds and smells of a spring night and the strobing lights of the ambulance. In the distance, a coyote howls, eerie and lonesome. Maybe I shouldn't have asked that question.

Kevin shrugs. "I'm not sure. He was so sick, and he was gone so fast, I really couldn't think straight." He's quiet for a moment, then, "I guess it wasn't the right time."

I guess not. It never is.

He turns toward me, suddenly all business. "We should call for a tow."

"Yes."

So he does. As he makes the call, we walk toward the ambulance. He puts his other hand under my elbow. I fight the impulse to sink into him. It would be better if I pulled away. I don't, but it would be better. After a quick exam, the EMT determines I only have a few bad bruises, and he assures me I'll be fine as long as I take it easy for a few days.

Once that's done, Kevin asks, "Did you call someone to come pick you up?"

I look down at my phone. "No, I didn't. Not yet."

"It's kind of late. Come on, I'll get you home." Kevin jerks his head in the direction of his black-and-white patrol car. As I get closer, I see it's covered with the dry spots you get after a rainstorm and what appears to be cat paw prints.

"Do you have a cat?" I take a deep breath as we walk around to the passenger side. This could change everything.

"Two. And a dog. You?"

"Oh, I have a dog. A golden retriever."

"Really? Me too."

"Hmm." *Interesting.* "I bet they'd get along."

"I bet they would." He's silent again—longer this time—then turns and looks right into my eyes. "Do you think Jake was right? That when you know, you know?"

"Um … I think God can do miraculous things. But I also think it's that you will one day look back and say, 'Yes, that's when I knew.' Not necessarily in the moment."

"So, I guess we'll just have to go on a date to find out."

"A date?"

"Sure." He grins and opens the car door. "We'll start with one."

And he waits for me while I slide in, smiling. A well-used Bible rests on the console between the seats, and I have to move over a pair of hiking boots at my feet. Suddenly, everything feels just right.

As Kevin strides to the other side of the car, I lean across and unlock his door. Seconds later, he thanks me, plops into his seat, and starts the engine. He glances over at me, still grinning.

Then, as God is my witness, that man winks at me again. What a goof. A beautiful, wonderful goof. And I feel like Samantha Baker getting into a red Porsche with Jake Ryan.

Wow. This guy definitely has potential.

THE END

Study Questions

1. The main theme of *Altared* is God's goodness—and how that relates to being single. For most of the series, Uli doubts that God is good because of the struggles of her life. She believes a good Father would want His children to be happy. Can you relate to Uli's doubt? If so, in what way?

2. While on vacation in Belize, Uli becomes increasingly upset when she feels Catie and Jolene don't support her engagement to Cole. Who do you think was right in this situation? Should friends support friends even when they believe they're making a mistake? Why or why not?

3. How long should you wait before talking to someone you've had a fight with? What are some biblical examples of "mending fences," as it were?

4. Have you ever come to the realization that you missed the difficulties your friends have faced because you were so caught up in your own problems? Did something—or someone—help you see the truth of that? If so, what changes did you make as a result?

5. What's the bravest thing you've ever done?

6. Have you lost either or both of your parents? If yes, how old were you? How did that affect you as an adult? (*I, Sharyn, relate most to Uli. Though I lost my mom, not my dad, when I was in high school. She had breast cancer and passed away the year I graduated. As a result, I've had a hard time trusting God. I felt if He could take my mom from my family and me, He could do anything. Any person I loved could die … even a husband. In many ways, I believe that's at least part of the reason I've remained single.*)

7. Have you ever felt exposed? Maybe not like Catie did that night on the beach, but, somehow, you were in a situation that left you feeling naked. What were the circumstances and how did

233

you handle it?

8. Why does it take Catie so long to let Tess back into her life? What do you think it is about her heartbreak over Brian that bothers her the most, especially once she seems to have gotten over it?

9. What kind of sacrifices are you willing to make for the people you love, whether physical, emotional, or personal? Would you give up an organ? A career? A romantic relationship? Discuss the benefits of making deep sacrifices.

10. Can you, like Catie, attend the wedding of someone you once had feelings for? Why or why not?

11. Why does Uli have such a hard time letting Cole go? How much is that tied in to their sexual relationship? Would things have been better if she'd never slept with him? Why or why not?

12. What did you think of Catie's comment that she can sometimes feel the absence of the man she believes she's meant to be with?

13. Do you struggle with your weight? What are some things you've tried? Would you see food poisoning as a good thing if it led to long-term weight loss? Why or why not?

14. In chapter thirteen, Uli believes things are starting to look up—she's losing weight, getting married, and interviewing for an ideal job. But, eventually, each one falls apart. How could she look at these events in a different way for a healthier result? What did you learn from that?

15. Jolene makes the difficult decision to leave her work at Cocoon House in order to be closer to her daughter and grandchildren. Do you think she made the right choice? Why or why not?

16. Is it easy or difficult for you to share the Gospel with others? If it's difficult, have you found ways to do so anyway? When's the last time you told a stranger about your faith?

17. Have you ever felt abandoned because you were the one single in a group of couples and families? What would you have done if, like Uli, you'd gone to an activity, such as an amusement park, only to have everyone go off in their groups and leave you to spend the day alone?

17. Jolene doesn't handle it very well when she finally learns about Trevor's past. How do you respond when you find out someone you love has kept significant information from you?

18. If you've ever dealt with cancer—whether you had it yourself or a loved one did—you know how painful it can be. How do you think Catie handled it? Was she right to choose to be near family during chemotherapy?

19. Uli finally comes to this conclusion: "Even with my broken heart, God is good. Even with cancer, He's good. Even if I never marry … and Catie never marries … or neither of us has children or someone we love gets sick and dies, He's good. I can't look for proof of His goodness; it doesn't work that way. I have to start with the foundation that He is good … and then trust that everything else makes sense within that framework." How did you respond to that?

20. What did you think of Catie's serendipitous meeting with Jake's brother, Kevin? Has she finally found love? Is it realistic to believe that every single person who wants to get married will? If you said yes, do you have scriptural evidence to back that up? Or share scriptural evidence that you believe proves otherwise.

21. Looking back at your life, what are some ways God has shown Himself to be a good Father?

Uli's Orange Jell-o ~~Salad~~ Dessert — Oh, You Decide

It's really pretty simple. And delicious. Kind of like a creamsicle dish with fruit in it and pudding on top.

Start by dissolving a large (4.3 oz.) package of orange Jell-o in two cups of boiling water. Next, add one 6-oz. can of frozen orange juice (I usually end up adding half of a 12-oz. can), 2 small cans of mandarin oranges, drained, and a 20-oz. can of crushed pineapple with the juice included.

Stir everything together and pour into a 9x13 dish. Chill until solid.

Now, here's the good part—and the reason you'll probably call it a dessert. Beat one package of instant vanilla pudding with 1 cup of milk until it sets. Then gently fold in an 8-oz. container of Cool Whip. Spread that on top of the Jell-o and chill until it's time to eat.

I'd devour the whole thing if I could!